Amalgam-Man:

Burnt Crispy

A Novel by

J. Matthew Neal

Amalgam-Man: Burnt Crispy

Printed in the United States of America
by Dunn Avenue Press
Muncie, Indiana 47304
ISBN 978-1-7349372-6-8

Novels by J. Matthew Neal

Specific Gravity

Ontario Lacus

Americium the Beautiful

Stella Scura: Dark Star Rising

- *Book One: Glory of The Great Dame*
- *Book Two: A Little Girl Grows Up*
- *Book Three: Science Squad Unite*
- *Book Four: First Family*
- *Book Five: Now I am become Death*
- *Book Six: A Child Once More*

Amalgam-Man

Amalgam-Man: Burnt Crispy

As a fan of mystery novels, I was drawn to this one because of the concept of a mystery involving arson, a museum, and a rare camera. The camera belonged to Drake Fowler, a famous photographer, and when its authenticity comes into question, Rudbeck suspects he is involved. Due to a rough childhood, he usually felt like an underdog, but now he sees himself as the champion of the common man, helping people whenever he can. He's an eccentric man, and most people just humor him, hoping he'll stay out of the way.

J. Matthew Neal delivers a suspenseful mystery filled with academic intrigue and superhero flair. The action is dialogue-driven, the pacing steady, and the characters are engaging and deeply developed. Rudbeck is not a dangerous vigilante; instead, he's a likable protagonist navigating real-world responsibilities alongside crime-solving. The language is clever and humorous.

Overall, Amalgam-Man: Burnt Crispy, the second novel in the Amalgam-Man series by J. Matthew Neal, is a fast-paced mystery that blends science, suspense, and satire. It includes insider knowledge of medicine and academia, along with a touch of comic book charm. Despite the heavy subject of science, it's an easy read. Readers looking for a cozy mystery with depth, intelligence, and quirky charm will appreciate the balance of suspense and humor.

— *Sandra Cruz, Reader Views*

Dr. Dan Rudbeck is a talented academic physician whose career advancement has been limited by his abrasive, politically incorrect manner and penchant for excessive interest in eclectic areas outside of medicine that detract from his regular duties.

His greatest claim to fame came in high school when he created the fictional character Barclay Dixon, a vastly talented Renaissance man, a living amalgam of all things excellent—the amazing Amalgam-Man. He has found that his life hasn't paralleled that of his creation. Unfortunately, his multiple personal shortcomings have resulted in him not achieving the status he desires.

Two years ago, he uncovered a complex healthcare ransomware scheme and became a regional hero. He married his old college sweetheart Jayna, and life seems good in Staffordsville, Ohio.

However, his life is turned upside down when not one, but two large buildings in Staffordsville are burned down in the same week, using an accelerant so ubiquitous no one besides him would think of it. In addition, the loss of a legendary, rare camera on exhibit at one of the buildings has him concerned that foul play is at hand.

The motives behind the fiery destruction of these two unrelated buildings seems unclear, but Rudbeck is on the case. Can he draw upon the wisdom of the Amalgam-Man to solve this crazy mystery before time runs out?

"She does him good, and not harm, all the days of her life."

— Proverbs 31:12

"It does not matter how slowly you go, as long as you do not stop."

"He who learns but does not think, is lost! He who thinks but does not learn is in great danger."

— Confucius

Prologue

Saturday, October 4, 2025
Dubois County, Ohio
State Road 128
2217 hours

Dubois County Sheriff's Deputy Ronald K. Wolford was on his usual nightly patrol headed west down Ohio Highway 128 on the cool, dry Saturday evening in early October. He was detail-oriented, and his rural patrol route was methodical, thorough, and somewhat predictable. He was no maverick, and he'd learned long ago that being methodical and following a routine led to far fewer mistakes. The higher-ups always had their eyes on the rookie—especially one who had his eye on a leadership position one day. There was a big conference football game in town that night, and he would likely run into something that required his attention. More often than not, that "something" involved excess alcohol.

He then spied the broken-down brown and orange bus on the side of the road about a half mile from the county line. Twenty-three-year-old Ronnie had wanted to be a police officer for as long as he could remember, and he went to the police academy as soon as he earned his bachelor's degree with honors in criminology from Ohio State.

Police work wasn't a popular career choice nowadays due to political issues and diminished prestige among the public. However, he still wanted to make it his career and help others in his community. He had only been on the job a few weeks, but he somehow knew he would encounter something unusual tonight in the sleepy Ohio county of his birth, and he didn't want to screw up.

As he drew closer, he saw the Bowling Green University bus driver outside as he activated his flashing lights and parked in front of the bus.

He exited his vehicle and approached the driver, who was nervously smoking a cigarette. "What's happened, sir?" he said to the short, middle-aged, overweight man.

The uniformed driver shook his head as he exhaled a puff of smoke. "Right front tire blew out. I've got the tire service coming out to fix it. Take an hour or so, the guy said."

"You guys coming from the evening football game?"

The driver nodded as he took another drag from his cigarette. "Yeah. I guess it's better to have issues here on the local highway than out on the interstate, huh? Weird, we always have the tires checked before leaving. Never had this happen before."

"I suppose so. It would've been worse for a tire to blow out there. Everyone inside okay?"

"Oh, sure. There's a restroom and everything in there. One other thing, though, and I'm glad you stopped by . . . these two fellas saw it too. Something you probably want to investigate." He watched as two passengers walked off the bus and approached him. One extended his hand.

"How you doing, Officer?" the tall Black man said as they shook hands.

"Good, very well, thank you. Looks like you all have some problems."

The athletic, fortyish man laughed. "Well, we'll get home okay, but some lady has way worse problems than us."

"What do you mean, sir?"

"There was just a woman who tried to get on our bus; we'd

never seen her before, and she wasn't with our group as she was wearing a Central Ohio sweatshirt, which is dangerous to wear with this crowd since we lost."

The deputy laughed. "What was the issue with her?"

"She was walking down this highway for some reason and just happened to find us because we broke down, but there's nothing out here. She's extremely drunk or on something else, and we told her this isn't her bus. She then left after we told her she was in the wrong place."

"Yeah, that's right," the other, shorter passenger said. "I could smell the booze. The gal was hammered."

"What'd she look like?"

"Slightly above average height and weight, maybe forty-five or so, dark hair and eyes. I would say she was Asian or part Asian."

"Where'd she go?"

The taller man pointed westward down the highway. "That way. This was about five minutes ago, so she can't have gotten very far. I was just about to call you guys, and then you showed up."

"Thanks for letting me know. I'll go track her down right now. Take care, and I hope you guys get home soon."

Wolford returned to his modified Ford Explorer police cruiser, drove slowly west, and eventually saw the dark-haired woman staggering slightly on the shoulder about a half mile down the road. He pulled up behind her, exited the car, and approached her.

"Ma'am, hold up a minute." The woman stopped, turned around, and stared at him. "Hello. I'm Deputy Wolford of the Dubois County Sheriff's Department. So that you know, my body-cam is audio and video recording you right now."

She looked at him blankly for several seconds. "Nice to meet you, Sheriff, sir." She pointed at his badge. "I like shiny things."

"May I ask where you're going, Ma'am? This road leads out of town, and it's unsafe for pedestrians to be alone, especially after dark."

The fortyish, five-six woman looked at him, opened her mouth wide, and finally smiled. "I'm going back to the medical school, sir," she said proudly with slurred speech. "Gotta grade me some papers that are due the day after tomorrow."

"If that's the case, you're going the complete opposite direction, and you're a good fourteen miles from campus. How much have you had to drink tonight?"

"*Drink?* I haven't had anything other than pop. Why . . . why would you say that, Mr. Policeman?"

"Ma'am, I'm three feet from you, and your breath reeks of alcohol. The people on the Bowling Green bus pointed you out to me and said you tried to get on it."

She shook her head. "Don't know about any Bowling Green bus. I just want to get home."

"Where's home?"

"Close to the medical school. That way." She pointed west.

"I already told you that's the complete opposite direction of where you want to go. What's your home address?"

She thought for about two minutes. "Don't remember, but I know where home is, I promise. That way." She then pointed south, in a different direction, nowhere near town, but still wrong. "You can give me a ride, right?"

"Yes, Ma'am, but I can't give you a courtesy ride unless I know where we're going; you have pointed to 'home' in two vastly different directions. And I think you're too inebriated to go home now, anyway."

"Well, just leave me alone, and I'll get there. I didn't do nothin' wrong."

He grabbed her right arm gently. "I can't do that. I know you're not driving, but it would help me to know how much alcohol is in your system or if something else is going on. Will you do a portable breathalyzer test?"

"Well, I guess so. Does it hurt?"

"No, you just blow in a little tube, that's all."

She nodded. "I suppose it's okay."

"Okay, let me hold your arm as I don't want you falling over." He escorted her back to his cruiser, pulled out the yellow PBT (preliminary breath test) device from his duty bag, and put a disposable mouthpiece on the end. "Ma'am, it's like blowing up a balloon. Can you do that for me?"

"Huh. I'll try my best." She took a deep breath and put her mouth over the white mouthpiece.

"Okay, blow in. Blow, blow, blow. Good job." He looked at the readout and couldn't believe his eyes after the result flashed on the screen fifteen seconds later. "Holy crap. You blew 0.394 percent, which is almost five times the legal limit. I've never heard of one that high. Ma'am, I'm worried about your safety." He looked at her disheveled clothing—rumpled blue jeans and dirty, cola-stained college sweatshirt. "Do you have a purse, wallet, ID, or phone?"

She felt for those items in her jeans. "I guess . . . not. Must've lost them." She laughed, almost falling over.

He steadied the drunken woman with his left hand. "What's your name?"

"Um, it's, uh . . . Sybil, I think."

"How do you spell that? With a C or an S?"

"Heck, I don't know, sir. I gots me a PhD in medical genetics, but can't spell worth a damn. Thank God for AI and spell check."

"What's your last name, Sybil?"

"Huh?" She looked at him, opened her mouth wide, and laughed. "I know it . . . I know it as well as I know my own name. It's on the tip of my tongue."

"Ma'am, you don't know your last name?"

She shook her head. "I guess I forgot it, sir."

"Okay. Ma'am, you're clearly extremely intoxicated and wandering down a highway late at night. You're alone and can't tell me where you're going. You've got no ID and don't even know your name."

"May I ask . . . what I've done wrong?" she asked with extremely slurred speech.

"Well, Ma'am, you're really impaired to the point of almost passing out, and you're lost, wandering down the highway in the wrong direction, and you're almost out of the county. You have no ID and don't even know your own name. I'm terrified that if I leave you out here, something bad will happen to you. So, for your own safety, I'm arresting you for public intoxication until we can figure out who you are and deal with this situation safely."

"Hey, I'm a professor at the medical school is who I are." She pointed to her chest with her right thumb. "I be an important person."

He looked at the disheveled, intoxicated woman's attire and wasn't convinced that she was a medical school professor. "Maybe so, but that's irrelevant right now, Ma'am."

"But I haven't had anything to drink! Am I going to jail? I've heard it can be a fun experience with an opportunity to meet new friends."

He shook his head. "Public intoxication is just a ticket, so, no, you won't meet new friends tonight, and please don't make friends there if you ever go, but right now, let's get into the back seat of my vehicle so I can take you to the emergency room for medical clearance, and then we need to go to the station to do some paperwork. I can't just leave you out here."

She looked up at him with a stuporous grin. "Do I at least get a mugshot? I want mine on my sweatshirt."

"No, Ma'am. You can be released to a sober adult, otherwise, you'll need to sleep it off at the station if the ER releases you. I'm worried about your safety and health. Do you have any medical problems like diabetes, seizures, or anything? Take any medications?"

"Not that I know of. Can I call somebody on my phone?"

"No, because you've lost your phone."

"Oh, yeah, I forgot. Can't do that, then." She laughed.

"We need to get off the road because we're blocking traffic, but you can call someone when we get to the hospital. Who do you want to call?"

"Huh. The one named after the big yellow flower, you know."

"Sorry?"

She thought for a couple of minutes. "It's under R, for Rudbeck."

"Dr. Rudbeck?"

"Uh-huh."

"Which one—the medical doctor or the artist and professor?"

She held her right hand up high. "Do ya think I need an artist right now? The big guy. Dan Rudbeck. I can't think of his other name. Malgy something or other. He's kinda famous."

"Okay, yeah, I know him. We'll call him as soon as we get to the small hospital down the road, and maybe he can help." He opened his cruiser's rear right door, helped her get into the hard plastic seat in the rear compartment, fastened her seat belt, and closed the door.

They then drove the three miles to the Palatine Community Hospital emergency room, where he stopped the car and helped his inebriated passenger out. He held her by the arm as they walked to the entrance, where a triage clerk greeted them.

"What you got for us tonight, Deputy Wolford?" the fortyish, overweight clerk asked.

"Medical clearance before we go to the station, Tonia. This lady's pretty intoxicated."

Sybil stared at the clerk and held her right hand up. "I have not had one drop to drink. He is terribly mistaken."

"Sure, Ma'am. Heard that one before." Tonia smiled. "Okay, Ronnie. I'll take you back to room six. No other patients here right now. It's been slow tonight."

They went back to the patient room, where a nurse came in to take vitals and a lab technician came to draw some blood per police protocol, and Wolford let her make a phone call to Dr. Rudbeck after he found the number of the answering service, which would hopefully connect her to him.

He had arrested a few intoxicated folks in his brief law enforcement career, but this was one for the books.

AAAAA

Rudbeck Home
2105 Winthrop Street
Staffordsville, Ohio
2320 hours

Rud·beck·ia \ rəd-be-kē-ə \ noun
Any of a genus (*Rudbeckia*) of North American chiefly perennial composite herbs having large, showy flower heads with mostly yellow ray flowers and a usually conical scaly receptacle.

Dr. Daniel Rudbeck and his wife had just gone to bed. The massive fifty-eight-year old with a gray receding hairline picked up his ringing smartphone and answered the answering service number. "Hello?"

"Malgy? It's Sybil. I'm at the hospital and need your help. You're the only one who can."

"Sybil? Sybil Tegler? What's wrong? Where are you?" The caller ID was from the university answering service that connected them, so he didn't know the location. "University Hospital?"

"No, the sheriff arrested me, and I'm in the Purpletime emergency room."

"Purpletime? What?" He thought for a few seconds as his

thoughts became clearer. "Do you mean Palatine? Why are you there, and why did they arrest you? Are you okay?"

"They say I'm drunk as a skunk, but I don't even drink, and I'm going to the clink, I think."

"Why do they think that? Did they do a blood alcohol level?"

"The policeman did a breath test with some yellow thingy which was super-duper high, and he said I should be dead, but here I am, a woman barely alive, he says. They want to do some other tests on me. Can you come over here? They said I could have my own doctor come."

The officer had certainly used a portable roadside breathalyzer. They were pretty accurate in helping make roadside judgments, although the results weren't admissible in court.

"But I'm not your—jeez." He sighed, knowing he was stuck. "Okay, I'm on my way." He was a board-certified medical toxicologist, and it wasn't unusual to be consulted on weird cases in the emergency room on occasion, but not for someone who was just drunk. It was a bit unusual in that he had known Sybil for several years, and didn't know her to drink, and certainly not to excess.

On the other hand, there was always a first time for everything, and it was probably better he go than someone else who might ignore minuscule details that might be important later. Things were not always as they seemed, he learned long ago. Sybil was a bit peculiar and had some personal problems, but he'd also had his share of personal issues. He was always there to help out those less fortunate and misunderstood by others, and she deserved the benefit of the doubt.

"Where are you going, Dan?" his pharmacist wife asked sleepily as he put on his golf shirt and pants and gathered his wallet, phone, ID badge, and keys.

"I have no idea why, but I gotta go to the Palatine emergency room."

"Huh? Palatine has a toxicologic emergency? Organophosphates from a farm pesticide or something?"

He shook his head. "Nothing so esoteric. One of the medical school basic science faculty was taken to their ER by the police for medical clearance. I don't know the whole story, but she sounds pretty drunk."

"The police need your rarefied expertise for an intoxicated

person? Sounds pretty routine."

"I don't know, but it sounds kind of weird. Nothing I get involved in is routine. I'll see you later, I guess. I have no idea when I'll be home. I'll try not to wake you when I return."

He grabbed a diet cola from the refrigerator for a small jolt of caffeine as he didn't have time to make coffee, then went out to the two-car garage of his modest home and fired up his red Ford Expedition. At least he had acquired a new one last year, a rather extravagant wedding present from his new wife, but it was sorely needed; it replaced the antiquated blue one that was in such bad shape that it was often dropping rusty pieces of metal on the road; his friends said that the old "blue bomb" had terminal leprosy and needed to be euthanized. Most of the residents and even some of the medical students drove better cars than that. His wife, ex-wife, and daughter finally convinced him that he needed a new ride.

Unlike his fictional character Dr. Barclay Dixon (who lived in a spacious Beverly Hills mansion and drove multiple foreign luxury cars), he didn't care much about his image; his daughter and second wife didn't care about image, either. This, coupled with his abrasive personality and eclectic interests outside of medicine, led to his academic career not having the stratospheric trajectory he had hoped.

Lately, though, things were looking up a bit, due to his behaving better these days and making a new physician friend in rather high places. The second trip through married life had helped immensely in helping him shape up and be less immature.

Palatine Community Hospital was a tiny hospital at the west edge of Dubois County in the small Ohio town of the same name, and it took him about fifteen minutes to drive there from home. The hospital was a rural triage station, only had eight inpatient beds, and didn't care for any really sick patients, who were transferred to Staffordsville University Hospital or Columbus. In addition to the inpatient unit and emergency department, there was a small pharmacy (which his wife also managed), an outpatient physical therapy unit, and patient education center.

He pulled up to the emergency entrance, parked in the on-call physician space, walked in, put on his ID badge, and asked Tonia where his patient was; the university health care system owned it, so he was credentialed there, and most people even in little

Palatine knew who he was.

She took him back to room six of the twelve-room emergency department, as only one patient was there. He wanted to ensure that her behavior wasn't just due to ethanol, as one couldn't make assumptions, so he had the secretary order a toxicology screen, levels of methanol and ethylene glycol, and a routine chemistry panel. He approached the sheriff's deputy, sitting in the chair next to Sybil's bed.

"Hi, Deputy, I'm Dan Rudbeck."

The tall, muscular, dark-haired deputy offered his hand. "Nice to see you, sir; you're quite well-known in this town."

"Sure, I remember you, Ronnie, from some of the career days at the high school. Glad to see you with the sheriff's department after you finished college, as we need more good men like you on the force. So, what's up?"

"First thing—I know she called you, but I must ask—do you recognize this woman?" He nodded after looking at the passed-out female with matted-down black hair and rumpled clothing sprawled out on the patient bed.

"Sure, she's Dr. Sybil Tegler. She teaches and does basic science research in genetics at the medical school. She's been here for about six years."

"Huh. She's really a doctor, then?"

He nodded. "A PhD professor. Medical genetics."

"Yeah, she said that, but I wasn't sure it was true. You can guess why."

He nodded. "She's quite a sight, for sure."

Wolford took out his pen and clipboard. "How do you spell both names? Sorry, but she has no identification."

He told him the spelling. "Was she driving? How in the world did she end up all the way out here?"

Wolford shook his head. "No, it's the weirdest thing. There was a Bowling Green bus on the side of Highway 128 with a flat tire coming back from the Central Ohio football game going west, and I stopped to see what was going on. The driver and several passengers said that Dr. Sybil had tried to get on the bus, and then she started walking down the highway out of town after they told her it wasn't her ride. I found her ten minutes later, wandering down the highway almost at the county line, and I arrested her for her own safety after her PBT came back sky-high.

If it weren't for them pointing her out to me, she'd still be walking down the highway, or run over, or whatever."

"That's pretty bizarre, and she's lucky you found her." He tapped the woman on the shoulder. "Sybil? Hey, it's Dan Rudbeck. You awake?"

She looked up sleepily. "Huh? Rudbeck? Shit, I've got a headache. Can I get an Advil?"

"Sure. Sybil, where's your ID and personal belongings?"

"I don't know, Malgy. Must have lost 'em. Hey, I'm going to jail! Did you bring my bail money? I heard jail food is pretty good, and I'm hungry."

"Look, Sybil, you weren't driving. Public intoxication is just a ticket in Ohio, right? He looked toward the deputy. "I'll have them get you a meal tray."

Wolford smiled and nodded. "I already told her we only have to go to the station for some paperwork, unless she has to stay here or get transferred to the bigger hospital."

"Sybil, Deputy Wolford detained you only because you were endangering yourself by wandering down the highway, and he did the right thing. Someone could have easily hit you. Deputy, she just has to get her ticket, then she may go?"

"That's correct, Dr. Rudbeck; she has to come down with me and fill out some stuff and get her citation, then we can release her to a responsible, sober adult; otherwise, she has to sleep it off at the station, as I can't let her loose in this condition. It can be you, given that she lives alone."

He wasn't sure how Jayna would take the news of an intoxicated, dirty house guest she didn't know, given her conservative religious beliefs about drinking alcohol (he wasn't a fan of it either). "That okay with you, Sybil? You can come to my house until you feel better."

"Okay, Malgy. I trust you."

"Sybil, where the hell were you that you got so wasted? Some faculty party in one of the suites? Whoever gave you all that booze should be ashamed. I've been to several events with you and never saw you even drink at all."

"That's the thing, I didn't have anything to drink. I did go to the ball game but just had some pop."

"Regular or diet?"

"Regular. I don't like zero sugar pop. Why is that important,

Malgy?"

"It might be. Did you have anything to eat?"

"A large popcorn with extra butter, a candy bar, and a couple of hot dogs."

Not a very healthy meal. "Any chance you picked up someone else's drink that might have been spiked with something?"

She shook her head. "No way. The friend I was with just had some bottled water."

"Could someone have slipped some alcohol or something else in your drink?"

She shook her head. "I don't see how that could've happened."

A blood alcohol level that high would've required multiple drinks anyway, but, like the police, he had learned to be skeptical of excuses that didn't make sense. The nurse came in and showed him the initial lab results.

"Oh, come on now. We all make mistakes, Sybil, although your lab blood alcohol is 0.41 percent." That value was over the lethal threshold (0.40 percent) established by the National Institute on Alcohol Abuse and Alcoholism. "To a non-drinker, it would certainly be lethal. I don't get it. The rest of your toxicology screen is negative."

"I am dead serious, Malgy. I didn't have nothin' to drink."

He frowned. "That's impossible. I can smell it on your breath, which would probably burn right now if I tried to light it."

"Is there any way I could be intoxicated without having consumed liquor?"

He thought for several minutes, noting that she was sometimes forming fairly complex sentences, but not others, although her speech was very slurred. He then noted that her evening "meal" of popcorn, candy bars, hot dogs, and regular soda was very high in carbohydrates.

He was a specialist in weird stuff, and his new theory was also an explanation for her apparent high tolerance for ethanol, because she was exposed to it all the time. "There is one possibility, but only about a hundred cases have ever been reported in the literature. I've only seen one in my entire career."

She sat up and smiled, which was interesting because a few minutes earlier, she was almost incoherent and now seemed nearly alert. "Really? Do I have it?"

He made a "T" sign with his hands. "Time out, Sybil. There's a ton of testing we must do first that will take several days at least to get the results."

"Can you give me a hint as to what it is?"

"It's a rare condition where your own intestinal flora ferments carbohydrates to ethanol, producing a state of intoxication without having consumed alcohol. It's called auto-brewery syndrome. Have you ever had any bariatric or other intestinal surgeries? They place you at higher risk for the condition."

She shook her head and lay back on her pillow. "Nope, no surgeries, no medicines, and I never heard of that condition. What now, Malgy? To the jail? Do I get to wear an orange jail suit? That would be cool. I also want a mugshot for my sweatshirt. That would give me some street cred with the students, to get busted."

He laughed. "You're *not* going to jail or getting a booking photo, and I don't believe advertising this unfortunate incident on your clothing or getting jail street cred is a great idea with you going up for tenure soon. It's a bad enough situation already. I'm thinking now that we should admit you to the big hospital until we can get this figured out, then we can run some tests." He looked towards the deputy. "We can send her to the medical school hospital; then she can come get her citation after she leaves, right?"

Wolford nodded. "I guess that would be okay, or I can bring it by her room tomorrow evening on my next shift. I can't give it to her now, as she isn't coherent enough to sign the ticket. Good call about going to Uni—she's probably too drunk to keep at the station."

"Okay, Malgy. I gotta stop by home and get some things, though. I'll need some clothes since I don't get to wear a jail suit."

"Why do we need to do that, and how are you going to get into your house? You don't have any keys, and the hospital has gowns for you to wear, and I can get you some orange scrubs from the hospital laundry if you desire the inmate look."

"Key's under the mat, if I can find it. It'll take just a minute. I want my own jammies."

He rolled his eyes. "Well, okay. I guess it isn't too far out of the way." She didn't know her address, but the hospital had her information on file. The lengths he went to in order to please his faculty were extraordinary.

AAAAA

About ninety minutes later, he had returned to his red Ford Expedition after dropping Sybil off at the main hospital and handing her off to the resident admission team, after they had stopped at her house and obtained her personal items; he had given them explicit instructions on her diet and what additional tests to order (it was good to be the boss), and he proceeded to drive home and least get three hours more sleep before getting up again.

Dr. Daniel Andrew Rudbeck was the Director of Internal Medicine at Staffordsville University Hospital and assistant dean of Central Ohio University College of Medicine—Staffordsville, a regional campus fifty miles southeast of Columbus. He was an unusual quasi-celebrity in his hometown of about 72,000 people, and instantly recognizable to most locals. He was a board-certified medical toxicologist and head of the university's fellowship program. Due to his esoteric expertise in poisons, he was frequently involved in cases involving the Dubois County Medical Examiner and the Staffordsville Police Department, where the leaders of those areas were quite familiar with him and not always welcoming of his intrusiveness into legal affairs. However, he had an exceptional talent for uncovering clues others could not, so they had a begrudging tolerance for him. The Medical Examiner often told him that even a broken clock was right twice a day.

But the six-three, 245-pound, fifty-eight-year-old physician's most extraordinary claim to fame came in high school when his 60,000-word novel "Amalgam-Man" featuring the incredible Renaissance man Dr. Barclay J. Dixon, an MD/PhD who was board certified in multiple specialties and was an expert in all things—not just medicine, science, and the arts, but the ladies as well. This over-the-top book won first place in the 1981 Ohio High School Literary Society contest, but that was just the beginning for Amalgam-Man.

Despite a failed high school play he created based on the character, a TV movie of the week and subsequent TV series followed, thanks to a good friend's cousin, a Hollywood screenwriter. Back in the early 1980s, he was upset that the TV series was a parody of private investigators, but today he tended to laugh at it, knowing that it was quite an accomplishment back then to have a TV series last two seasons; he did get credit as the creator. He had hoped to actually be in an episode, but that never materialized due to his needing to perform "real" work (trying to become a physician, a fairly time-demanding career).

Today, that accomplishment wasn't such a big deal, with over 1,500 TV channels, more than twenty streaming services, not to mention social media, and AI-created videos. Three longer novels followed (The Prince of Oaks, The Lightning Giant, and The Sulphur Shadow), with little financial success; he had created his own publishing imprint, Amalgam Press, as no major publisher was interested in these lengthy literary masterpieces. Too intellectual for the dull masses, he thought. Amalgam-Man had run his course, it seemed.

People had often ridiculed him because of his creation, but he laughed all the way to the bank as he had made enough money from those improbable ventures to graduate from college and medical school with minimal debt, as, unlike Dixon, he didn't come from money; he considered that quite an accomplishment.

He realized long ago that his real life wouldn't parallel that of his fictional character, created by the pubescent, one-dimensional mind of a sixteen-year-old. His diverse creative qualities made him unique; in the years that followed, his eclectic, unfiltered projects were almost his undoing in the buttoned-up world of academic medicine, and his success with Amalgam-Man was not to happen again in other ventures.

Because of his abrasive, often politically incorrect nature, he was frequently passed over for promotion because of the fear of what embarrassing things the loud, ungainly man might say or do. He had made several politically incorrect videos with the residents for their graduation banquets over the years—which might have been okay if he were in his late twenties, not his late forties.

His outrageous video skits often made fun of the administration, which was problematic since he *was* part of the administration. Some of them were quite elaborate, such as "The Resident Who Wouldn't Die," in which the other residents tried to get rid of an incompetent and disliked colleague, but he kept returning from the dead after each cliffhanger "chapter" where he met a different doom. The best attempt to "destroy" him (unsuccessful as he somehow returned afterward after each chapter) was when he launched a flaming dummy off the tenth-floor hospital tower into the creek below. His firefighter cousin (now the fire chief) was none too happy about that, and both she and his first wife Charlotte thought his time should be better spent on academic pursuits rather than wasting time with those activities.

Other skits, like the elaborate and expensive to produce "Ward Trek," poked fun at various pejorative patient stereotypes, such as "gomers:" patients who were so undesirable they were weaponized and fired like torpedoes from the enemy ship; his famous line "our shields can't take another hit from those damn gomers" in a British accent was immortalized on social media after some of his videos leaked out. His daughter (ten at the time) was given a small part as an alien in that one, to her mother's chagrin.

As usual, he didn't listen to his ex-wife, cousin, or former executive coach, Elizabeth Beckwith (who gave up on him). He even had to meet with Human Resources a couple of times for "sensitivity training" due to some of those productions and a disparaging patient term he coined long ago: P^3 (P-cubed, or "Piss Poor Protoplasm"). So there was a price to pay for doing as he always pleased.

He was well-respected in his field nationally, as he had authored several review books on toxicology aimed at medical students, residents, and fellows. Not one to leave well enough alone, he then further diversified his academic portfolio by writing a humorous medical text called "Toxicology for the Unmotivated"—using Barclay Jarvis Dixon, MD, PhD as a pseudonym. It contained many photos of scantily-clad young women (mostly attractive student nurses he had paid). This manuscript, as would befit any tome written by the early 1980's-era, politically incorrect Dixon, was clearly sexist, even by mid-2000s standards.

TFTU was famous as an underground book and was actually considered a pretty good text if one ignored the outrageous extraneous material; but, despite the *nom de plume*, in the end most academicians knew only one person who could've possibly written it, as the unusual combination of medical toxicology expertise, high-quality model photography, and fine writing skill was pretty unique. Whenever he thought he'd destroyed all the copies in the hospital (before e-books), another bootlegged copy turned up in the medical library or a resident's pocket. TFTU was readily available as a download from the Internet and was a constant reminder that things released into the public domain would remain forever.

However, the book got rave reviews and made him a legend with the male medical students and residents, but with administration and his conservative then-wife (who didn't appreciate all the photos of his early-twentysomething "models" in bikinis or their underwear while demonstrating medical equipment or playing "patients")—not so much. His second, very Christian wife was also not a fan of that fine contribution to medical science. His daughter, however, thought it was pretty funny.

His typical, unorthodox academic process was one step forward and two steps backward—a quality piece or two of scholarly work followed by something far less productive, with occasional distasteful excursions like TFTU and obnoxious video skits requiring extensive cleanup.

Another thing that the higher-ups had disdain for was his stochastic antics around accreditation site visitors, which could cause big problems for the hospital if offended. He hated arrogant behavior and made no bones about telling them off if he felt they disrespected people possessing inferior genetic material beneath their hallowed academic standards. He was also fond of joking around, and he discovered that most of those folks had their sense of humor purged by the accrediting body they were a member of.

He didn't care, but those incidents didn't help his career. He had learned to be more compliant in that regard and more help than liability. It didn't hurt that he uncovered a corrupt medical education board site visitor two years ago who was involved in a massive hospital ransomware scheme. So, on occasion, he was right, and his hunches saved multiple healthcare systems billions of dollars.

And yet he was always a champion of the common man, the underdog, because he often felt like that himself. That was one reason he wanted to help Sybil Tegler, who wasn't terribly popular and seemed sad most of the time without many friends. Her little Highway 128 intoxication adventure would not sit well with the university higher-ups come review time.

The blue-collar physician had been known to get into heated arguments with his colleagues about things he thought were right, and had no tolerance for physicians or administrators who treated people under them disrespectfully. He was sincere and didn't tolerate any unethical behavior. He had uncovered a crooked election for medical staff president a couple of years ago that many others would have let slide. The stakes were relatively low, but he felt no crime should go unpunished.

But his most rewarding activity was mentoring medical students, residents, and fellows because he had the uncanny ability to get more out of an average performer than they could get out of themselves. Part of that was because he was no superstar himself and had made his share of mistakes; he realized that many great mentors, like stellar athletic coaches, were people who could relate to the masses, and true superstars seemed to lack that quality.

People had come to admire his integrity, and some probably feared his potential instability; he was a large, loud, powerful man who had learned to box quite well from his Golden Gloves champion father (one of the few good things his dad did for him). Altercations with him weren't desired by people with any sense.

His office was cluttered with old cameras (he was a photography buff), vintage action figures, various photographs, dozens of small gifts graduating students and residents had given him, a couple of his regionally famous daughter's surreal watercolor paintings, and other random stuff. He loved to tinker with gadgets, and his dream was to have a specialized suit for paramedics in the field, which would contain its own air supply, have augmented strength, and offer dozens of poison antidotes and medical treatments for patients in the field.

The AM-1 prototype, a lithium-powered carbon-fiber exoskeleton of shadowy Ukrainian origin, had been used once, when he flew in on a medical helicopter to save his old college girlfriend Jayna from carbon monoxide poisoning with his novel CO scavenger neuroglobin-44. While that rescue succeeded, the cost of this complex device was unfortunately prohibitive to mass produce (given the suit's microprocessors) and likely had limited utility for everyday use.

After that, he became a regional hero and was offered a prestigious job in Chicago as Director of the American Board of Physician Education. However, he decided to turn it down and stay in Staffordsville to pursue his renewed relationship with Jayna.

Jayna Marie Blackwell was one year behind him in high school, and they dated seriously in college—although she had gone to Ohio State and he to Xavier. He was going through some immense personal problems then with his father's alcoholism, and, due to his low self-esteem at the time, he "ghosted" her and broke contact, and wondered why she didn't want anything to do with him when he finally called her again over a year later. He found out later she had seriously thought they might eventually get married and was worried that something had happened to him. Later, he realized that it was incredibly selfish, that she deserved to have an explanation and closure to the situation. At that point in his life, he had difficulty meeting his emotional needs. He felt like a complete failure.

Jayna was a devout Christian who lived in Texas for nearly three decades after marrying a man eleven years her senior, Dallas attorney Samuel Claymore, whom she had met at a church mission trip shortly after graduating from pharmacy school. She had three sons with him (one of whom, Robert, was dating his daughter). Sam died of fulminant COVID pneumonia in 2021, and she moved back to Staffordsville to take a job as director of the pharmacy after her position in Dallas was eliminated due to a hospital merger. Her first encounter with him was awkward, but they eventually started dating after she realized the immense personal problems he had dealt with and how he had changed.

Like many Texans, she owned firearms and was an expert markswoman. She was markedly different than his first wife, the elegant, upper-crust French-Canadian forensic pathologist Charlotte Boisseau, who was a wonderful person, but somewhat self absorbed and essentially concerned about her image (his political incorrectness and overall abrasiveness were not conducive to climbing the social ladder that she craved). After their divorce nine years ago, Charlie married more "mainstream" chemical engineer Jeff Garrett and lived in his old house, while he purchased a smaller ranch house nearby.

In contrast, Jayna didn't care much about her image or climbing the social ladder. It took a while for her to get back with him, given their past history and how he had suddenly disappeared from her life decades before. But underneath a shy exterior and her conservative persona, she was highly passionate and amazingly fun-loving and, eventually, became more accepting of his alter ego's persona than Charlie ever was, despite not having much enthusiasm for Barclay Dixon in their youth. That wasn't surprising, as Barclay was a sexist womanizer of the early 1980s; rumor was that he had slept with 25,000 different women (an average of eight women per day over ten years). Jayna didn't care too much for that particular trait or his alcohol and tobacco addictions. Like Jayna, he completely abstained from alcohol (she for religious reasons; he because of his dad's alcoholism and probable genetic predisposition to addictions himself).

They married in a small Methodist church ceremony one year ago, and she moved into Dan's modest house on Winthrop Street. She still owned her old house on Barker Street for when her children came to visit, although she and Dan planned to move to a new home and sell hers eventually.

Chapter One

An elegant bar in a five-star hotel
2130 hours

Amal·gam \ əmalgəm\ noun
1 : an alloy of mercury with another metal
2 : a mixture of different things

Dr. Barclay Dixon walked through the sophisticated, decorous bar, looking for companionship, as several young ladies smiled and winked at him. He was used to such attention from the fairer sex, given his movie-star looks, vast wealth, and impeccable taste, but he had become bored with women in their twenties and thirties, despite their youthful vitality. He was looking for someone with a little more maturity and greater intellect than his usual dates. Such a woman could be hard to find. Mature women could also be quite dangerous, he had learned. Danger was a fact of life in his business. Sometimes pleasure and danger went together.

He then spied the familiar, exotic-looking, purple-haired

woman sporting a pale lavender evening gown, and he couldn't believe his good luck. Or was it bad luck, considering who she was? He never knew for sure with this character. He decided to roll the dice and headed to her at the bar, knowing he might regret it in the end—and it really might be his end if he wasn't careful. Hopefully, it would be enjoyable in the short term, since this might be his last night on Earth.

"Well, if it isn't my old friend, Ms. Alexandra Nina Volkova. We had fun tangling when you had on that purple leather catsuit at our last encounter. Pound for pound, you are quite the grappler. I realize now how much I like wrestling. Wrestling pretty women, that is. Guys—forget it."

"Why, the famous, erudite Dr. Barclay Dixon is in my midst," the mid-fiftyish woman said in a thick Russian accent as she turned towards him and sneered. "I see that medicine is only one of your many interests now that you have also taken on being a secret agent and have become a thorn in my side."

"Now, that's not a very nice thing to say."

She smirked. "Oh, I forgot I am in the company of the amazing member of *Homo sapiens* composed of mercury alloy, a workmanlike material suitable only for lowly dental fillings. Or is it *Homo erectus?* Mercury is toxic, so that you know. Just like you." She stared back at her drink and stirred the ice cubes with her manicured right index finger. "Don't you have somewhere more important to be, Dr. Dixon?"

"I have to go where my talents are most needed. May I buy you a refill, Ms. Volkova? It looks like you're drinking whiskey on the rocks, and that stuff will melt your red nail polish clean off. What happened to your vodka martinis? You Russians sure know how to scarf that Stoli down."

She puffed out her small but nicely curvaceous chest. Good things often came in small packages, he remembered.

"How dare you perpetuate such disparaging stereotypes about my great people?" She hummed a few bars of the Russian National Anthem and held up a half-filled glass of amber liquid. "Iced tea, Dr. Dixon. I allow no substances to impair my mind these days, as I constantly must be on my toes to deal with the likes of you. Get with the program since it's not the 1980s any longer."

"Yes, I finally gave that up, along with my expensive pipe

habit. Can't smoke it anywhere these days, anyway, as it makes me feel like a criminal. Vaping didn't seem like a good thing to take up; there's no elegance or class about it. There was just something comforting about the ritual of firing up a fifty-thousand-dollar Dunhill Briar pipe filled with the finest aromatic tobacco flown in several times weekly by my custom tobacconist."

"I know what you mean. I stopped smoking expensive French cigarettes years ago as I am concerned about my health. Still, I did not think that mere money was an issue to the eminently successful Barclay Dixon, a master of high finance, medicine, and the arts."

"It's not, but I have learned over time that addictions are not good."

"Humph. Does that include your addiction to amorous dalliances?"

He shook his head. "Of course not. That is a biological necessity, not an addiction."

"A matter of opinion. That particular addiction is apparently incurable." She rubbed his balding head. "Well, the great Barclay Dixon is losing his thick, luxurious hair. This cannot be possible. And some gray! It makes you look distinguished, you silver fox."

"Hair loss is a sign of high testosterone, you know."

"I see, how special for you. I have heard that recent medical studies say too much testosterone is bad for your health."

"Even more reason why we should live life to the fullest right now, before my time runs out. Therefore, let's go to my opulent hotel room."

The purple-haired woman sneered at him. "As usual, you waste no time getting down to business. What shall we do there? Watch Robot Monster? Play Scrabble? Eat popcorn?"

"If you don't know, you're not as smart as I thought."

"I must disagree with you. I'm way smarter than you think."

"At least the mini-bar tab will be cheaper now that you've stopped drinking Stoli."

"We must see if the concierge has a Scrabble set on hand."

He nodded. "Probably. I doubt they are in high demand."

"I hope Robot Monster is on pay-per-view. It is my favorite. Its soundtrack was done by famed composer Elmer Bernstein, whose mother was born in the great Soviet Union."

"I agree, that was a fantastic soundtrack."

AAAAA

First Methodist Church
3445 W. Oldman Street
Staffordsville, Ohio
0925 hours

Dan and Jayna took their places in the choir of First Methodist Church, the oldest church of that denomination in Staffordsville, although it was one of the smallest. The town had grown since it was built, and many individuals wanted to go to the larger churches with their greater prestige and resources.

Jayna and her family had belonged to that church when she was growing up, and it only seemed natural that she would want to go there when she returned to town three years ago.

The building was old, built in the 1900s, and wasn't large or fancy by today's standards. It had beautiful stained glass windows, and the outside architecture and indoor wooden accents had a quality not often seen today. But it wasn't new and shiny.

Having faith in his life now was comforting, as he certainly didn't have it growing up. He rarely set foot in a church when he was a kid, and it was obvious his parents didn't. His dad, Bobby, probably lived the most un-Christian life one could lead. Bobby had alcoholism and had been in jail for DUI or fighting in bars numerous times. He knew all the bail bond agents in town who were necessary for bailing out his dad at all hours of the night. Not something to be proud of.

Bobby was also known to abuse cannabis and illegally obtain controlled substances like opioids and benzodiazepines, which got him into even greater trouble with the law.

Bobby was also verbally and physically abusive to the family, but that stopped when he became old enough to take care of his dad; after he kicked his dad's butt a couple of times, he never did it again. He talked about those traumas with his psychologist, Deanna Palmer, as he wasn't proud of having to do those things.

His mother, Carolyn, wasn't very evangelical, and he always felt that might have helped her deal with his dad. They were both gone now, may they rest in peace. He didn't see his older sister, Becky, very often, as she had left town right after high school to live in Minnesota, where she didn't have to deal with her parents' dysfunctions. He never was upset at her about leaving, as she deserved to have her own life, even though that left him as the person to take care of all the problems.

He enjoyed being a choirist, although he knew the two reasons the church leadership asked him were: (a) he was married to Jayna, a pretty good soprano and organizer; (b) he was one of the few true basses in the area, and had a fairly good natural singing voice. The normal bass range was E2 to E4, but he could easily get down to C2 and sustain that note. He did release a CD of "Amalgam-Man's Greatest Hits" about fifteen years ago, which did not earn any recording awards.

Jayna insisted he get a voice coach, and he found a suitable mentor at the nearby university, who helped him with his music reading and vocal range, so that he at least became a passable bass in one of the choir's fifteen members. They were glad to have him, as his distinctive voice and popularity in the community probably helped increase the size of the congregation.

After the service, they always helped serve at the church social hour; in early October, it was still nice enough outside to have it in the courtyard. He enjoyed the simplicity of it all, with the focus being friendship and socialization rather than climbing the corporate or academic ladder to put one more notch in his belt. He used to fly first class all the time, and belonged to all the airport lounges (Commander's Club was his favorite, with its free food, WiFi, drinks (wasted on him because he didn't drink), and other symbols of pseudo-luxury).

He always thought that was the kind of life he wanted, but he found it lacking in the end, as the people were superficial and cared only about their own career advancement. First Methodist Church may not have been fancy, but it was full of kind, caring people who followed God's Word. He was happier now than he had been in a long time, with the type of life he never thought he wanted. They lived in his modest home on Winthrop Street and had everything they needed.

After the church reception, they drove to a small café to have a light lunch (his meals were much lighter today than in the past, due to his desire to keep his weight down). He was still contemplating the events of the past twelve hours, with a drunken Sybil Tegler found wandering down Highway 128. He needed to go in and check on her and decide on further testing, which might take a few days to arrange. Hopefully, she could go home today or tomorrow and return in a few days after a follow-up was arranged. Living close enough to the hospital (five minutes) was good, so going there on a Sunday afternoon wouldn't take long.

Hopefully, he and Jayna could relax the rest of the day without any new emergencies. He had a hunch it would be a busy few weeks ahead. There was just something unsettling about the whole Tegler thing.

Chapter Two

A Dark Old Warehouse
Somewhere in Columbus, Ohio
Saturday, 1322 hours

Dr. Daniel Rudbeck's superlative mind contemplated the wonders of the universe as he pulled on the handcuffs holding him to a padded metal chair that was bolted to the floor on the cool October afternoon. The blindfold the woman had put on him kept him from seeing anything, but he could hear his wife next to him, breathing calmly.

"You okay, Jayna?"

Silence for a few seconds as he could hear metal clacking against metal next to him. "What's that, eminent polymath Barclay Jarvis Dixon? 'Am I okay?' What the heck do you think?" Jayna Claymore Rudbeck sighed. "I'm blindfolded and shackled to a metal chair bolted to the floor, so, no, I've had better experiences, you big dummy. This event is not turning out to be the convivial afternoon you had promised."

"Sorry you don't find it enjoyable and relaxing . . . a chance for meditation, mindfulness, and to get away from it all. Leave those responsibilities and worries behind. You might end up in email jail for letting them pile up and overloading your inbox. Hey, I made a joke! Email jail, get the irony?"

"Oh, sure. I'm glad you think this is relaxing and funny. I try to indulge your eclectic interests and unusual activities, but you always have to carry things to the extreme; you never have any middle ground. This is like something from one of your crazy novels or the TV show."

"What a stupid question. Anything worth doing is worth doing correctly, and my novels are fine literature for the intellectually elite."

"Yeah, right. When you wanted to do an escape room, I thought it would be something simple and fun that we could all enjoy, not creepy and weird, but, no, no, not for *you*. You had to find the most challenging one possible, right?"

"Why, of course. Such sinister suspense adds to the realism. Why would we want something that's too easy?"

"I really feel that some weirdo is going to come in, chop us into little pieces, and have a grisly barbecue with our remains. Maybe my remains—you would be too tough and fatty to chew on. They would spit you out."

"I resent that, as I am the prime sirloin of human beings. There is no finer quality."

"Oh, come on, Bonus Mom," Dr. Genevieve Suzanne Rudbeck said, who was sitting next to Jayna in a similar simulated predicament. "Lighten up. You know that Barclay Dixon always must have the best of everything, including excitement and adventure. Creepy and weird is right up his alley."

"No comment," Jayna said.

"Well, arguing isn't going to help, so how do we get out of this fix before the kidnapper comes back?" he asked. "I will never live it down if we don't escape before time runs out."

"Shut up, Dad, I'm thinking," Evie said. "My handcuffs seem to be attached to the chair back with some kind of weird lock."

"Mine is attached to the chair by what seems to be a regular padlock. Big deal, as I don't have the key. The chair is heavy metal and bolted to the floor," he said. "Even I, with my titanic masculine strength, can't move it. However, nothing is ever hopeless where I am concerned."

"I said shut up, moron from whom I received half my DNA—naturally, you can't break hardened steel, and the elegant intellect of PhD shall prevail over the crude brawn of MD this day. But mine doesn't feel like a padlock. It's something different. Almost cylindrical."

"Now, Evie, you shouldn't call your father a moron," his very Christian wife said sarcastically. "Honor thy mother and thy father. Exodus 20:12."

"You're right, that's far too generous and an insult to morons. He's an idiot with an IQ less than twenty-five, at least for today."

"That's better," Jayna said softly.

"However, the device affixing my cuffs to the chair isn't a padlock, but some type of wire is coming from it. I don't think it's a bomb, but I guess it's something important, or it wouldn't be there."

"Escape rooms often have dummy distractors. It may not do anything at all to waste our precious time," he said confidently.

"Dad . . . this is your first one, you said, so you don't know anything about it. But I assume you two don't have that wire?"

"No, but what do you think it is?" Jayna asked. "Be careful."

"What, an escape room is gonna explode or electrocute me? It feels like an insulated electrical cable for charging a phone or something. Chill, and let me pull on it to see what I find, as someone has to get the ball rolling. The ticket to escape has to be something one of us can actually do." He heard a loud "kerplunk" a few seconds later as a heavy object hit the wooden floor of the old jail cell.

"What was that?" he asked.

"At the other end of this wire is a USB-C connector, which I must have pulled out of a power bank. The lock holding my handcuffs to the chair is therefore electromagnetic. When I disconnected the power, it immediately unlocked and fell to the floor. I'm loose from the chair but still cuffed and blindfolded. It's a start, I guess."

"I can't feel the keyholes," Jayna said. "Usually, I can twist my hands and feel them on the other side if they're applied with the keyholes opposite my hands. I'm pretty flexible, but these bracelets only move in one direction but don't rotate, as there's no chain between the cuffs."

"How would you know anything about them?" Evie asked curiously. "You're a smart lady, but *that's* not a topic I would expect you to have expertise in. What gives?"

Jayna sighed. "Evie, you were an only child. I grew up with three older brothers and raised three very rambunctious sons, so we played lots of cops and robbers with me always being the one who got 'arrested' since I was the smallest, and I always had a secret hidden key our cop uncle gave me so I could 'escape' from the plywood 'jail' we had in the back yard. We were free-range kids with essentially no adult supervision growing up, so we did pretty much whatever we wanted when we didn't have school, as long as we were home for supper."

"Yes, those were the days. Also, don't forget that you were really arrested two years ago for shooting an accreditation site visitor with your Glock. Luckily, we had proof he drew first, and you were exonerated," he said. "I always hated that rotten bastard, and he's rotting in prison now. Most people just dream of shooting those SOBs at the accreditation board, but you actually did it."

"I will always cherish the experience of shooting Roland Okdar in the hand," Jayna said sardonically. "Anyway, if yours are like mine, they're hinged, and you can't rotate your hands, which will make it impossible for you to get yourself free even with the key since the keyholes are on the other side where your hands can't reach."

"But if I had the key, I could undo yours since I am at least mobile now."

"Yes," Jayna said. "But we don't."

"Well, it would be nice to have the key. There has to be one somewhere," he said. "They wouldn't do this to us if there's no way of getting free."

"If it's in the room, it will take me forever to find it while blindfolded." She paused for a few seconds. "Hey, wait a minute. There *is* a small object tied to the side of the chair with a string, but it doesn't feel like a key," Evie said. "Some type of magnetic key, maybe?"

"No," Jayna said. "I could feel they were mechanical cuffs when our female host put them on me. Describe the object as best you can."

"It feels like a skinny, flexible piece of springy metal, maybe one-eighth inch in width, and approximately two inches long.

There's a tiny handle on the end where the string's attached."

"That's a *shim*," Jayna said excitedly. "You should be able to get free with that."

"A what?" Evie asked. "Never heard of it."

"If you don't have the handcuff key, it's often possible to use a thin piece of metal to jam between the ratchet and the pawl and disengage the two so that the cuff arm becomes free. Easy peasy, especially since they supplied you with a tool designed for that specific purpose, but most people would have no idea what it's for or how to use it."

"Why not just give us the key?" he asked.

"That would be too easy. You wanted challenging—this is it, Dan. Can't have it both ways."

"You have experience in this, too?" Evie asked again. "Your diverse skill set makes you the perfect mate for my dad."

"This day, I'm not so sure about the latter. I'll tell you about it at lunch, assuming we survive and don't *become* someone's lunch, except for your dad. No one will consume him. Yecch."

Evie laughed. "So, what do I do now?"

"Take the metal strip and insert it gently between the ratchet and the pawl on your other cuff. You may need to close it a little bit to get it to go in. With some force, it should slide right in, disengage the two, and release the cuff."

"The ratchet is the part with the little teeth that can get tighter?"

"Yes, on the swinging arm. The pawl is the part on the inside with teeth that cause it to lock."

"The teeth are all the way in on both sides, though."

"Doesn't matter, just stick it into the groove."

"I'll try. I have large hands for a girl, and these things don't allow for much flexibility. I just don't want to drop it." Several minutes passed. "Okay, it worked, Jayna! That's amazing. I had no idea you could do that; it's like in the movies. It'll be easier in front with the blindfold off for the other one."

"Wow, this is tough," he said. "We got our money's worth."

"Be quiet, Dan," Jayna said. "Now take mine off. Your dad's are probably an oversized model, but they should work the same way."

"Hey, why does she get loose before me?"

"Silence, Dan. I'm closer to her. I also have better fine motor skills."

"Huh? Since when?"

Jayna sighed. "I thought Barclay J. Dixon knew everything, including all details of human biology and neurology, since he was an MD/PhD who was board certified in ten specialties—"

"Thirteen. Internal medicine and eight subspecialties, surgery, neurology, radiology, and emergency medicine."

"Oh, my bad. But all people, regardless of size, have roughly the same number of touch receptors in each fingertip—about three thousand. But mine are more tightly concentrated in less surface area, because my hands are smaller than yours and Evie's. So, I have more touch receptors per square millimeter, giving me better fine sensorimotor control than y'all. It's a biological fact that women are typically superior at fine, detailed motor tasks."

"While I am clearly superior at the 'big' motor skills, like heavy lifting and smashing things," he roared in his deep bass voice. "Need those too, hon."

"Doesn't help us much now, does it?" Jayna said harshly.

"Well, no . . . but we may need them later," he said quietly.

"Doubtful we will run into some zombies you need to punch out, Dad. Okay, I'm loose from the other one. Here, let me take yours off," Evie said. A few minutes later, he could feel Jayna removing his. "I am being kind to you when I should just leave you here, Dr. Dixon."

"That wouldn't be very nice. And your complex descriptions of everything are eating up our precious time."

"I'm just acting like you. Okay, now that we're all free, now what?" Jayna asked, growing impatient, as Evie retrieved her eyeglasses from the table. "We still need to get out of this jail cell and then out of the room."

"Here." He found a hole in the wall containing a small, clear plastic tube. Inside was a rolled-up index card.

"What's it say, Dad?"

He put on the reading glasses on a lanyard around his neck. "It reads 'HFMC QMVT CMBV.' Gibberish." He thought for half a minute. "It may be a Caesar cipher."

"A what?" Jayna asked.

"A Caesar cipher replaces each plaintext letter with a different one. What do we get if we replace the letter with the one after it? I for H, G for F, etc."

"IGND RNWU DNCW. More gibberish," Evie said.

"Try the one before. G for H, E for F, etc."

"*GELB PLUS BLAU,*" his daughter replied.

"German, there ya go. Yellow plus blue."

"Luckily, Amalgam-Man is multilingual. Except in French," Evie said.

"You are lucky to have me. Well, that was easy. Evie, you're the expert on colors. The answer is—"

"Green, of course," Evie said. "That's simple."

"Yeah, but what is 'green' the key to now? There has to be something else, and this room isn't all that big." Jayna looked under the old wooden table. "There's something taped under this table." She removed the tape and laid it on the table.

"It's a cylindrical Kryptex lock which requires a five-letter word to open. Green opens it, I bet." He pulled apart the cylinder, and a large, heavy metal key fell out. "It looks like it could fit in that jail door."

Jayna put the old key in the jail cell door, which unlocked it. "Well, that gets us out of here, but there's still another door to go, with a four-digit digital combination lock."

He looked at the digital timer on the wall. "Twelve minutes to go before the bitter end. How many combinations?"

"9,999, of course, duh," Evie said.

"Right. Too many to guess," Jayna said. "We need to find a clue."

"Let me look in here." Evie went through some drawers in an old chest and found various items, including a bag of gummy candies, some playing cards, a dozen assorted keys, a pencil, a pad of paper, and several small toy animals.

"We want something that has four categories," Jayna said. "The keys must be a distractor, as they don't go to anything. There are four suits of cards, but that doesn't help."

"Looky here," Evie said. "There are four different types of gummies: little bears, pineapples, worms, and rabbits." She separated them into groups. "Nine bears, four pineapples, eight worms, and three rabbits."

"What if there was a zero in the combination?" Jayna asked.

"My guess is they wouldn't include that. Anyway, the combination could be 9483. The possibilities are that, 4983, 3849, and so on. That would be 4! or twenty-four different combinations."

"Or another Caesar cipher where you add or subtract from that," he added.

"Seems overly complex to accomplish in the allotted time," Jayna said. "Evie, you write down all twenty-four while I try them all."

8493 was the ticket, as it opened the door, and they were free, with three whole minutes to spare, which would've been more had his wife not given expansive explanations for things like finger touch receptors. For a very introverted individual, she could be far more talkative than he at times, with a sharp intellect that matched his.

"I guess it was kind of fun, at that," Jayna said. "Thanks for arranging it."

"Oh, *now* I get thanks, huh? Twenty minutes ago, you were both calling me names, and you were going to leave me in there. So, lunch is on me," he said.

"That's so magnanimous of you, Dad. You can pay the tab, but Jayna and I will get to pick the venue as we have solved most of the clues. We'd be dead meat by now if not for us, or at least embarrassed by not escaping in time."

"Hey, wait a minute—"

"Evie's right, Dan. We're the ones who got us loose. Jayna mostly."

"I did contribute to solving the German puzzle."

"Yeah, that was so complicated," Jayna said. "But it was essential, and everyone did their part to the best of their ability, which counts. Some of us have more ability than others."

The two women looked at him intensely. "Okay, okay, I can see I'm outnumbered. Working Guy's Buddy is out of the question, I guess."

"That place is off limits to you anyway," his wife said, pointing at him. "I have spies out there telling me if you frequent that place."

"Amalgam-Man is a master of disguise. You'll never know."

AAAAA

Super Sprouts Café
University District
Columbus, Ohio

"This place is really nice, Evie," Jayna said as she took a bite of her avocado toast. "Do you come here often?"

"Yeah, Rob and I come here a lot after work. They have really good stuff. Right, Dad?" Evie said, laughing.

"Truly outstanding, ladies. I must come here more often." He took a bite of his gourmet peanut butter and jelly sandwich, the closest thing to "comfort food" available at this exclusively plant-based upscale casual restaurant in Columbus' University District. "Simply delectable."

"Do I detect a note of sarcasm in your voice, Dan?" Jayna asked softly.

"Oh, no, no, Heaven forbid. I need to eat better, which is healthier than the tenderloin or burger I would've had at Working Guy's Buddy."

"Well, I think it's simply wonderful," Jayna said, taking a sip of iced tea. "I wish we had this in Staffordsville."

"So, Jayna, you said you had a story to tell about the cool trick you instructed me on."

"No, she doesn't," he said. "It has no practical use."

"Yes, I do, and I saved the high school spring play with that skill, so it does have use. On that day, you were useless."

"How in the world did you do that?"

He held his hand up. "Jayna, you don't—"

"Quiet, your offspring needs to know this. Evie, we were doing a big production of Guys and Dolls in my junior year, and I was the dramatics student production manager, as I was a better organizer and director than actor. Guess which senior was playing the policeman on the beat?"

"Barclay Dixon, of course."

"Certainly, although it was only a small part, which was the best he could get after the abysmal failure of his 'Amalgam-Man' play. Dan was talented at many things, but acting wasn't one of them.

"It was about time for Dan to go on for one of his few scenes with the others, and we wondered where the heck he was. Not that his role was vital, but cute Debbie McGuire was one of the female leads, and she was missing, too. Your dad had the hots for her, so I suspected they were together and up to no good. I went outside the auditorium and heard Debbie yelling for help from the gym. I ran to the gym and then saw where your stupid dad had tried to play Harry Houdini and had handcuffed himself and Debbie to the door, and they couldn't get loose."

"He didn't have the key? What a dweeb."

"You don't have to tell this story, Jayna. It's embarrassing."

Jayna stroked his cheek. "Oh, but I must, dear, to fully explain why knowing you teaches one about so many interesting things. Your genius father did have the key, but he had put their cuffs through the door handle in an orientation where it was then impossible to get it into the keyholes at that angle—great spatial awareness, Rudbeck! Glad you aren't a surgeon. What a great way to impress a girl!"

"I clearly was not as focused as I could've been on the right things."

"That was obvious, given your infatuation with Debbie. Our uncle was a cop, and the cuffs we played with at home were real police ones that he gave us, not the toy ones most kids have. I lent them to Dan as a prop and told him quite sternly *not* to play around with them beforehand. However, did he ever listen? Could he, with his testosterone-saturated Barclay Dixon brain, *possibly* resist playing cop and persuading a pretty girl to try them on within five minutes of me giving them to him? *Noooo.*"

He smiled. "Huh. No red-blooded young man could resist doing that with such a fine lassie. Debbie was a real cutie pie."

"Yeah, right, your romance ended so well. I then remembered something from messing around with them at home, pulled out a bobby pin from my hair, and broke it off the end. It's a bit smaller in width than a true shim, but I'd tried it at home, and it worked. I then did that trick on them by shimming Debbie's bracelet and got her out. Your dad could release himself with the key after the other bracelet was free from the door handle. We barely made it to the stage on time, and we never did tell anyone else what happened."

"At least you didn't lend him a real gun. How did it end up between Dad and Debbie?"

Jayna shook her head. "Not so great. She didn't speak to him for a long time. Would you, after that debacle?"

"I would not. I can't think of a worse 'date' than that." She punched him in the shoulder. "Way to go, Casanova."

AAAAA

Later that afternoon, he sat down at his desk in his home study and began looking at the police bodycam video Ronnie Wolford had recorded during his interaction with Sybil Tegler a week ago. He watched the conversation with the bus people who maintained that Sybil had tried to get on the bus and then wandered westward along the highway. He then watched Wolford's initial interaction with Sybil and how she was staggering down the road.

He also observed some inconsistencies in her speech throughout the encounter. He had watched a fair number of those police bodycam videos on the Internet, and most of the intoxicated arrestees were consistent in their slurred speech.

Sybil's speech seemed appropriately slurred at all times, to be sure, but the word syntax, pronunciation, and grammar were often excellent at times. Maybe that was normal for someone of her high education. She seemed to forget things like her name, but remembered other details. He also noticed again that she seemed to form complex sentences at times, and went from almost passed out to completely alert within a few seconds. He had to contemplate what all those things meant, as this was seemingly not your average intoxicated person.

When they got to the ER, Wolford briefly tried to do sobriety tests that he would generally do in the field, but decided to do them in the ER since they needed to wait on lab work.

He then watched on his tablet the HGN (horizontal nystagmus test), which should show alarmingly abnormal conjugate eye movements in someone that intoxicated. If Wolford had done it outside in the dark, there would be little detail; but in the well-lit examination room, he could easily see that her eye movements appeared normal. Her dark brown eyes contrasted well with her sclerae, even in the ER. What the hell did that mean?

He was no police officer, but he knew enough neurology to interpret what he was seeing: she was tracking Wolford's hand movements perfectly without any abnormalities; this was evidence against intoxication. This tracking was a neurological reflex, and abnormalities couldn't have been faked. The man whose mind was always going a mile a minute would have to think about this new information to determine the reason.

He was in deep thought when he was interrupted by Jayna, who came in wearing a white slip and her hair in curlers, rudely interrupting his essential contemplations.

"Dan, you need to start getting ready for the Youngswood museum event; it starts in an hour. Your other things can wait."

"Okay, I'll get ready. Just working on some stuff."

"The Tegler public intoxication case? Haven't you obsessed over that enough? I know she's one of the med school faculty, but who really cares about a professor who got plastered at the football game?"

"There's just something about it that's really weird."

"There's always something with you. Well, the weirdness will have to wait until later." She pointed towards the door. "Get your big tail in gear and put the OCD to rest for a while."

She was right; it was time to get ready, but he didn't know if he could shut those thoughts out of his mind for the evening.

His final task before showering was to go through the day's mail. He discarded the junk mail, then opened an envelope that contained a small packet of flower seeds: *Rudbeckia hirta,* or black-eyed Susan. He smiled as he looked inside and saw a small piece of paper with an eight-digit number, -3280.8504, and a riddle: "I work this many hours in a year, ever since my birth." He had no idea what that meant. A lot number for the seeds? It had no significance to him. The negative sign was curious. A typo, maybe?

Regarding hours worked in a year, the standard was 2,080. The significance of that number made no sense either.

Jayna would happily plant the seeds next spring as she liked gardening and large, bright flowers. But why would someone send him ubiquitous *Rudbeckia* seeds worth only a few dollars? He thought of someone's idea of a little joke as he put them into the middle desk drawer. He was not good at throwing anything away, and you never knew when you would need something.

Chapter Three

Youngswood Cultural Center
Staffordsville, Ohio
1820 hours

Jayna had the valet park her blue Toyota Camry as they walked into the Youngswood Cultural Center, a two-story arts museum on the west end of town. The Camry seemed out of place among the Cadillacs, BMWs, Mercedes, Teslas, and other high-end vehicles that most patrons drove, but he didn't care. He had gotten past his obsession with his "image"—something his therapist had helped him with. Also, no one worried about a Toyota Camry being stolen. They walked in, he wearing a tailored black suit with white shirt and black tie, and Jayna wearing a strapless crimson evening gown.

He and Evie had been donors, of course. It was the year's art event for Dubois County, where the mayor and most of the high-society types in town (as many of those individuals as there could be for a small college city of 72,000) gathered to dine on fine cuisine in the attached conference center. He wondered if he was really considered a "high-society" type these days or if he and

Jayna had only been invited due to the presence of his phenomenally talented daughter.

Probably both these days, as he, Jayna, and Evie had recently been to the White House for dinner and even stayed overnight in the residence, as the President was actually a fan of his offbeat novels and was impressed by his giving his carbon monoxide antidote neuroglobin-44 to the world for free. He didn't tell any of his colleagues about that trip, but a photo of him and President Mendoza in the Oval Office leaked to the national press a few months ago. *That* raised quite a few eyebrows.

One of Evie's watercolors was exhibited, which was valued at $15,000, but she had donated it to the museum, given her generous and affluent nature. She came in with her boyfriend, Jayna's youngest son, Robert Claymore, who was one year younger than her. The statuesque five-eleven redhead, in three-inch heels, stood eye-to-eye with her handsome, sandy-haired, six-two date; she was wearing her typical pure black-and-white outfit: white strapless chiffon evening gown with black polka dots, black hose, white clutch purse, white hairband, and black pumps. Jewelry: obsidian earrings and necklace, of course. Robert wore an appropriate black suit with a white shirt, tie, and shoes.

"Rob, how are you?" Dan asked, extending his hand to the wiry Robert Claymore.

"I'm great, Dan, thanks. I really enjoy attending all these things with Evie. She's opened up artistic doors for me I never could've imagined."

"Lots of cool stuff on display here."

"Yeah, there is. Mom, Evie told me about your fun afternoon at the Columbus escape room. I'm sorry that I wasn't able to be there."

"It was an unforgettable experience, Rob," his mother said. "It really did exceed my expectations, as it was quite challenging. The owner said we were the first group to get out of that one in time. Life with Evie's father is never dull, that's for sure. We'll have to do it again, maybe at a different place."

Mrs. Eleanor Raymond, the museum director, came up to them. "Dr. Rudbeck, it's so nice for you to make an appearance here. We are so honored by your presence."

He smiled. "Why, thank you, Ma'am, it's a privilege to be here, and to be recognized for my many contributions to—"

He stupidly ignored that the heavyset, gray-haired woman had veered off in the other direction and that Jayna had poked him in the ribs with her right elbow, as she often did when he was being clueless.

Mrs. Raymond looked at him and smiled. "I'm sorry, sir, I meant the lovely professor Dr. Genevieve Rudbeck." She turned back towards his daughter. "Thank you for donating one of your famous watercolors to the museum." The short, stocky museum director reached up and hugged Evie.

Evie smiled. "You're welcome, Mrs. Raymond. It's an honor to have my painting here along with the work of other greats such as Drake Fowler. I shouldn't even be in the conversation."

"Nonsense. You've been coming here since you were a little girl. It's only fitting that one of your unique paintings be exhibited here. You are clearly our most famous local artist, after all."

Evie shrugged. "I don't know about that. I'm fortunate to have certain gifts that help."

"Well, you are fantastic. Good to see you, and I'll talk to you in a little bit at dinner."

After about fifteen more minutes of mingling, they sat down to dinner, and Fowler was seated at their table with Mrs. Raymond, Evie's mother Dr. Charlotte Boisseau, and her husband, Jeff Garrett. Fowler was a handsome-looking, tall man, likely in his sixties, with salt-and-pepper hair and beard.

Evie was seated next to him and offered her hand. "Mr. Fowler, it's such an honor to meet you. I can't believe I'm really here with you in the flesh at your table."

"Thank you, Genevieve. What a beautiful name. French, isn't it?"

"Right. My mother is from Montreal, and I have dual citizenship and speak fluent French." She blushed, being in the company of such a famous photographer. "And call me Evie."

"Thanks. Evie, your paintings are singular. I have two of your watercolors myself, and I've never seen anything like them. The colors are simply astounding. Even simple objects take on an ethereal quality."

"Thanks, Mr. Fowler. May I call you Drake?"

"Of course."

Evie took a sip of diet cola the server had brought. "Drake, I consider you to be the Henri Cartier-Bresson of the modern era, and I admire your adherence to the analog medium—pure photography, which favors using the entire tonal range of a photograph. Not many people do that these days, given all the extra steps necessary to use film. No tricks with computer manipulation, which is as it should be."

"Thanks, Evie. I still love using it, especially with good old ISO 400 Tri-X. There are newer emulsions out there, but Tri-X gives me qualities I can't find in any other medium."

She nodded. "You are right about that. I have processed a lot of that film back in the day in my dad's old darkroom with D-76 and Microdol-X. I loved the smell of all the chemicals and the enlarger workflow, with Dektol, print fixer, burning, dodging, etc. It was truly a unique craft, largely lost in this modern era of digital image manipulation. It was also a meditative time, as one had to shut out most light and interruptions for several hours. It was hard enough to make a photo, and you really had to think about what you were shooting. Only thirty-six exposures per roll, not the ten thousand on a digital storage card."

"Me as well. I admire your work, too, but photography is my full-time job. It's my understanding, however, that painting isn't your vocation, yet you're immensely successful at it. You do work in the art field, I presume?"

She smiled. "Not quite. I do have a master's degree in fine arts, but also a PhD in astrophysics, and I'm an assistant professor at Ohio State. I research binary stars and have an interest in dark matter. I am investigating some odd gravitational perturbations in the central Alaska area that seem to grow slightly yearly."

"That sounds awfully complicated. Is that phenomenon due to climate change?"

She shook her head. "No. I don't know what to make of it, if it's anything at all."

"Wow, I sure don't know much about that. I've never met a combination artist and astrophysicist before. But they say you can see far more colors than normal people, in addition to your own natural artistic abilities. Is that really true, or just an urban legend?"

She laughed. "Yes, it's true."

"Can you explain that?"

"You're an old-school film photographer, so I assume you understand the chemistry of how color film works, although you primarily shoot in black-and-white."

Fowler nodded. "Of course. There are three color layers, each sensitive to a primary color—red, green, or blue. Each layer contains silver halide crystals and dye couplers. When exposed and later developed, it creates an image that approximates what we see with our vision, when the three layers are combined in chemical processing. Film, however, can't even begin to approach the human eye's dynamic range."

"Correct. In our retinas, we have cones that, in normal people, can distinguish about a hundred different colors each, which is a lot, as humans have better color vision than most mammals. The combined red, blue, and green cones allow us to see 100^3 or one million colors.

"However, I am a tetrachromat—one of the handful of women with a full functional set of yellow cones, which allow me to see 100^4 or one hundred million different colors. This has been demonstrated with sophisticated scientific testing. I don't have a reference point as to what you see, but photographs from digital cameras come very close to helping me understand that, as the extra 'color channel' doesn't exist. My dad tried making a 'four-channel' digital camera, but it wasn't advantageous. I can also see a little bit into the ultraviolet range, which makes flowers and plants appear markedly different. That is hampered a bit by the fact that our lenses block out most ultraviolet light."

"Are there any other species that have that characteristic?"

"The trait is found in several aquatic animals, such as goldfish and the mantis shrimp, and mammals like reindeer." She laughed. "*Rudbeckia* species, like the black- and brown-eyed Susans, ironically, are quite spectacular to me and quite different than what you see. I can see the 'landing strips' in flowers that pollinators such as bees detect."

"At least your parents didn't name you Susan Rudbeck." Fowler grinned.

"Ah, but they *did*—my middle name is Suzanne." She laughed. "My eyes are blue, though, not black or brown."

For a young woman with four sets of retinal cones who could see one hundred million different colors and even a bit into the ultraviolet spectrum, her absolute preference for monochromatic outfits and accessories was perplexing to most. It wasn't an effort to be different (like him, she had that tendency at times), since she had shown that penchant for her clothing and toys as a toddler; his theory was that she was overwhelmed by colors most of the time, and black-and-white clothing was one way to shut it out. She was similar in her choice of automobile (a gray 340-horsepower souped-up Hyundai sedan).

"I would guess you could spot forgeries, then."

"Fine art forgeries?" She nodded. "Of course. I have done consulting for several museums and federal agencies. I can detect subtle differences in pigments that most people and imaging modalities cannot. This works best, however, for paintings where I've seen the original. I have an eidetic memory and can remember exactly things I've seen."

"Have you been to many museums?"

She nodded. "Of course. All the major ones in the United States and Canada, as well as the most famous museums in London, Paris, Rome, and Florence."

"Will those observations hold up in court?"

She shrugged. "Not really, as there's no way to prove what I see. However, my observations can prompt further testing, which can prove my examinations, such as carbon dating."

"Carbon dating? That's incredible." Fowler took a bite of his wheat roll. "How does that work?"

"The quantity of radioisotopes remains constant throughout time, but the amount of carbon-14 in the world increased tremendously in the mid-1900s due to the dawn of the 'atomic age' and all the nuclear tests, which led to a spike in the isotope in any modern-day carbon-based pigments. So, for an antique painting, it's pretty easy to tell if it's fake, since the carbon-14 content would be higher than it should be from pigments in that era. For newer paintings, it's harder."

"Is your condition genetic?"

She nodded. "Yes, in many cases. My mom, across the table, is a pathologist and has the ability to a lesser degree than I; she can see perhaps twenty times the colors you can, as she has only partial yellow cones."

"Wow, what a talented family." He stood up and extended his hand to Evie's five-nine mother. "Drake Fowler, Ma'am."

"Charlotte Boisseau. It's wonderful to meet you."

"I can see where Evie gets her height and stunning good

looks."

"Thanks, Drake." The fair-skinned redhead blushed like her daughter did earlier. "If I use real glass slides and not electronic images, I can see things no other pathologist can. I have also helped the Secret Service identify counterfeit money. Evie can do that easily as well."

"I've never heard of this ability. Are there any men with this talent?"

Charlie shook her head. "No, it's found only in women."

"Why's that?" Fowler asked.

"The ability requires the genes to be active on two X chromosomes. Even then, extremely few women with the genes have any degree of true tetrachromacy because the genes aren't always functional; mine are only partial. There are maybe ten women like Evie in the world."

"Does this ability help you with astrophysics, Evie?"

"Maybe a small amount, but not to a large extent. Most imaging is electronic, and false color is applied, so it has more application to painting than astronomy. It does help with my income, though. I make about three to four times my academic salary with my paintings."

AAAAA

After an elegant dinner and engaging conversation about art and photography, the table contingent went on a museum tour with Fowler and finally arrived at his prized Ukumat 2200, at the main museum display in the atrium.

"That's it, Drake? The famous camera you used to take street photos?" he asked. "It gives me goose bumps just to look at it."

Fowler nodded. "Yes, that's it. My old friend. It has never let me down, after over a million exposures."

"Surely you had a backup?" Robert asked.

"I did, but I never had to use it."

"Did it ever need service?" Robert asked. "Most shutters last only a hundred thousand exposures or so, and I can't imagine the millions you must have taken."

"Once in a while, it needed some lubrication. Nothing major. It's hand-built to a different standard than most cameras could ever hope to be. Hopefully, it has half a million more exposures left in it."

"It's beautiful and has an incredibly long shutter life. And you used a 50mm f/1.4 Zeiss Planar lens to take most of your photos," Evie said. "Occasionally, a 35mm f/2. Nothing exotic in terms of focal length—just ultra-high quality prime optics. Superb."

"That's right, you have an excellent memory."

"And eye for perspective. Skill and dedication to the craft, not fancy equipment, is the key to fame and fortune." She pointed to her father and frowned. "My dad here, on the other hand, has terminal EAS."

"*EAS?* Oh, no. I'm so sorry to hear that, sir."

Evie laughed. "Relax—EAS, not ALS. 'Equipment Acquisition Syndrome.' He wouldn't be caught dead without the latest and greatest high-speed mirrorless zoom lens or fancy fifty-megapixel body with the newest processor, Drake. He likes the equipment more than taking pictures, and I've seen him trade in cameras he had never even used. It's incurable and gets worse every year."

"Nothing wrong with having the best equipment," Fowler said.

"Sure. I have an Internet blog on new photo equipment, I'm certain you've seen it."

Fowler shook his head. "Sorry, I don't really keep up on the latest equipment, Dan. As you can see, I have relatively simple needs and hardly ever use a digital camera. The oldies are just fine for what I do."

"Right, and you're living proof that you don't need a wide array of the latest fancy lenses to take prize-winning photos," Robert said. "It's the artist, not the brush, they say."

"Unfortunately, some of us do need the latest and greatest," he said. "We have little talent, so we have to buy a game. Kind of like golf clubs or tennis rackets." He looked at the famous camera that had taken over a million photos. It was wonderful in its simplicity compared to his fancy mirrorless cameras that could shoot sixty frames per second and take over 3,000 photos on a single charge. "*Life is really simple, but we insist on making it complicated.*"

"That's a good quote, Dan. Confucius, correct?"

Evie laughed. "You know your stuff. None other where my dad is concerned. Confucius is sort of his mentor."

"Sometimes I need less complexity in my life. A simple camera for a simple life."

Yet, on this night, he had an ominous feeling that his life was to become more complicated, not simpler.

Chapter Four

Rudbeck Home
2105 Winthrop Street
Staffordsville, Ohio
0247 hours

A sleepy Jayna answered Dan's cell phone several hours later. His CPAP machine was running and he often didn't hear his phone, but he did notice it going off this time. He didn't often get calls in the middle of the night, but it seemed to be becoming more common lately.

"Hello? Yeah, he's here. Just a minute."

He woke up sleepily, removing his mask and turning off his CPAP device as he took the phone. "Oh, no, it's not the ER or police station with another drunk faculty member, I hope."

"It's Sandy, so I doubt that." She handed him the phone and tried to go back to sleep.

"Sandy? What the heck does she want?' He took the phone. "What's up, Chief?" he asked his fire chief cousin.

"The damn art museum burned to the ground," Sandy said. "All of that famous photographer's exhibits and everything else have been destroyed."

"Huh? What . . . did you say? The Youngswood Arts Museum is gone?"

"Yes, that's what I said."

"The paintings, too?"

"Yeah, Danny, I said everything. The building was largely wood and drywall, so it's all burnt down."

"Holy shit, no kidding? But . . . we were there just last night!"

"I know."

"Was anyone inside when it happened?"

"No, luckily not. Do you remember anything weird about the event?"

He sleepily thought for a minute. "No, not really, but I'll ask the others. And, I'll be happy to lend my expertise to the police."

"That's great, but don't be too intrusive. I know how you like to meddle and get involved in things. I just thought you should know before you go in tomorrow."

"Thanks." He hung up the phone and sat on the side of his bed, wiping matter out of his eyes.

"The art museum burned down? Seriously?" Jayna asked as she took a sip of bottled water.

"It's gone, and we were just there last night. Anything suspicious that you recall?"

She shook her head. "Not at all. It was one of the most uneventful shindigs I've ever been to. Most of the patrons were people we knew from the community, medical school, or hospital."

"Then why did it burn up? Something is weird here."

"You can't do anything about it now, Dan. Things happen. Go back to sleep."

"Okay, maybe you're right." It was just bizarre, the event with a drunken Sybil Tegler (a professor never known to drink), and now this. He also couldn't stop thinking about what he thought was a normal horizontal nystagmus test that the sheriff's deputy had done, and there was no way he was getting back to sleep.

He knew for some reason that there would be something else coming up soon. He had mentioned his mentor's quote on simplicity, but there certainly was nothing simple about this night.

AAAAA

Jayna had a special room in their home, one dedicated to her first husband, who had died of COVID-19 pneumonia several years ago. He rarely went in there, as he felt it somewhat awkward. Dallas attorney Samuel Claymore was eleven years her senior and was a loyal and wonderful husband for over twenty years, and fathered her three sons; their youngest, Robert, was dating his daughter. He knocked as she opened the door around seven AM the next morning, on the third anniversary of his death.

"Are you okay, hon?"

She wiped some tears from her eyes. "I'm all right. Just a little bit sad today."

"I know, and I'm sorry. Can I help?"

She nodded. "You already have. I appreciate having this space to honor Sam, Dan. That does help immensely. Rob is around, of course, but Tom and Andy couldn't make it up this year. I'll meet up with them in Dallas in a couple of weeks. Eric, Greg, and Aaron aren't too far away and we'll meet up for dinner next week." Her three older brothers all lived within sixty miles; her parents had both passed away several years ago.

He stroked her on the right cheek with his hand. "You don't need to thank me. This is your home, too."

"Most husbands would find it a bit awkward. That and my changing my middle name from Marie to Claymore."

"I don't, and I'm not most husbands. I've been through pain too." He gave her a hug. "He was your spouse for over two decades—of course, you want to honor and remember him, and his name is a part of you and your sons. I would never want you to forget that. Does doing that lessen our relationship in any way?"

"No, it doesn't."

"Of course not, because he's part of who you are, and I love everything about you. Sam was a comfort and loyal partner to you for over a third of your life, and he's the father of your three wonderful sons. I wish I had known him, Jayna. He seems like he was a great man. I'm so sorry about what happened to him."

She started crying. "I often wonder if we hadn't gone to a certain place, eaten from a particular restaurant's take-out, done this or that, if he'd still be alive. I guess we can't go back in time and worry about such things. The hardest part is that the boys and I never really had a chance to say goodbye. He developed fulminant ventilator-dependent pneumonia almost overnight and had to be sedated. He was never conscious again."

"I'm sure he knows how you feel, Jayna.You were the best wife he could've ever had."

"I hope so. I know there is a Heaven, and he must be there looking down on us." She wiped tears from her eyes. "Would he approve of us and our marriage?"

He nodded. "I'm sure he would've wanted you to be happy after he was gone. You can't help that he died."

"I know he would. The boys are happy for me, too. I worried that they thought I had maybe married too soon after he died and was being disloyal to their father, but I told them about our history. All three of them gave their blessing to us, Dan. They know that marrying you doesn't remove my memories of Sam, and you've been a wonderful source of comfort for me, to help me through the loneliness. That isn't the boys' burden. They need to get on with their own lives."

"I try to make up for all the lost years, Jayna."

She stroked his face. "Oh, I've forgiven you for that long ago, Dan. You did the best you could at the time with your issues I didn't know about. I was hurt inside for a long time, but I got over it as it made me stronger. We can't fret over what can't be changed."

"Come on, let's run to the grocery before work, since the kids are coming over for dinner tonight. I promise not to buy a bunch of unhealthy stuff."

She smiled at him. "Right, you'll just sneak your junk food in the cart while I'm not looking. You think for some reason I won't notice it."

He thought about how fortunate he was to be able to comfort his wife, and how they ended up together after all these years, back in their hometown, after the stupid way he had treated her. He may not have achieved all the things he had wanted in his professional career, but that was okay, as he was at peace with himself.

He had learned that most people never get a second chance, but she finally gave him one. He was lucky that his first real love became his last.

AAAAA

Evie and Robert came by for dinner at Dan and Jayna's house that evening, where eggplant Parmesan was being served (prepared by Evie, quite the culinary enthusiast), along with Caesar salad, asparagus, and some other vegetarian sides. Robert said grace as they held hands and had a prayer in honor of his father, Sam, on the anniversary of his death.

"I assume everyone saw the news about the museum," Dan said as he took a bite of French bread after applying a generous portion of butter.

"Yeah. Man, that's so bizarre, Mom, about the museum burning down," the sandy-haired Robert said, taking a bite of his Caesar salad. "We were just there. It's so scary, as it could've happened while we were there."

"Well, at least the famous camera wasn't lost," Evie said, wearing her typical casual ensemble of gray sweater, black jeans, white headband, black sports watch, and black high-top Chuck Taylors, as she sipped her black coffee. She avoided the white Chucks since they had a red stripe on the bottom, which she found intolerable. Evie reached for the serving plate. "Anyone want some more eggplant?"

"Huh? Wait a minute—what do you mean?" Jayna asked loudly. "Your dad just said the whole place burned up, and you're talking about the eggplant! That thing was priceless, I heard. Fowler took most of his famous photos with that camera."

The tall, freckled redhead shook her head. "Yeah, I know the museum burned down, my lovely stepmama, which is truly tragic, but about the camera . . . I don't believe the one there was the actual one he used, but merely a replica. It's not uncommon to have replicas of extremely valuable items at lower-end museums, because of the lesser level of security."

"*What?* That seems somewhat unethical," Jayna said sternly. "People went there to see the real thing, so it was a gyp for everyone who donated money to be there."

Evie laughed. "Trust me that 99.99 percent of folks there would never know the difference, Jayna. Did you know, Rob?"

Robert looked up in surprise. "I would've never even considered that, no. I was just in awe to have seen it, replica or not. It's legendary."

"How do you know it was a fake?" he asked.

Evie sighed. "Replica is a more appropriate term than fake,

Dad, but I actually saw it once, at a museum in Paris. The color of the one here was a little off."

"Color?" Robert said. "It was metallic, there was no color."

Evie smiled. "Oh, yes, there was. You just couldn't see it."

"Maybe the one in Paris was the replica." He took a bite of his asparagus. "Is that possible?"

Evie shook her head. "No way. They wouldn't allow that at a high-profile museum."

"Are you sure about Fowler's camera, Evie?" Robert asked curiously.

"I can't prove it quantitatively; as you know, there is no imaging modality that can entirely reproduce what I see, but . . . *oui*. The exterior of the original was made with an alloy consisting partially of cadmium and had a slight greenish tint to me. I didn't say anything, as it would seem logical not to have had the hallowed camera of fame actually there. It was interesting that he was asking me about my ability to detect forgeries, though. I wonder if he was digging for whether or not I suspected the camera, or just making conversation?"

"Maybe," he said. "Were any of the paintings or Fowler's photographs forgeries?"

She shook her head. "*Je ne pense pas.* Any modern pigments would be apparent to me, and I'm sure they were all genuine. Many modern pigments look the same to you, but not to me when compared to ones from a hundred years ago. A few million down the drain there, too. I can't tell if a photograph was original, though. Monochrome silver grains look all the same to me, and their technology hasn't changed in over a hundred years. But the paintings there weren't really worth all that much."

"Except the painting of yours that was lost. Sorry," he said.

Evie laughed. "*Je vais y survivre, papa.* I'm not exactly in the poorhouse. I sure don't spend it on my clothes."

"So, if his Ukumat didn't burn up in the fire, he still has the camera, or he had already sold it under the table and is trying to collect insurance money. But wouldn't the insurance company know that the camera might be a replica, as Evie said?" he said.

"Not necessarily, if the insurance rider was made out for the full amount," Evie said. "They might ask for proof of authenticity, but that would be possible to fabricate if dishonest people were involved. A small museum like ours might not have even asked for a COA." She took a bite of eggplant.

"Mom, you said you used to work in Uncle Aaron's insurance office during the summer during college. Did you have any policies like that?" Robert asked.

"For museum items? No, those policies are highly specialized. Aaron mostly implemented auto and homeowners' policies. However, I did recall one time when a lady tried to say a jewelry item was stolen to get the insurance money, but we wouldn't do it because she filed no police report. It turns out she still had the item and lied about it; filing a fraudulent police report would've gotten her in even more trouble. So, yes, people do dishonest things because they are entitled and think insurance is 'free.' It's not, and everyone pays higher premiums in the end."

"How much is it worth?" he asked.

Vintage photographic equipment connoisseur Robert thought for a moment. "I did some research on it before the event. The original Ukumat 2200 with the cadmium casing is one of the ten rarest purely mechanical 35mm single lens reflex cameras in the world, as it had a very limited production. His original—ten million bucks, easily, maybe twelve."

"Are you kidding, Rob?" he asked.

"Nope—people will pay outlandish prices for things like that, it's crazy."

"How much is a Ukumat 2200? Not the one Fowler used, but just if I wanted one to mess around with?" Evie asked.

"A functional camera—which is just the standard model—maybe four or five grand, which is what a good condition used model would go for at EKH Camera or another reputable online dealer, although even those don't turn up that often. Given the digital revolution, the company stopped making them in 2001 but still continues to service them. The 2200 was the last completely mechanical model, so they're always repairable. The subsequent models, like the 2400 and 2600, had some electronics that couldn't always be replaced due to the unavailability of printed circuit boards. But a skilled machinist can always craft replacement mechanical parts."

"A fair amount of naturally occurring cadmium is radioactive. If the real camera was burned up and Evie's wrong, there should be some beta decay in the remnants, and we will likely find the shell of either camera. Titanium cover plate, Rob?"

Robert nodded. "Yes, it would be high-end materials, Dan. Titanium for both, but with the cadmium plating on the genuine article. Titanium has a melting point around 3,000 degrees Fahrenheit, so it should be intact. That particular camera was from a very limited production of twenty-five."

"If it was a replica, then, there would be no decay." He thought for a few seconds. "I . . . have an idea that is marvelous in its simplicity and execution that will determine which camera was there."

"Oh, no," his wife and daughter both replied in unison. "We don't even want to know."

Chapter Five

Youngswood Cultural Center Remains
Staffordsville, Ohio
0742 hours

Early the next morning, on a bright and sunny Tuesday, Staffordsville Police Lieutenant Brian Eppard sighed and slapped himself in the face as he saw the large, ungainly, balding man wearing slacks and a golf shirt ramble to the Youngswood fire scene, as the other officers greeted the man and let him through like the local celebrity he was.

"Up bright and early, I see. I thought it would take you at least another day for you to get here, Rudbeck, given your massive responsibilities in the medical, literary, and entertainment worlds. Wouldn't want you to miss hosting your insightful radio show."

"I am, as always, where the action is, Lieutenant. Didn't the police chief promote me to special consultant to the Staffordsville Police Department?" He pulled out his official ID badge.

The tall, fiftyish, balding Black police lieutenant groaned. "Ugh, don't remind me. But your unpaid duties are by special invitation only. I don't remember sending one to you for this, and I can't see how it involves the medical field."

"Then you should be glad I showed up, as you never know what knowledge I might have that you can use. '*The gentleman holds justice to be of highest importance. If a gentleman has courage but neglects justice, he becomes insurgent. If an inferior man has courage but neglects justice, he becomes a thief.*'"

Eppard, a snappy dresser who was wearing a gray suit with a white shirt and blue tie, looked at him in disbelief for several seconds. "Man, that Confucius stuff is deep, and it'll take me the rest of the morning to figure out what that even means—something about thieves and being insurgent, whatever that is, but it doesn't sound good. However, it remains to be seen whether or not I will be glad for your timely arrival."

"You will be glad after I find some evidence you can use."

"Yeah, I can't wait. Hey, guess what? The jail is looking for a new doctor after the last guy croaked a week ago, and you came to mind."

He nodded sadly. "Yeah, good old Burt Quimby. It was his time at age eighty-nine. He was a legend."

"Yeah, Quimby had even more jobs than you and coached the boys' basketball and girls' softball teams, too. Retirement just wasn't for him. But given your vast understanding of the criminal mind, I thought that would be a great job for you. Those inmates could use your talents."

Correctional medicine was actually a legitimate medical specialty now, with its own board certification exam. He had thought about it once, as it could be an interesting specialty, but not right now, given his other responsibilities.

"Yeah, it would be a fascinating job, Brian, but I think my plate is rather full right now."

"What a pity, it would be right up your alley. But when do you have time to do your actual work, Rudbeck? Isn't there some statewide poison control emergency you should be dealing with, novel poison antidotes to discover, a mission-critical budget issue to solve, literary masterpieces to write, radio shows to broadcast, or some politically incorrect movie to create you can post on social media?"

"I haven't made a politically incorrect movie in over ten years. And they were for local entertainment only, not to post on social media, although the occasional one may have leaked."

"Oh, sorry, my bad. The one where you launched the flaming dummy off the tenth-floor hospital tower was indeed a *tour de force*. See, I learned some French, just for you. I'm sure your firefighter cousin loved that movie. The alternate universe where the tobacco companies took over healthcare was also great. I laughed my ass off."

"No, she didn't like it at all. And investigating wrongdoing is part of my actual work as a high-level administrator."

"Oh, ignorant me, I forgot everything is now within your domain." Eppard pointed to the yellow instrument in his hand. "What the hell is that?"

He looked at Eppard. "It's a radiation detector; what did you think it was?" he asked with a puzzled expression.

"Do I look like a fricking scientist, Rudbeck? When the hell would I have used a Geiger counter? I can't keep track of all the crazy gadgets you have around, like your thermal camera, metal detector glasses, high-tech super-suit, and many others. Why do you have that here, anyway? Did a thermonuclear weapon create this fire?"

"Of course not, but Evie thinks Fowler's camera was a replica because the color was off. She says the original one would've had a slight radioactive signature. While her observations won't stand up in court, the radiation measurements will."

Eppard opened his mouth wide. "A radioactive camera? Holy shit, that doesn't sound very safe. Who the hell would make something dangerous like that, and wouldn't the radiation expose the film and ruin it?"

"Relax. It's low-level and not harmful, and wouldn't expose the film. Some lenses used to be made with thorium-doped glass, as thorium has an extremely high refractive index and can produce very high-quality optics. More modern, improved materials are used now."

"Damn, that's good to know; some of these younger officers and firefighters may still want to have children." Eppard scratched his balding head and adjusted his thick, dark-rimmed glasses. "Well, I give your daughter way more credit than you. So, if it's a fake, you must suspect foul play, as I surely knew only you would."

"I don't know, Brian, but it's always possible. Don't you think this building burning up is a bit odd? Central Ohio isn't a place in the country known for excessive fires. It isn't even that dry out."

Eppard nodded. "Right, it's a weird coincidence you were on the guest list last night. The museum was only eight years old, so there shouldn't have been any structural or electrical issues. Were any old enemies from your novels in attendance, Dixon? That Russian lady spy? I heard she was there. Maybe she did it to get revenge."

He laughed. "Funny. I'm sure she would like to do him in sometimes."

"I guess you're really gonna go through the burned remains looking for radiation with your little toy?"

"That's about it, yeah. The particular radiation I'm seeking only goes a few inches, so it will take me a long time."

Eppard shook his head. "Damn, that's messed up. But go ahead and have fun and leave me alone. It will get you out of my hair for a while, at least."

He spent the next three hours scouring the burnt remains but failed to detect any beta decay. He had procured some cadmium alloy of the same composition and thickness as the camera casing, which he had used as a control and could detect at six inches.

Using a sensitive metal detector he had also brought, he eventually discovered a burnt camera fragment with part of the top plate; the glass pentaprism had melted. But it *wasn't* radioactive.

So, it seemed more likely than not that the camera that had burned up was a replica, as his daughter had said, and she was almost always right about visual observations. Evie said it wasn't uncommon to have a replica rather than the priceless real thing at small, regional museums, so that alone didn't prove criminal activity—but it was a possibility he had to consider, given its value.

This theory, of course, was contingent on the actual camera being still around somewhere, as it could be sold for a large sum of money (under the table, of course, as news of the "real" camera having burned up would be all over the news soon). Surely, some eccentric folks would pay good money to have that in their collection.

He knew that the fire department wouldn't know if arson was a factor for a while, but he had his opinions, which weren't always valued by the police or his fire chief cousin, as he had sent them on some wild goose chases several times in the past—which both of them were quick to remind him of.

Yet, he had been right two years ago when he uncovered a massive healthcare ransomware scandal involving the national medical education board and a corrupt accreditation site visitor after the president of the medical society died mysteriously at a social event. He was hailed as a hero for uncovering that corruption and for having saved Jayna from a fire by resuscitating her with his unique carbon monoxide antidote, which he then gave to the medical world for free, even though he could have made millions of dollars from it. A condition of his gift was that big pharma sell the drug with no more than a two percent profit over cost. Even the President of the United States got wind of that and recognized him for it.

He was labeled a fool for giving something away like that, which could've made him rich, but that wasn't who he was, and he didn't have the opulent lifestyle of Barclay Dixon. After that event, they offered to make him the director of that board, but he declined, as that would have meant moving to Chicago.

Arson was one of the least often investigated and least prosecuted criminal offenses, mainly because the evidence in most cases was circumstantial. From his limited legal knowledge, he knew that circumstantial cases were difficult to prove in court. And although he had some theories, he had no actual evidence of any wrongdoing. Not yet, anyway.

Sandy's arson team had the accelerant-detecting canines out there yesterday, and he didn't want to be in the way of that. The first American arson dog program was developed in 1985, and while the animal couldn't identify the substance, of course, it could narrow down the focus to a certain area, so that definitive lab testing could be done. Arson dogs could detect gasoline, for example, in quantities of 0.001 drop, which is better than some electronic detection means.

Another tool for detecting accelerants was the VTA, or vapor trace analyzer, which could detect hydrocarbon traces of accelerant residue in the air. All these technologies would be utilized to determine if foul play was involved, which seemed unlikely at first glance.

But what if there was a sinister motive for burning down the museum? That's how his mind worked. What could it have been? He knew that from writing his novels, there were six primary reasons for arson: destruction of evidence, insurance fraud, revenge, suicide or homicide, to make a political statement or induce fear, or because of a psychiatric disorder. There was an extraneous benefit to writing fiction, after all.

He was pretty sure there was no political statement to be made by torching the art museum, and there was no revenge motive he could think of; that left insurance fraud as the most likely culprit, with Fowler's camera and photographs at the focal point of the mystery.

He shared his latest findings with Lt. Eppard and headed to his office at the university hospital, and to take his wife to lunch, as remembering the passing of Sam was a bittersweet time for her.

AAAAA

Brian Jerome Eppard was one of two lieutenants at the Staffordsville Police Department. Brian was born in Akron to a police sergeant father and registered nurse mother, and he knew from high school that he wanted to follow in his dad's footsteps. He had an older brother and sister, who went into accounting and nursing, respectively. But he knew he always wanted to become a cop. Many tried to talk him out of it, telling him he was too smart to be a mere police officer, but he never wavered from his goal to become the best officer he could be.

After high school, he went to the University of Akron, where he majored in criminal justice. He then pondered his options: city police department—large or small city; state trooper; federal agent (i.e., FBI, DEA, ATF, etc.). After completing the police academy, he decided that he could make more of a difference in a smaller city, and he liked smaller college towns, so he joined the Staffordsville Police Department as a patrol officer. Two years after joining, he decided to further his education by obtaining a master's degree in public administration from Central Ohio University, as police leadership positions for Black officers still were not plentiful, and he wanted to stack the cards in his favor come promotion time.

Brian was a stellar officer and made sergeant after six years and lieutenant after five more, earning several awards in the process. He was involved in the criminal division and was always on the scene investigating serious crimes in the community. He also had a reputation for being hardworking and trustworthy, albeit slightly sarcastic and prickly. He had an impeccable record and had even been contacted about joining the state police or the FBI, but he declined. Like his father, he married a registered nurse, and together they had a son and daughter. He was on track to become captain in a couple of years when the current captain retired, and he would likely become police chief someday if he stayed in town.

His wife worked in Staffordsville University Hospital's intensive care unit and had frequent interactions with one Daniel Rudbeck; Brian and Dan had met several times at some hospital events, and the lieutenant had learned of the Amalgam-Man's interest in areas outside of medicine, which included intrusion into solving crimes for which he occasionally provided helpful information.

Dan the Amalgam-Man had an interest in almost everything, was always hanging around, and initially was quite bothersome to Brian; eventually, the police lieutenant developed a deep respect for him, as he was pretty intelligent and always wanted to do what was right, although Eppard would never tell him that. Brian was always curious how the Confucius-quoting Barclay Dixon managed to do any actual work, given his bouncing around all the time from one thing to another, seemingly with the attention span of a squirrel.

After the Amalgam-Man amazingly brought down the Roland Okdar hospital ransomware scheme a couple of years ago, the police chief made him an unpaid "special consultant" to the police department, which gave him even more access to Eppard; Brian accepted this and learned to count on him as a friend who would always help him when needed. Brian always listened to him now, even though he could be very irritating, remembering that no one took him seriously about the ransomware crime when he was right all along. Uncovering that scheme saved multiple healthcare systems billions of dollars.

There were other times he was wrong, though, and sent the police on some wild goose chases, like when he sent them to raid a church's coffee roasting business because he thought they were making methamphetamine. No one could be right all the time, however. Eppard would always continue their sarcastic banter, which they had had for years, as it could be pretty entertaining.

AAAAA

Staffordsville Arts Foundation
455 W. Washington Street
Staffordsville, Ohio
1550 hours

"Thanks for meeting with me on short notice, Mrs. Raymond," he said to the overweight museum director at her makeshift office in the Staffordsville Arts Foundation near downtown, since her regular office was in ashes.

"Sure, Dr. Rudbeck. I'm still just overwhelmed at all this and how the museum could've burned down right after the event." She took a sip of coffee. "But I'm a bit confused. What is your official role in this? No one was poisoned. That's what you do, right? You're a poison doctor?"

He pulled out his city-issued police ID. "Normally, yes, but I'm also a special scientific consultant to the Police Department and assist in the investigation using special sophisticated detection methods."

"I see. I don't know that I have any information that the police don't already have. I've already spoken to them. Do they have any information about the fire, like what could've caused it? What are the things that crooks use to start fires called?"

"Accelerants, like gasoline and kerosene."

"Did they find any of those?"

"It's a bit early to say definitively, but nothing so far. The dogs and instruments together would've found something big already."

"I hope it was just an accident and that someone didn't do it intentionally. That would be horrible."

"I understand, Ma'am, and the fire and police departments will continue their investigation. My main question today is regarding Drake Fowler's camera, which was on display."

"Sure, his famous Ukumat . . . it's horrible that it was destroyed, and I'm sure he's devastated. What about it?"

"I just need to know if the one on display was the real camera or a replica."

"*Replica?* My word, why would you think that?"

"You *are* aware of my daughter's exceptional visual gifts, I assume."

She nodded. "Of course. I've known Genevieve for over twenty years."

"She doesn't believe it was the real camera. She's seen the original in Paris."

"I don't mean to disagree, but Mr. Fowler told me it was the genuine camera. I don't have any real way to verify that, but why would he lie about it? Any other evidence it wasn't real?"

He nodded. "The original camera had an outer casing made of a very weakly radioactive metal, and fragments of the camera I found in the rubble didn't have that radioactivity."

"Would the radioactivity have been removed by the fire?"

"No, Mrs. Raymond. Radioactivity is a fundamental physical principle that cannot be altered by burning, freezing, or other known means. That's why it's useful here."

She shook her head. "I have no way of knowing if it was real or not, only that Mr. Fowler said it was. You're from here, Dr. Rudbeck, so you understand—this was just a local showing at a small museum to recognize local patrons and artists like Evie, and we were unbelievably lucky to get the famous Drake Fowler to come to our modest little place for free. I didn't ask for a certificate of authenticity or anything as I thought that would be rude given his graciousness to come here for free, and I took him at his word. Even if it was a replica, no one would have known the difference."

She was right about that. "One more question: I assume all the museum pieces were insured? I'm sure *those* folks would know the difference."

"Of course. The eminent Worthington T. Brick Company of Philadelphia insures everything, as they specialize in such items. It all would've been covered." She took a sip of coffee. "Does Evie suspect any other irregularities, like art forgeries?"

He shook his head. "No, she doesn't believe so. She's pretty adept at detecting those."

"One good thing. So, what happens next, Dr. Rudbeck?"

"We need to finish our investigation and take the next steps. One final question: Were there any surveillance cameras installed in the building?"

She nodded. "Yes, but all that was surely destroyed in the fire. I'm afraid there isn't any record of anything, sadly."

"You're probably right. Were those files stored locally or in the cloud?"

She shook her head. "We don't have a fancy setup. They would've been video files on a local hard drive in the basement on the server. It was a pretty old computer, still in use from the old museum before this one was built. We depend on philanthropy and try to keep our expenses low."

He stood and offered his hand, which she took. "Thank you for your time, Mrs. Raymond. I will contact you if I have any more questions."

Unbelievably lucky to get Drake Fowler to come for free—right. Unbelievably gullible museum director is more like it, Eleanor Raymond. It just seemed logical that Fowler was involved in the fire, but he had to put the pieces together. Why the hell else would such a famous photographer come to a hick town museum in central Ohio?

As usual, he would have to convince his colleagues of the things only he could see. For that, he would need evidence. Gathering evidence the Rudbeck way would invariably ruffle some feathers.

AAAAA

The next step in his crime-solving investigation would be to learn more about the famous photographer Drake Fowler. Born Dennis Lloyd Fowler in Philadelphia in 1960, he became interested in photography at an early age, as his father owned a large camera store. In high school, he was the photography editor for the yearbook and newspaper and was always present at school events, taking photos. He even had a side gig covering random events with one of the Philly newspapers. He had access to the best photo equipment available and went to Columbia University on a scholarship, where he majored in fine arts with a concentration in photography.

He remained in New York after graduation and had a brief career in photojournalism, working for the New York Times and other newspapers. He was excellent at all areas of photography, including landscapes, but his true love was street photography: walking around New York, taking various photos of people. He had experimented with and had mastery of view cameras and medium format, but his true love was 35mm. His career took off in the early 1980s, when digital photography was still a crude concept. He became tired of equipment that broke down and wouldn't last, so he purchased a handmade Ukumat 2200 from Germany, which, coupled with a 50mm Carl Zeiss Planar lens, was his expensive but operationally simple tool of choice to make his legendary photographs.

He became even more famous in the 1990s and 2000s as a correspondent for Time and Newsweek. His famed street photographs of everyday life had a certain human quality, a gritty edginess that few others could ever match. His eye for composition was unparalleled, and his use of available light was legendary, especially in an era when ISO 400 film was about the fastest to go without excessive grain. Fowler was also a master in the darkroom, although most of those close to him stated in interviews that he was so good at composition and lighting that he didn't need much retouching.

In the 2000s, digital cameras hit their stride, and Fowler tried them all (mainly because manufacturers sent him cameras for free, hoping he would adopt their models). He never really cared much for digital, though, even in the 2010s and 2020s when most felt that digital imaging overtook film in terms of sheer resolution. Quality, however, was a more subjective term that wasn't easily decided in the "analog vs. digital" arguments. "Pixel peepers" who examined solely technical data (he fit into that category, as he was more interested in the equipment than actually taking photos with it) would conclude that digital was superior; "traditionalists" like Fowler countered with the argument that analog film had greater dynamic range than digital sensors, although that gap was narrowed by sophisticated processing software.

Fowler also felt the contemplative nature of analog imaging was essential to producing the ideal photograph. Taking a picture took careful planning, and one only had limited exposures on a roll, so the process differed from a digital camera that could shoot 120 frames per second.

These were all facts widely available in books and interviews. Still, he wanted to learn more about this famous man and why someone of his stature would come to a small museum in Staffordsville to exhibit his famed camera and photographs. He had learned from Robert that Fowler had a close friend who grew up ten miles from Staffordsville, and he thought maybe that was the reason.

He also had seen videos of Fowler in his forties, living high in his Manhattan apartment, throwing large, lavish parties in expensive venues whenever possible. Fowler was also now divorced from his third wife, so all those activities would stretch the bank account of even the most affluent of individuals. Like Sybil, Fowler was another individual who seemingly couldn't live within his means, although he had far more resources than she did.

He needed some help digging up dirt on Fowler, and he knew just the person to do it: his old friend Jake Fisher. He and Jake had gone to high school together, and his school photographer buddy was now the director of information technology for the hospital. However, he and Jake also shared a love of photography, and Jake was the director of audiovisual services at the hospital until he took over the IT department. Jake, like him, had specialized knowledge that he knew could help here.

Jake also likely knew a lot more about Fowler than he would because of his interest in analog photography; Jake was also a master of "data mining" information on individuals from various sources, earning him the moniker "Jake the Rake;" Jake loved photography and would know places to look for information he didn't.

It was time to set up a meeting to see what information Jake could turn up on Drake Fowler. He was certain there were skeletons in his closet that would make him a prime candidate for burning down the Youngswood museum.

Chapter Six

Melvin P. Biggerstaff Medical Sciences Building
Central Ohio University College of Medicine
0955 hours

Dan went on his weekly rounds to the Biggerstaff Medical Sciences building across from the hospital. The Biggerstaff building was named after Dr. Melvin P. Biggerstaff, the founding dean of the medical school and a large benefactor after his death. The building housed most of the preclinical faculty (biochemistry, genetics, physiology, anatomy, cell biology) and their research facilities. The large three-story building (plus a full basement) was only twenty-five years old but had a variety of ills that were very atypical for a young building, which most of its residents quickly pointed out.

He had an appointment to meet Dr. Jack Meach, the head of the biochemistry department, for their monthly meeting. He was sure to hear about the poor quality of the building during this encounter; he and Meach didn't get along that well. Not many people liked the crusty, obnoxious department head, but he brought in a lot of research money, which meant a lot in the university world; Meach was also fully tenured, meaning he would be tough to get rid of—and Meach knew it. It wasn't a battle he was willing to fight just yet. Meach was in his early sixties and, hopefully, would be retiring soon.

John Charles Meach was a native of Cleveland, the son of medical school professors at Case Western. He earned his bachelor's in biochemistry at the University of Pittsburgh and his doctorate from Johns Hopkins—then, as today, one of the most prestigious programs in the world.

Meach had academic positions at various medical schools in Ohio and Pennsylvania over the years and had a stellar basic science research career, mainly focusing on the mechanisms of hypoglycemia recovery in mice and other diabetes-related projects. He earned tenure after only five years and became a full professor in eight—far ahead of most of his colleagues. He had many prestigious grants and was clearly the high earner in his department. He was somewhat disappointed that he ended up in less prestigious Staffordsville rather than Columbus or another large city, but, like him, his abrasive personality didn't endear him to the administration at any institution he worked at.

But Dan Rudbeck had many friends, and his issues with career stalling had more to do with his eclectic outside activities, many of which were politically incorrect. Meach was more talented, but just a nasty guy no one liked. He truly disliked very few people, but the man he was about to see was one. He entered the large office with a sense of dread.

"Jack, how's it going?" he said, shaking the shorter man's hand as he entered his office.

"I guess okay, Dan. Want some coffee or pop?"

"Diet if you have it." Meach handed him a can of diet cola from his small refrigerator as they sat in his dark brown lounge chairs. "How's research going, Jack? You always seem to have a lot of grants going, even in this era of federal cutbacks. Lots of money is coming in from the pharma companies for some of your basic drug research, so you're doing way better than most. Anything new?"

Meach pointed a finger at him. "How about we talk about what's not new: I hate this goddamn piece of shit building, Malgy. It's only twenty-five years old, and something new is wrong with it every week. The water main bursts once or twice a year, creating a scenic waterfall in the lobby, resulting in a massive re-routing of pedestrian traffic and mass confusion. We even had a couple of Canada geese who somehow got in there and were swimming around in the lobby, shitting that yellow crap all over the place. Do you know how badly that stinks? Those obnoxious assholes are a protected species, too, so we can't even shoot them, and they attack if you get too close. If some kids were in there, tearing up the place, we could go after them, but not those honking bastards. It's like they know it, too."

"Correct. Canada geese don't have anal sphincters and are a significant nuisance, but they're protected under the Migratory Bird Treaty Act. It's sort of like diplomatic immunity for a bird. You didn't hear this from me, but they also can be quite tasty when prepared properly; one local motel restaurant advertises their Tuesday night special as 'roast beef of the skies.' You should try it for a fancy night out on the town."

"Whatever; thanks for using your encyclopedic knowledge of stupid-ass stuff to give me an ornithology and culinary lesson. The fucking HVAC never works in summer, and the heat's always broken in the winter. It's the planet Mercury of buildings—it's either burning hot or freezing cold, with no middle ground. And let's not even talk about the damn bugs or the mice."

"You use mice in your experiments, right? Now you need to buy fewer of them."

"Oh, you're so funny. The mice have to be from a specific lineage, Rudbeck. You don't know anything about animal research. Don't be such a dolt."

"*Specific lineage?* That sounds pretty racist to me, Jack. Be careful I don't report you to the DEI mouse police."

"I also know enough about insecticides now to get my own exterminator's license."

"Now *that's* a talent you can use anywhere; having a side hustle is good. At least the place is new enough that we don't need to worry about asbestos."

"Funny again. You're a true comedian, Rudbeck; you should do stand-up. Your office hasn't been flooded several times, has it? You wouldn't be laughing then."

"Confucius emphasized finding strength and resilience in adversity, suggesting that focusing on positive emotions and maintaining a positive outlook is more beneficial than dwelling on the negative. I also don't feel that experiencing it personally makes it any more real. But, yeah, I hear you. I wish I knew a good solution."

"Sure you do. You're the administrator of this area, so why don't you fix it? Or have you just become another damn suit around here with his head up his ass? Maybe your ancient Chinese buddy can. Those stupid quotes you spout all the time—what a pile of crap."

He stood up to his full height and pointed a large finger at Meach. "Watch it, Meach. I don't need to take that shit from you or anyone else. I work my ass off around here, but I'm not a magician, so shut the hell up and offer some constructive suggestions for a change. I know that's impossible for you."

"Maybe you do have to take it. Are you going to make me shut up?"

"Step outside, and I'll show you. I don't think you want that."

Meach broke eye contact with him. "Okay, you win, big guy, but, of all people, I never thought you'd become a corporate drone, Dan."

"I'm not. It's a sixty-million-dollar building, and the original contractors are long gone, so we can't get restitution from them. Our contractors have fixed what they can, so what do you want me to do as a solution?"

"Well, I know one. I want to burn this SOB to the ground, and we could collect the insurance money."

"You do realize my cousin is the fire chief, correct? Jack, that may not be something you wish to say, especially since the Youngswood Arts Center burned up last week."

"Aww, I'm just kidding, Malgy."

"Don't kid about stuff like that. That plan is also not very practical." He sighed. "I get so tired of how everyone misunderstands how things work. This is a university, Jack, not a private business. We're self-insured, so we would just be taking money from ourselves in the form of an insurance fund, a separate company. Things don't work like that, man. You're a department head, so you should know those details."

"Okay, but we could've built another building for what all the repairs we've made cost."

"Good advice to take under consideration. As usual, this has been a great meeting, Jack. I can't wait to do it again. Thanks for the can of pop."

He left the meeting, again with a bad taste in his mouth after meeting with the regional medical school campus's most disliked department head. He hated the Biggerstaff building too, and he couldn't recall a young building with so many problems. There were buildings over a hundred years old on the main campus with far fewer issues.

Unfortunately, he didn't have a solution today for the chronically ill building with multisystem organ failure, which was dealt a crappy hand in the building lottery; it was the P^3 (Piss Poor Protoplasm) of edifices. The best plan was to try to develop a long-range *pro forma* for a new building sometime in the next five to ten years. That would take significant fundraising and politicking, as government funding was harder to come by these days.

AAAAA

Working Guy's Buddy Bar & Grill
901 S. Fremont Street
Staffordsville, Ohio
1210 hours

After that fantastically upbeat meeting, he traveled to his best-loved one-star restaurant. He sat at his usual old wooden booth at Working Guy's Buddy, waiting for his monthly lunch with his favorite cousin. His autographed photo was at the front, not for doing anything exceptional, other than eating a two-pound cheeseburger in ten minutes. This exhibit of his obnoxious behavior was one reason Jayna refused to go there—the other was that the only vegetarian option was onion rings, and deep-fried, breaded vegetables didn't qualify. Ah, he would leave the fine dining to different places.

Sandra Jeanne Arnold was his first cousin on his mother's side, and they were only a year apart in age—she was a year younger. He was far closer to Sandy than his sister Becky, as he and his sibling were much farther apart in age, and Rebecca Elizabeth Rudbeck felt her little brother was very annoying at times, which he was. The omnipresent family dysfunction in their earlier years was also not conducive to family togetherness. Many other people felt him irritating, but Sandy always tolerated him and even looked up to him at times as a role model.

Sandy was also a childhood friend of Jayna Blackwell, as they were the same age and lived only two blocks apart; Sandy's older brother Will was the same age as one of Jayna's brothers, Eric, and they were good friends. Sandy and Jayna had become close again after Jayna returned to Staffordsville from Dallas after Sam died.

How's it going, Danny? His cousin gave him a fist-bump as she sat down. The fifty-seven-year-old city's fire chief was a trim five-eight and 140 pounds, and had grown out her hair a bit and dyed it blonde.

"I'm pretty good. Weird about the Youngswood museum, huh?"

Sandy nodded. "Yeah, tell me about it. I'm getting too old for this type of thing. I can't remember anything like that ever happening around here."

"Any clues?"

She shook her head. "Way too early to tell. It'll take weeks to sort it out, and we may not find anything at all. The insurance company will likely have to eat it. Considering what the Fowler camera is worth, assuming no wrongdoing is found, that'll be a pretty penny."

"Yeah, ten million dollars right there. It just seems suspicious that Fowler would have picked our museum for an exhibition. It's was a nice place, but hardly up to his standard."

"What's your implication?"

"Evie claims the camera on exhibit was a replica, as it differs slightly in color from her vision of the real one, which she saw once. The real camera had a top plate made of a slightly radioactive alloy, and the camera pieces I recovered from the remains had no radioactivity. Fowler could have burned the museum up to collect the money; then he would still have the real camera to sell on the black market."

"That's an awfully wild theory, Danny, and you're going to have to put together a lot of pieces to make that legal argument. You know Evie' observations won't hold up in court."

"I know, it's just a hunch." He took a bite of celery, which was healthier than fries or onion rings. "Laurie and the girls doing well?"

"Oh, sure. Adrienne will start teaching high school social studies close to here, and Carrie is thinking about veterinary school."

"That's great. Carrie always did like her critters. She'll make a great vet."

"Laurie will probably work three or four more years, then retire. The teachers' pension in Ohio is pretty good."

"What about your pension? You should be eligible soon."

She nodded. "Yep, about the same time, and I'll retire too, then Laurie and I can travel more. What about you, Danny?"

"I don't know. I like what I'm doing and don't know who would replace me. I don't see myself retiring in the next few years."

"Evie still dating Jayna's youngest son?"

He nodded and smiled. "Yeah, they're an attractive couple. He's very laid back, which is good for her, as she can be pretty intense."

"Just like her dad. You and Jayna doing okay?"

He nodded. "For the most part. Like any couple, we have issues. I'm just so glad we could get past our personal problems, as I thought I'd lost her forever. She still gets emotional about Sam—he only passed three years ago. I think the worst part of that is she never had a chance to say goodbye to him. His coronavirus pneumonia was so fulminant that he had to be on a ventilator and died within days of diagnosis. She regrets whether she gave it to him, if he got it from somewhere they went, and so on."

"I guess everyone has regrets, Danny. We all do." She took a drink of her diet soda. "You're looking trim these days."

"Well, Jayna has adopted a vegetarian lifestyle, and Evie and Rob don't eat meat either, so that leaves me the odd man out. Also, I have been hitting the gym and swimming quite a bit."

"Good for you. Still in counseling?"

He nodded. "Yeah, I've been seeing Deanna Palmer in Columbus now for over ten years. She has helped me a lot in dealing with my anger issues with my dad and such. She's used to dealing with physicians. We aren't an easy bunch to work with."

"I can only imagine. Things okay with you and Charlie?"

"I guess so. I do more administrative stuff now than toxicology, so I don't see her as often as I used to. We go out to dinner with her and Jeff every month or so."

"I still think that would be awkward."

He shook his head. "It's really not, Sandy. Charlie and I broke up on good terms, and I was even at their wedding. We always put Evie first and ensured she understood our divorce had nothing to do with her. I'm lucky to consider Charlie one of my closest friends. I don't have a lot in common with Jeff, but he's a nice guy. I'm just glad we can continue to have a good relationship. I'm over my regrets about us, as I'm much happier now." He took a bite of the grilled tenderloin with mustard the server had brought; he had given up his beloved mayonnaise-laden breaded variety these days. "You talk to Beck much?" Becky was his older sister, whom he was never particularly close to; she had recently divorced from her second husband, Tim.

"Some stuff on social media. I don't really hear from her a whole lot, Danny; we were never all that close. When's the last time you saw her, anyway?"

"At my and Jayna's wedding, a year or so ago. Not since then. She's talked about coming down sometime soon to visit some friends here and in Columbus."

"You can't fix everything, you know. She dealt with your dad in her own way by leaving for the Twin Cities. You're such different people."

"She's still my sister, and I care about her. I know she probably still struggles with finances and likely has some substance issues of her own. I can't help but feel that she resents my success. I worked very hard to get where I am, and if she had asked me for help, I would've done so."

Sandy took a drink of her diet cola. "People have to work things out their own way, Danny. I know you do. You were the one who weathered most of the abuse from your dad, dealt with his affairs after he died in his drunken car crash because Aunt Carolyn was incapable, and took care of her when she was sick. You have nothing to feel guilty about. She made her choice not to be around. If she resents you for some reason, it's her problem, not yours."

"I guess so. I've learned that not everyone is going to like me, and that may include family. I have just learned to rejoice in all the good things I do have."

"Atta boy, Danny." She punched him in the shoulder.

He finished his robust meal and thought about some unusual testing he needed to do with Sybil Tegler at the research center tomorrow morning. To be prepared for the residents ' and medical students ' questions, he would need to brush up on all the latest literature on auto-brewery syndrome.

Chapter Seven

Staffordsville University Hospital
Clinical Research Center 2 West
0803 hours

The next morning, he came into the patient room at the medical school inpatient research center, where Sybil lay in a bed as a nurse was inserting an IV into her left hand. He had an internal medicine resident and a medical student following him, taking notes about any utterance from this giant of internal medicine and toxicology.

"How are you today, Sybil?" he asked, noticing she was much better groomed and dressed than at their last encounter. That wouldn't take much, as she'd hit rock bottom after the Bowling Green football game.

"Pretty good. Surely better than a week ago."

"That's for sure. Do you remember any of that evening?"

"It's just a fog. Did I make a spectacle of myself?"

He laughed. "You could say that. You insisted on getting an orange jumpsuit and having your mugshot printed on your filthy sweatshirt with pop spilled all over it."

She shook her head sheepishly. "I don't remember any of that. How embarrassing."

"Well, you were five times the legal limit, so it was amazing that you could even talk and were still alive, let alone recall anything you said or did. You also tried to get on a broken-down Bowling Green bus, which is how the sheriff's deputy found you in the first place."

"A bus? I don't remember that either. So what is it we're doing today, Malgy?" she asked.

"Carbohydrate challenge—the gold standard for diagnosing auto-brewery syndrome."

"Yeah, you mentioned that, but you said it's a pretty rare condition."

He nodded. "Correct. Some microorganisms preferentially metabolize sugar to alcohol—the most common being simple brewer's yeast, *Saccharomyces cerevisiae.* The microorganisms supposedly creating the alcohol utilize carbohydrates, of course, as a substrate for fermentation. The night the deputy found you wandering down the highway, you had consumed an extremely high-carbohydrate meal and a large regular pop, which could easily have precipitated it." He held two bottles of orange liquid.

"What are those?" she asked, pointing at the bottles.

"Each contains 100 grams of glucose, for a total of 200 grams. We'll give this to you, measure your blood alcohol level, and measure your breath alcohol content over several hours."

"What if I do have this weird syndrome? What do we do? I can't work or function being essentially drunk most of the time."

"As I said, the syndrome is caused by microorganisms, usually yeast, that ferment the carbohydrates to ethanol. In the literature, the yeast can easily be eradicated with antibiotics and antifungal agents. You will also need to modify your diet. Do you usually eat a lot of carbs?"

She nodded. "Yeah, I like to eat potato chips."

"You'll need to eat fewer carbs and cut out the chips and regular pop. They aren't good for you anyway. You are a little overweight and at risk for type 2 diabetes."

"That's a bummer."

"Well, you'll have to do that and a high-protein diet. We'll also need confirmation of the microorganisms in your gut."

"Is there a blood test for that?"

He shook his head. "No, we need a physical sample."

She frowned. "You mean a biopsy? How do we do that?"

"Endoscopy."

"Huh. Which end?"

He smiled and pointed to her mouth. "This one. Don't worry, you'll be sedated with propofol and likely won't even remember it." He nodded. "You have someone in mind?"

She nodded. "Sure. Dale Stephens is a friend of mine."

"Dale is a good choice. I'll contact him if your results warrant it."

"Do I have to stay in this bed?"

He nodded. "Your blood alcohol level may become extremely high, so, yes, for your own safety, we don't need you up and staggering around. Up with nursing assistance only to use the restroom." He picked the bottles up from her tray. "Okay, they've drawn your initial studies, so bottoms up, Sybil." She then drank the two orange-flavored bottles of liquid and lay back in the bed. "How was it?" he asked.

"Just like orange pop."

"With a lot more calories."

"But it wasn't that sweet."

"Sucrose is in most pop, not glucose. It's sweeter than glucose."

Over the next several hours, the lab technician came in to draw vials of blood as she watched shows on her tablet after being advised that answering texts and emails on her phone and laptop in an intoxicated state might not be a good idea.

At the end of the four hours, he and his entourage returned to the room. "How do you feel, Sybil?"

She twirled her finger in a circle. "Whoa. Really woozy. Like the day the officer found me wandering down the highway."

He nodded. "That's way more carbs than you would likely consume in any regular meal, so I expected that."

"So, when do I get the results back?"

"Hopefully in about an hour or so. I think you probably need to be in for observation tonight, as you shouldn't go home in this condition."

"I agree, Malgy. I was binge-watching some shows on my tablet. I won't get into trouble buying stuff online or answering messages."

"Okay. The team and I will be back in about an hour."

Seventy minutes later, he returned with several more members of his entourage, as many residents and students wanted to see this infrequent medical condition.

"Well?" she asked.

"The results of your blood ethanol levels are consistent with auto-brewery syndrome, Sybil. Your levels went up markedly after the carbohydrate challenge. Not as high as in the Palatine ER, but up to 0.372 percent."

"Dang. Was there any alcohol present in my system at baseline?"

"Yes, 0.021 percent, which isn't over the legal limit for an adult, but not an insignificant amount, but it demonstrates how sensitive it is to carbohydrates in your diet."

"So, what do we do?"

"I'm sending over a prescription for an antifungal agent, which you can start taking after your small bowel biopsy. I've contacted Dale, and he can do it tomorrow morning while you're still here."

"Okay, Malgy. I trust you. I'll start taking it tomorrow."

"I'll check on the biopsies the day after tomorrow, after the results are in." For some reason, the rare diagnosis of auto-brewery syndrome seemed too convenient, but he didn't have a theory on what else it could be, or what it had to do with the museum fire, if anything. He kept thinking about Deputy Wolford's normal horizontal nystagmus test in the Palatine ER and how that particular fact didn't fit in with the others.

It was now time to visit the Medical Examiner's office, where its leader always welcomed him eagerly with open arms.

AAAAA

Dubois County Medical Examiner's Office
University Hospital
Staffordsville, Ohio
0840 hours

"OMG. Whatcha need, Malgy?" Dr. Charlotte Madeleine Boisseau, head of pathology and the Dubois County Medical Examiner, said as she peered at some documents on her desk, seemingly knowing who had burst into her domain by his noisy, ungainly gait, with all the finesse of a bull in a china shop. One didn't dare break anything or mess up this place, or severe consequences would follow. He knew this lady knew how to wield multiple sharp tools and could cut you up with precision.

"How'd you know it was me? You didn't even look up from your important work."

"I would know those rapidly moving size fifteen feet anywhere. It's like the Sasquatch entered my domain."

"And how did you know I needed anything, Charlie? Can't I just stop by to say hello?" he asked his tall ex-wife, who peered up briefly from her electronic microscope, frowned, then looked back into it, clearly disinterested in whatever emergency this frequent intruder to her domain had.

"'*L'histoire se répète toujours.*'"

"Sorry, I'm a little rusty with my French."

"That figures. 'History usually repeats itself.' As in your history of bothering me about yet another urgent mystery to solve, lest the world be destroyed."

"Yes. '*Study the past if you would define the future.*'"

"Exactly, wise, ancient Confucius. Now, if we're done exchanging quotes, I have much work to do. I know you're a man of leisure with infinite time for his extramural projects, and—"

"This is pretty darn important, Charlie. I need to know the results of biopsies on Sybil Tegler's small intestinal contents."

"Sure, I anticipated you would want that." The freckled, redheaded pathologist handed him a report. "Large concentrations of *Saccharomyces cerevisiae*, which is quite unusual for a small bowel biopsy."

"Brewer's yeast. So, she had a significant overgrowth of that, which fermented the sugars to alcohol."

"Auto-brewery syndrome? You think she might have that?"

He nodded. "It's the best theory I have. Sybil swears she doesn't drink, but she was hammered in the ER after the police took her there when she was found staggering down a deserted highway after the ball game a week ago last Saturday. She tried to board a broken-down bus going back to Bowling Green, but was told to get off, and she kept walking west until she was almost out of the county. Either she has ABS, or she's lying. She permitted me to talk to the friend she was with, who said they were nowhere near any alcohol."

"It's a pretty rare syndrome, but you seem to specialize in rare stuff."

"Is there any way to fake these biopsy results?"

She looked at him and frowned. "Fake them? What do you mean?"

"I mean, could they be from someone else?"

"I suppose it's always possible for someone to have switched the samples, but that would be a lot of trouble. Why in the world would you think that?"

"I always consider every possible angle in my sleuthing."

"And that sleuthing often gets you into trouble, and I just don't want it getting me into trouble also, as Amalgam-Man's sleuthing usually costs a lot of extra time and money I don't have."

"Aww, come on, Charlie. The truth is more important than mere time and money."

"Tell that to the administration. Anyway, I've never heard of anything like that happening in my nearly thirty years as a pathologist."

"That doesn't mean it's impossible now, Charlie. Can you do enzyme studies on this biopsy?"

"*Enzyme studies*?" She scratched her head and nodded. "I . . . guess so, but which ones, and what the heck for?"

"Tegler's half-Asian. I want to check the levels of *ALDH1*, *ALDH2*, and *ALDH3* isoforms."

"Aldehyde dehydrogenase deficiency?"

"Yeah. Up to half of East Asians can be deficient. Affected individuals can't metabolize alcohol hardly at all."

She sighed and rolled her eyes. "Sure, I know all that, Malgy, believe it or not; you aren't the only one with medical knowledge. But do you have reason to suspect that abnormality?"

"She doesn't drink."

"Neither do you, and I don't believe you have that condition. Your father's family wouldn't have survived long with that enzymatic abnormality, which might have been good. No offense."

"Agreed." He nodded.

"But isn't that information already in her medical record? Surely she would've been tested for that."

"Yes, and it says she's ALDH negative per aldehyde breath test, but no genetic studies exist. I have access to her records since she asked me to take over her care."

"And you think that's also falsified?"

"Maybe."

"Oh, my, Malgy. Your paranoid suspicions also aren't a reason to do three thousand dollars' worth of tests. Tegler's a medical geneticist who surely knows if she has the disorder or not."

He laughed. "It's just a hunch, come on. If you don't do it, I'll just find another way."

She sighed. "What was her blood alcohol content in the ER?"

"0.41 percent for the Palatine blood draw. It increased to 0.372 percent after a 200-gram glucose challenge from a 0.021 percent baseline."

The slender fifty-six-year-old put her hands on her hips, as she often did when her ex-husband went down a bizarre path of no return. "Dang, Malgy, that's over five times the legal limit. Most normal people would be unconscious at that level, and someone with ALDH deficiency would be dead long before that, especially if she had *S. cerevisiae* producing ethanol in her gut."

The wheels were turning in his head. "Is it possible for someone to introduce *S. cerevisiae* into the biopsy *after* it was taken?"

She nodded. "That's also theoretically possible, but would require multiple accomplices along the way to help, including the gastroenterologist. You can't just stick it in there—you'd have to introduce it in precise steps to make it look real. Again, you describe an awfully convoluted caper if you believe she burned the museum down. For instance, how would Sybil have known that the Bowling Green bus was going to break down right there so she could pretend to get on it? From what you just said, that's the only way the police found her, right? The bus passengers pointed her out? That seems like a pretty random event."

"I guess so. But I am an expert in convoluted capers, that's why I am what I am."

"'I yam what I yam?' Popeye the Sailor Man? A bold declaration of your unwavering personality? You could do it by eating a bit more spinach, at that, seafarer." She laughed.

"I resent that, Madam Medical Examiner. I eat mostly veggies these days."

"I seriously doubt that. Maybe at home, but I know you sneak to WGB at lunch with Sandy to eat those burgers and tenderloins at lunch."

"But, about this event, I am just trying to consider all options, even those you feel improbable."

"And how could she have known Wolford would be down that way around that time? The whole illusion that you postulate depends on that."

"His patrol is likely fairly predictable. I need to check that out, but I guess that he comes down that route almost every evening at the same time."

"I guess anything is possible. Okey dokey, but you owe me big on this one, Malgy."

"You can add it to my list of IOUs. I know it's pretty long."

AAAAA

He returned to his office to answer some messages and emails, and then set out to find as much new information as possible on Sybil Annette Tegler (née Thompson). She was born in Dayton to firefighter father Jim Thompson and high school biology teacher mother Annette Wang; she had a younger sister, Winifred, who was a paralegal. With a little digging, he found that Sybil had gone to Beavercreek High School, a large Dayton high school with enrollment 2,300. He found a copy of her senior yearbook and saw that she was in the school band and science club—nothing unusual.

She then went to Wright State on a scholarship sponsored by the Dayton Fire Department, given her stellar academic standing in high school. She completed a dual major in chemistry and biology and, like her mom, obtained a teaching certificate and taught at a nearby high school.

She then met Henry Tegler, an accountant near her high school, and they started dating and were married a year later. A son, Thomas, arrived a year after that. Seven years later, she decided on a career change, and she was accepted into the PhD program in Medical Genetics at Ohio State, which she finished five years later after the small family moved to Columbus. She applied for a faculty position at the Central Ohio University College of Medicine and was given a position at the Staffordsville branch.

He was on the search committee for that position, and remembered that she was somewhat quiet and shy, much like his second wife. She didn't seem to have made many friends over her years at Staffordsville, but she usually went to all the requisite social gatherings. One thing he remembered is that she, like him, never drank alcohol. She was so concerned about it that she only drank from sealed water or soda bottles, and never punch from a serving table, for fear that someone might've spiked it. He never thought it was a huge deal; if he accidentally took a sip of spiked punch, he would just politely discard it, but she got really upset about it.

Her years at the Staffordsville branch weren't without some issues. She didn't make a huge salary as an assistant professor, but their combined income with her husband's salary should've been enough for a comfortable lifestyle in a small Ohio city. However, she started driving fancier cars and wearing nicer clothing, and some wondered how she could afford those things.

He was also on the faculty remediation committee and remembered some issues with her accessing online gambling sites from her Biggerstaff office. What people did in their off time was their business, but such activities on university property, using university equipment, were forbidden. The school firewall wouldn't allow access to those sites, but she thought using her smartphone as a mobile hotspot would work. It did allow access, but the university-owned PC still tracked her unapproved browsing habits.

She was called into the Dean's office and was told to stop going to gambling sites while on campus or risk probation or even termination. He didn't think a whole lot about it at the time, as several other professors and physicians (mostly male) had done the same thing and had even accessed pornography and other forbidden sites.

He didn't know if she was successful at gambling or not, but he knew that the house almost always won, and most habitual gamblers ended up losing a lot of money and often their relationships. When he'd learned a year ago that she was getting a divorce, he put two and two together and deduced that Henry had experienced enough of her severe gambling debts. He knew that Tommy lived with his father after the divorce.

The money issues could motivate Sybil to burn down the

museum in order to split the money with Fowler, who was too well-known to do it himself. He had to figure out how she did it, as many things didn't make sense. He eagerly awaited Charlie's report, which she would hopefully have the next day. As it stood now, he had a court date to testify on her behalf that she had auto-brewery syndrome. So far, he had no evidence to the contrary.

AAAAA

Dan Rudbeck's Office
Staffordsville University Hospital
0842 hours

He sat in his office at the hospital, answering emails and preparing for his 0900 appointment with a resident. Charlie called him right then on the videoconferencing app.

"Hey, what you got?"

"Negative on deficiency of any of the ALDH enzymes, Malgy."

"Dang. Okay, that was just a thought, but it makes sense she wouldn't have it."

"I know what you're going to ask next."

"What's that?"

"If *those* results could be faked. I suppose that's also possible in the same way the yeast biopsy could be faked, by having someone else's tissue instead of hers. I have no way to know for sure, other than doing DNA testing."

"I suppose that's out of the question."

"Without probable cause, correct. It would be far too costly, Malgy."

"Thanks, Charlie. I appreciate it."

Charlie raised an interesting question about the probability of that bus being out there at exactly the right time; that chance seemed small.

He found out, however, that Ronnie Wolford was meticulous and likely followed a set patrol schedule, which wouldn't be all that hard to obtain. About the bus, though—how hard would it be to rig a tire so that it would blow out at just the right moment? Was that even possible?

It might be time for the Amalgam-Man to step up his investigation a bit. But he needed to go to the courthouse to give some expert testimony on behalf of his colleague. He just hoped he was doing the right thing, but he had no concrete evidence to the contrary. Not yet.

AAAAA

Dubois County Courthouse
Circuit Court #2
State of Ohio vs. Sybil Annette Tegler
1005 hours

"Dr. Rudbeck, please tell us your qualifications," Judith Smalstig, the circuit court judge, asked him at Sybil's public intoxication hearing. Her attorney accompanied her, and the city attorney, Bill Westergren, was at an adjacent table. The trivial case was of absolutely no interest to anyone, so the small courtroom was otherwise empty at the hearing for this low-level offense. "We've discussed all the evidence, but I'd like to hear from you."

"I am a board-certified medical toxicologist at the university and a noted expert in certain rare conditions, this being one."

"And you are here on behalf of Dr. Tegler regarding her public intoxication citation?"

He nodded. "Yes, Your Honor. I believe Dr. Tegler has a rare medical condition called auto-brewery syndrome and was not drinking at the time of the event."

The slender, fiftyish Black judge took her glasses off and stared at him. "Say again, Doctor?"

"Auto-brewery syndrome, or ABS, is a rare condition where the body actually produces its own alcohol in the gastrointestinal tract. This occurs when certain yeasts or bacteria ferment carbohydrates in the gut, leading to elevated blood alcohol levels. In her case, as a biopsy proves, her small intestine has an overgrowth of *Saccharomyces cerevisiae* or brewer's yeast. I also did a carbohydrate challenge test that showed her levels went up markedly after a sugar load. I have the reports right here." He tapped the manila envelope he was holding.

"This is a treatable condition, Doctor?" the judge asked.

"Yes. Treatment includes antibiotics to eradicate the microorganisms causing the problem. She has started such and has begun to show some clinical improvement."

"So, you believe Dr. Tegler is not responsible for her intoxicated behavior and having a blood alcohol content five times the legal limit?" Judge Smalstig asked.

He nodded. "That is correct. While she shouldn't be driving until we eradicate the condition, she isn't responsible for it from a legal standpoint. Her counsel and I therefore believe her citation should be dismissed."

"Huh, that's a new one on me. Mr. Westergren? Any objections?" She looked at the overweight, fortyish city attorney."

The city's attorney nodded. "Sounds fair to me, Your Honor."

"Okay, then. Case dismissed." She struck her gavel. "Next case."

Sybil hugged him as they walked out of the old courtroom. "Thanks, Malgy. I know this would've been just a small fine, but it's better not to have it on my record. It's embarrassing for when I go up for tenure. I've had enough bumps in the road, as you know."

"No problem, Sybil. It's what I do. By the way, how are you feeling after a few days on the fluconazole?"

"Better. I seem to be less woozy than I was."

"Have you been using the portable breathalyzer I gave you?"

"Yeah. Every two hours." She handed him a logbook. "Mostly 0.03 percent or less. So when can I go back to work? I'm really getting behind on things."

He put his hand on her shoulder. "Hey, wait a minute. It will take a while to eradicate; probably at least another couple of weeks, and no driving for a while."

"That's okay; I only live about a mile away. The walk is good exercise."

"At least it's not walking out of the county down Highway 128 late at night."

Chapter Eight

Rudbeck Home
2105 Winthrop Street
Staffordsville, Ohio
0322 hours

Jayna sleepily heard his cell phone go off *again* in the middle of the night. She hesitantly poked her husband with it and went back to sleep, clearly not wanting to answer a third late-night call in two weeks.

"Dang it, what's up?" he asked sleepily after seeing the caller ID "Chief" and removing his CPAP mask.

"Danny."

"Oh, no, not *you* again. Hold on a sec." He turned the CPAP machine off. "What's happened now? Can't you leave your poor cousin alone?"

"Wake up, get your big ass out of bed, and get to the Biggerstaff Building pronto."

"Get my big ass to the Biggerstaff Building? That alliterative tongue twister is way too hard for me in the middle of the night,

Sandy."

"I mean it, Danny! No time for your jokes right now!"

"Huh? Did the water main burst again, or is the HVAC out? What the hell do you want me to do about it at three AM? I have many talents, but plumbing and heating aren't included in those. I'm so sick of that damn place. I'm going back to sleep."

"Well, guess what? You won't have to worry about it any longer. The whole thing has burned up."

"Wh-what did you say?"

"Yep. Burnt crispy. Two big damn fires in two weeks. That's a bit much for the Staffordsville Fire Department to handle and investigate. The overtime will kill the budget."

Jayna turned on the light. "What is it, Dan? The hospital again?"

"No, Sandy. She says the Biggerstaff building is on fire, and the interior has burned up."

"Huh? *Another* extensive building fire?" She sat up, somewhat confused, as she wiped matted-down blonde hair from her eyes. "Is . . . is that a joke? It can't be possible."

He shook his head and stood up. "That building is a running joke, but not in this case. Firefighters don't make jokes about fires."

"Who or how?"

"Don't know. Maybe it's for the best."

"You can't mean that, Dan."

"Was . . . anyone inside, Sandy?"

"Yes, we know of one person. He didn't make it. We haven't found any other bodies. Many lab animals were surely killed, though."

"Okay. I'm on my way. Again." He sighed. "Who was it?"

"Dr. John Robertson was sleeping in his office, as he often does, I hear, because he runs some of his instrumentation all night. They say he snores loud enough to wake the dead."

"So . . . arson, with a homicide . . . that's felony murder."

"You got it, assuming it's really arson. As you know, it will take a while to investigate, but it's statistically unlikely that two fires in two weeks are both accidental. The connection between the two is unclear, however."

"Right. I'm on my way, for whatever help I can give." These middle-of-the-night emergencies were getting a bit old. He again put on his clothes, made a quick cup of Dark Sumatra coffee in the Keurig (he didn't have time for his usual fresh-roasted dark roast pourover in the Chemex), and left to drive the three miles to campus. A few minutes later, he could already detect the scent of burning debris, but the fire had been extinguished by then.

Biggerstaff was a brick building, so the exterior was still intact, unlike the arts museum, but the entire interior had been destroyed. He looked at the smoldering building in amazement. Was it salvageable? As Fire Chief Arnold put it, it was burnt crispy, but it wasn't salvageable *before* the fire. He fully expected a parade celebrating the demise of the university's worst building tomorrow morning, to be led by Dr. Jack Meach as grand marshal.

The Biggerstaff building was also a more complex problem to sort out than the Youngswood museum, as the perpetrator couldn't benefit financially from the fire (the insurance "money" from a self-insurance fund would go to the university, so it was essentially paying itself). Destroying evidence, perhaps, or revenge? Killing Robertson from the physiology department? Who the hell cared about that morbidly obese, end-of-career, alcoholic loser, unless he had some dirt on the perpetrator? He again doubted there was a political statement to be made there, although he was sure many secretly cheered that the hated, cursed building was no more. Unfortunately, no one could talk to him now, and any evidence he had in his office was surely destroyed.

He then again thought back to the horizontal nystagmus test that Ronnie Wolford had done, and how it had appeared normal to him. He knew that it was pretty much impossible to fake that test, but overwhelming evidence pointed to the fact that Sybil was, in fact, severely intoxicated on that night, and the blood test proved it.

He forgot about that as he saw the smoking husk of what was once the hated, cursed Melvin Biggerstaff building. He thought about poor Robertson dying, and where all the occupants of that building were going to be relocated.

Ah, well, he was the one who wanted to be an administrator. Sometimes you get what you wish for. He just wished it wasn't at three AM.

AAAAA

Dubois County Medical Examiner's Office
Staffordsville University Hospital
1500 hours

Dan and his good friend, university cyber-expert Jake Fisher, went to the conference room at the Medical Examiner's office the next afternoon and sat, taking a swig of the gourmet coffee he had brought. Jake was a former audiovisual expert turned information systems specialist. Lt. Brian Eppard and Charlie were also seated in there for a meeting of Staffordsville's greatest crime-solving minds.

"Malgy, sorry to hear about the building," Charlie, dressed in a crimson pantsuit, said. "I can't believe it happened again."

"Well, I am, too, although many will be glad it's gone."

"I assume you're here to talk about Johnny Robertson," Charlie told the police lieutenant.

"Yeah, what else, Dr. Boisseau?" Eppard said. "This is the place for stiffs, is it not, or is business so slow that you're seeing live patients these days?"

She smiled. "To the point with sardonic wit as always, Brian. Preliminary cause of death is smoke inhalation, of course," she said as she took a sip of black coffee.

"Tox screen?" he asked.

"He was a drinker, I understand, and his blood alcohol content was 0.09 percent. Probably had a little nip at the office," she said.

"Slightly over the legal limit . . . but he likely could tolerate a lot, given his high tolerance for booze. So, not very impressive, really. Tegler's was over four times that," he said.

"Also . . . there were high levels of alprazolam in his system," his ex-wife said, handing Eppard a report. "I don't know what to make of that."

He nodded. "There ya go. Benzos and alcohol, a classic combination for disaster. Do we have a quantitative level?"

"It's not back yet."

"Do we know if the alprazolam was prescribed to him?" Eppard asked.

She nodded. "Yep."

"And do we know by whom?" he asked.

"Thomas Castleton, a local primary care physician, for anxiety attacks," she said. "He seems to be a well-respected physician."

"He would've been stupid to have taken that much alprazolam," he said as he took a bite of a jelly doughnut. "Especially if he was running an important experiment."

"Yeah, like no one ever did that," Eppard said. "Give me a break. Addicts do stupid stuff and overdose all the time. You said yourself he was a shitty researcher."

"He was, but that doesn't mean he overdosed on it." He took another sip of coffee. "I still am skeptical about why a famed photographer like Fowler picked our museum for an exhibition. What'd you find out, Jake?" he asked his friend, who acted like he was about to burst at the seams in excitement.

"A bunch of interesting stuff, so get this: The great Drake Fowler is damn near broke, despite being one of the most famous photographers in America."

"No way," Eppard said. "How did that happen, Fisher?"

"Bad investments, extravagant tastes, gambling, women, possibly some illicit substances—the good things in life. Even the wealthy have limits on their resources. With enough digging, I uncovered some bankruptcy filings in various courts, mostly in New York. His divorce proceedings are also a matter of public record, and a lot of it was in the news."

"So, he could have benefited from the insurance money from the 'loss' of his famous photographic tools and his photographs," he said.

"Damn right," the wiry, fifty-seven-year-old Jake said. "Sybil Tegler isn't the most prosperous person, either. Her online gambling has gotten her into a lot of problems, not to mention a costly divorce. You already know most of that, Malgy."

"So what's the connection here, folks?" Eppard asked.

"What do you mean?" Charlie replied.

"Two huge fires within two weeks. According to Chief Arnold, there hasn't been even one big fire like that in this county in the last eight years."

"Both fires can't be a coincidence, which is what you're saying," he said.

"Jeez, I don't want to start you on another investigation, Smokey the Bear Rudbeck, but, yes, that's my meaning. Two big fires in seemingly unrelated buildings, with no accelerant identified as of yet, although the investigation is ongoing."

"I can't think of any connection either—like anyone at the museum event who would work in or have access to Biggerstaff. Except me, of course." He thought for a minute. "Perhaps The Sulphur Shadow is the key."

"Huh? How's that, Rudbeck?" Eppard asked sharply. "You have some wonderful insight to share with us? Please continue."

He nodded. "Much can be learned from fine literature, such as The Sulphur Shadow, when someone poisoned the guy's CPAP machine. It was a time when Barclay Dixon decided to do medicine part-time and go into espionage."

"Just like you," Eppard said. "They say most authors write about what they know, and you know espionage, for sure."

"Don't interrupt my train of thought." He held his right index finger up. "Alprazolam can be easily aerosolized. Robertson had sleep apnea so badly that he had a second CPAP machine in his office, because he often slept there or napped on his futon. He didn't have a good relationship with his wife, who often wasn't home, so he really didn't have anyone to go home to."

"Yeah, I've read that wonderful contribution to literature, but you've again lost me, Dixon. You know we low-intellect, genetically inferior Neanderthal cops clearly can't function on your superior cerebral level. If only I could see the wonders and comprehend the things you can, my life would be so much better. Sadly, I am destined to live a life of ineptitude, not even knowing what I've missed."

"Don't be so hard on yourself, Brian. I found part of the plastic humidifier water reservoir from his CPAP machine. Most of it was melted, but I discovered trace amounts of alprazolam, although the water had evaporated."

"Alprazolam. A classic drug of abuse," Eppard said.

"It can be, yes; it's a benzodiazepine, but with other uses besides anxiety. Aerosolized alprazolam has been studied in clinical trials, as it's also a drug used to terminate seizures. Just like in The Sulphur Shadow, someone poisoned him with his own sleep apnea machine, although a more lethal agent was used there. He apparently died with the device on his face. The person could've done it knowing that it would be biochemically indistinguishable from the oral alprazolam he was prescribed."

"Huh. Would . . . he have maybe put it in there himself as a way to get more buzzed up?" Eppard asked.

He shook his head. "No, the alprazolam must be in a liquid form at a specific concentration, and dissolving pills in a solvent would introduce a lot of residue that I would have detected. If he had wanted to get high, there would have been many better-proven ways to do it than that."

"Just a thought. Well, I guess the team had better check the one at his home, too. What about the alcohol in his system, Rudbeck? Was that in his CPAP, too?"

"No, not in that reservoir, Brian. It would likely have to be heated to a temperature greater than the CPAP unit could supply. He was known to keep a large decanter of aged D.T. Darkkin & Sons whiskey in his office, so he probably did that on his own."

"The good stuff," Jake replied. "At least he went out enjoying the very best."

Chapter Nine

The next day, he had a new idea, and he drove to the police station to act upon it, as his OCD would not permit anything else once the idea entered his brain. He entered the old brick building and headed toward his friend Lt. Eppard's office. He entered, saw the tall lieutenant at his desk, and knocked on the open door.

"Brian, do you have a minute?"

Eppard sighed. "I will grant two minutes for you and your extraordinary cerebrum. What's up, Rudbeck?"

"I need your help. I have reason to believe that Sybil Tegler, or someone she was in cahoots with, arranged for that bus to have a blowout on Highway 128 that night, on the edge of the county, so that she could try and get on it."

"Have you checked with the tire service?"

"I did, and they say it was just a blowout."

"What do you want from me then, Rudbeck? Don't tell me. You believe someone planted an explosive charge in the tire in a sinister fashion to incapacitate the bus, and the service guy was paid off to cover it up, right?"

He put his hand over his mouth in astonishment. "You read

my mind, Brian! Of course, that's what I think."

"Come on, that's absurd. What do you want me to do, get a search warrant for that tire shop?"

"That would be a good start, yes."

"Good luck convincing a judge with that measly evidence. We'd get nothing else done if we investigated all flat tires; they happen all the time and aren't usually caused by criminal masterminds planting explosive charges." Eppard looked at his analog quartz wristwatch. "Your two minutes are up."

"They were going west, and the right front tire blew. The one closest to the shoulder."

"Yeah, so what?"

"I know from the police bodycam exactly where the bus was pulled over, and it would've blown out less than forty yards before that. Maybe I don't need a warrant for the shop, because an explosive charge would theoretically have left some traces of chemical residue on the road, right?"

Eppard paused for several seconds. "Well, maybe . . . only if there hadn't been a heavy rain or something to wash it away. It's not a super busy highway, so that might help you. I can't actually remember a case where something like that was measured, but I can check with Columbus or the feds."

He shook his head. "There hasn't been any precipitation at all since the event."

"You know this for a fact, Rudbeck?"

"Of course I do, as I always check all details."

"Again, what is it you want from me?"

"All I'm asking is to send a technician out there with me to test the area. What do you say?"

Eppard sighed. "I guess we could do that, since you are a man of leisure with all this free time and a vast technological arsenal at your disposal. Linda can collect gravel samples to see if there's any explosive residue. I will probably need some help from the university on your end to do fancy testing, though. We aren't really equipped for that here, and we certainly don't have the funds or personnel for another of your projects."

"Leave that to me. As you know, I have some connections in the lab."

"And I know you have unlimited time and funds, Dr. Dixon."

AAAAA

He and the lab technician drove to the blowout site on Highway 128 in the county's west end the next day. The skid marks led to where they stopped; the start of those marks was likely where the blowout occurred.

"Malgy, this is looking for a needle in a haystack. We're going to collect dirt and gravel from out here?" Linda Ashburn, the police lab technician, said. She was a thirtyish brunette, slightly overweight, and was wearing a set of coveralls, and clearly was not excited about her latest evidence-collecting assignment, as this "partner" was good at wasting time on fool's errands.

"Yeah, Linda. I know it seems like a lot of work and area to cover on short notice and with your other duties."

"That's right. Will we take it to your university lab to do mass spectrometry? We don't have the instrumentation for that."

"Yeah, no worries. My ex is fond of doing me favors."

"I'll bet she is. What are you hoping to find?"

"RDX from a C-4 charge." RDX, or royal demolition explosive, was the primary explosive component of C-4, a common plastic explosive used in military operations. "I suppose it could be something common like gunpowder, but that would be harder to engineer, more complex, and harder for us to detect."

They spent the next several hours collecting gravel samples from the shoulder and taking photos, as he realized this was a bigger endeavor than he had previously thought.

Finally, they collected the last of the gravel samples and loaded them into his vehicle to take back to the forensics lab, where a certain Medical Examiner's staff would eagerly be awaiting the specimens, which would undoubtedly require a fair amount of processing and use of the university chemistry department's mass spectrometer. He was certain they would give it A-1 priority just like all his other projects.

AAAAA

"Malgy, I think we've found something," Charlotte Boisseau said on the video call to her ex-husband two days later, at a rare moment when he was actually in his office. "Most of the stuff is typical asphalt. The primary component, of course, is bitumen, a sticky byproduct of petroleum, so there are typical peaks of that. But mass spectrometry shows trace amounts of a substance with exact mass 222.0343, which definitely doesn't correspond to anything in asphalt."

"That's the molecular mass of RDX."

She nodded. "Correct, you did your homework. I would have expected nothing less from Amalgam-Man."

"I don't think there would be any substances in asphalt of that mass?"

Charlie shook her head. "No, that would be very unlikely. I would need to verify this with forensic colleagues, but I would say that a C-4 charge blew out that tire at the place you collected the gravel."

"Guess I had better talk to the tire people and get the actual tire that blew out, since the one I examined certainly didn't contain any C-4. Something funny is going on here.

"Good luck. Another favor you owe me. Although you have nothing I need, so I guess it's another freebie."

"You will obtain great satisfaction after we solve the case, Charlie. Thanks."

Chapter Ten

Staffordsville Police Department
Interrogation Room
0920 hours

"Mr. Edwards, thanks for coming down." David Edwards, owner of ABC Tire & Towing, entered the small interrogation room where he and Eppard were waiting.

"Sure, Lieutenant, but I don't know what this is about or why the cops would want to talk to me. I'm just the owner of the tire shop."

"This is Dr. Daniel Rudbeck, special consultant to the department."

"Yeah, that's me. We met when I came into your shop yesterday. In particular, we want to talk to you about the Bowling Green bus incident on the first Saturday in October, sir."

Edwards shook his head. "I don't know what you mean. The evening of the Central Ohio-Bowling Green football game?"

"The right front tire of their bus blew out on Highway 128 around ten PM on its way back from the game."

"If you say so. Look, I'm the business owner and don't deal with every little thing. The tow guy would've taken care of it, because I was probably in bed."

"Well, we don't care about the tow. We want the actual tire that was removed," Eppard said.

"I told you what I told this big guy here when he came in with one of your cops. We gave him the tire, and they took it. That's all I know, Lieutenant, I swear."

"Then someone is lying, Edwards," he said. "The tire you gave us couldn't have been the original tire, as forensic analysis shows, the 'blowout' was too regular to be real. We also found traces of C-4 explosive residue on the asphalt near this purported 'blowout.' I'll ask you again—where's the original tire?"

"I told you that the one you took was the original, according to the technician."

"Look, Edwards, this is serious business," Eppard said. "There are several crimes tied up in this, and if you know anything at all, you're a co-conspirator and looking at felony charges. That exploding tire could've killed those occupants."

"I hear you, Lieutenant, but I'm the owner, as I said—I'm not there daily. The person you want to talk to is Eddie Phillips, my manager. He would've handled that."

"Okay, Mr. Edwards," Eppard said. "We'll get Phillips in here, but you'd better be telling the truth."

"I am, sir. Am I free to go?"

"Yeah," Eppard said. "We may want to talk to you again later, though."

They left the interrogation room, returned to Eppard's office, and sat down.

"What do you think, Rudbeck?"

He took a sip of coffee. "He's the owner, and it's very possible he knew nothing about this. It's not the largest tow and tire service in town but fairly large. I guess we talk to this Phillips guy to see what he has to say."

"Well, I'll have the guys get him in here."

AAAAA

Three hours later, he and Eppard re-enacted the same scene with Edward A. Phillips, the ABC Tire manager, a heavyset man in his mid-thirties. He sat down as the lieutenant began the conversation.

"Mr. Phillips, thanks for coming down. This is Dr. Daniel Rudbeck, a consultant to the department helping us with this investigation."

"It's nice to meet you both, but I'm unsure why I'm here."

"You're here because we have absolute evidence someone sabotaged the right front tire of Bowling Green University Bus #43 with a C-4 charge and blew it out on Highway 128 after the football game a few weeks ago. It caused the bus to be stranded on the westbound shoulder for about ninety minutes."

"I don't know about that incident, but why ask me?"

"Mr. Phillips: Someone at the tow company did this," he said. "It's only a matter of time before we find out who. You or one of the employees would've touched the blown-out tire when you fixed it out on the road. We'll detect the residue on someone's clothes. If not yours, then someone else's."

Phillips shook his head. "I don't know what you're talking about."

"Really?" he said. "Let me educate you: your company uses Reliable Uniform Service for your coveralls."

Phillips took a sip of burned police station coffee. "Yeah, so what, man? Lots of companies use that place for uniforms. Doesn't mean anything."

"'So what' is that I've obtained all the coveralls from your employees for the last two weeks. The technology we use can detect residue from explosives in trace amounts. Even if you didn't plant the explosives, the residue from where you handled the tire would be on there."

"That's a lie."

"Is it? As we told your boss, you're looking at felony charges as a co-conspirator if you don't come clean with this. We'll get a search warrant for your house, car, and everything you own until we find the evidence somewhere, Phillips."

"In that case, I think I'm done here until I talk to a lawyer."

"Go ahead, call him or her then, Phillips," Eppard said. "You've had lawyers before, haven't you?"

"What do you mean by that?"

"This is a police station. Don't you think we've run your record already? You did time for burglary in Columbus about ten years ago, so you know the system."

"Hey, I did my time, Lieutenant. Don't threaten me. Just because I screwed up in my twenties doesn't make me responsible for this."

"It just makes us less likely to believe you," Eppard said. "Better call that lawyer."

They could hold him for a couple more hours, but hopefully, Linda would have some new information momentarily. He and Eppard left the room as he went to find her.

AAAAA

He met with Linda Ashburn at the police lab thirty minutes later. "What'd you find out, Linda?"

She smiled excitedly. "You were right, Malgy. One of the uniforms that Phillips wore in the last few weeks has trace amounts of RDX on it, the medical examiner's office said. He must've gotten it on there when he changed the tire. The date corresponds approximately to the date the bus tire blew out."

"Is there any other way that could have gotten on it? Nothing in the shop? I'm no expert on auto mechanics and the products they use."

She shook her head. "No. He could've used no chemical product with a compound with that exact mass of RDX as a byproduct. So, unless he's detonating C-4 for some other reason, he's our man, Malgy."

"Time to call Eppard and get an arrest warrant for Phillips, who's still at the station. These warrants seem to be piling up."

***

Ten minutes later, he walked to Eppard's office to share the news about Phillips' shop coveralls and the RDX residue Linda found.

"So, David Phillips at ABC Tire & Towing was the one who set the charge in the tire and detonated it with a UHF radio transmitter when the bus got out of town, close to where Tegler had been waiting, so she could conveniently walk a few hundred yards to get to the broken-down bus. He replaced that tire with an identical one with similar wear and an artificial puncture hole. This gave her the perfect alibi, and the sheriff's deputy had a predictable schedule and came across the bus right on cue; the passengers, predictably, directed him to find Tegler staggering down the highway. And it was all documented on his bodycam—too well, as Wolford's normal nystagmus test was what prompted me down this path in the first place."

"Okay, I believe you, Rudbeck, especially since we know Tegler set off the transmitter that blew out the tire. Phillips maintains he simply got a message from an anonymous caller to arrange the tire deal, and fifteen thousand dollars was deposited in his bank account the next day. I'm amazed Tegler would have those kinds of funds."

"Unless Fowler helped out. We also have the person in Bowling Green to investigate, as the charge would've been placed there. The main purpose of Phillips was to swap the rigged tire to one that just had a simple blowout."

"It would be helpful to have the tire, but they must've disposed of it. No matter, I think we have enough evidence to proceed."

Chapter Eleven

Radio Station WEPL 1340-AM and 104.1-FM
1300 W. Adams Street
Staffordsville, Ohio
0900 hours

"Welcome to another edition of Rudbeck's Rounds, the medically oriented show designed to bring the public the best and most current medical knowledge. I am your host, Dr. Dan Rudbeck, from Central Ohio University College of Medicine. I am pleased to introduce this month's guest, Dr. Theodore Brannigan. Dr. Brannigan is Professor of Medicine at the medical school and program director of the hospital medicine fellowship program. Ted, it's great to have you on the show today."

"Thanks, Dan. I'm happy to be back."

"Can you tell us a little bit about your topic?"

"It's one that's a little bit in your realm, Dan, as it involves a toxic product. It's a disorder called aldehyde dehydrogenase deficiency."

"Tell us more about it, Ted."

"Well, as you know, a lot of people drink ethyl alcohol, which is found in alcoholic beverages. This substance, produced by the fermentation of various carbohydrates, is pleasurable to many people and results in a sense of euphoria due to its binding to certain receptors in the brain. At higher concentrations, it can cause lethargy and even death. Most people break down alcohol at a predictable rate, but aldehyde dehydrogenase or ALDH deficiency is a disorder where that doesn't work right, and toxic byproducts develop."

"Why is this disorder important?"

"Dan, there are several types of the enzyme aldehyde dehydrogenase, but the ALDH2 mutation is the most important and the most common single-point mutation in humans. It's found in very few Caucasians, but about 50% of East Asians have this mutation."

"So, you're saying it's very common."

"Absolutely. Alcohol is initially broken down by alcohol dehydrogenase to acetaldehyde, which is then broken down by aldehyde dehydrogenase to acetic acid, which is essentially vinegar, which is harmless and disposed of by the body."

"What happens in this ALDH mutation?"

"The toxic intermediate metabolite acetaldehyde accumulated in the bloodstream as it can't be metabolized further. This substance is toxic and results in facial flushing, lightheadedness, palpitations, and nausea. This reaction can occur at very low levels of alcohol consumption and can make an affected person quite ill."

"I remember a drug used for alcoholism a while back that caused similar symptoms."

"That's right, Dan, it was a drug called disulfiram, used as a deterrent for drinking alcohol. It blocks the effect of ALDH and causes similar symptoms to those with the disorder."

"Did that drug help people with alcohol abuse disorder, Ted?"

"Not really; it was just a deterrent and did nothing to address physiological processes in the brain. Newer drugs such as naltrexone and acamprosate seem to be better for that problem."

"How does a person know if they have the disorder?"

"That's a great question, Dan. People at high risk, such as those of East Asian descent, can undergo various tests. An easy one is breath testing, where the patient ingests a small amount of alcohol and measures acetaldehyde concentrations in the breath.

This is a quick method of identifying affected persons."

"Are there other tests, Ted?"

"There is a 'patch test' where a patch containing a small amount of alcohol is applied to the skin; flushing or redness indicates ALDH deficiency. The most definitive test is genetic testing, where we test the DNA to determine if they carry the gene. It is the most reliable method, but is also the most costly."

"Is there any treatment for this disorder?"

"Right now, the best treatment is for affected individuals to abstain from even small amounts of alcohol. There are experiments with gene therapy in progress, but this treatment would be quite costly for a condition whose symptoms can be avoided by abstaining from alcohol. It may explain the lower levels of alcoholism and high rates of abstinence compared to other ethnic groups."

"Thanks, Ted, for discussing this prevalent condition that I bet a lot of people don't know anything about."

"Thanks for having me on the show, Dan."

"Appreciate everyone tuning in, folks. Public service announcement: whether or not you have aldehyde dehydrogenase deficiency, don't drink and drive. Get a cab, Uber, or other transportation home. It's not worth the risk to you and others on the road.

"Join us next month on Rudbeck's Rounds when we will have Lieutenant Brian Eppard from the Staffordsville Police Department and hospital attorney Marianne Ellsworth discuss healthcare privacy as it applies to law enforcement and how to deal with requests from law enforcement regarding patients."

Chapter Twelve

Spacious Mansion of
Barclay J. Dixon, MD, PhD
1159 hours

Dr. Barclay Dixon entered his cavernous private dwelling around noon, hoping to fix himself a leisurely lunch from his well-stocked kitchen, when he realized his front door had somehow been opened. He was extremely meticulous, and it was impossible that he didn't close it fully when he left that morning.

This was not the first time that had happened, as Danger was his middle name; well, not really, but at least he was thinking of changing it to that. Clearly, his sophisticated high-end alarm system had been bypassed by an espionage expert and rendered useless.

Only a couple of his antagonists possessed such a combination of intellectual and fine motor skills, and his vast knowledge of encyclopedic details recalled that small hands possessed tremendous touch discrimination due to the finger receptors being packed into a smaller surface area. This latter characteristic narrowed down the potential list of suspects as he surveyed the home cautiously.

His keen sense of smell (matched only by certain K-9 officers and his high-end olfactometer) then detected the odor of expensive French perfume: *Baccarat Les Larmes Sacrees Eau de Parfum* at $7,500 an ounce. He remembered that scent, as he had an eidetic memory.

The person who usually wore it also had small hands in addition to an insatiable taste for life's finest luxuries. Luxuries were expensive, though, and everyone had to earn a living. Some did it with less honesty than others, and some items in his possession were priceless.

He then heard subtle noises from his opulent study and knew who it *must* be. Only one individual could simultaneously be so bold and smell so good.

He then saw the five-five purple-haired woman, wearing black leather pants and jacket with three-inch high heels, with a shiny magenta low-cut blouse underneath revealing the cleavage of her modest but perky breasts. My, those were fine-looking mammaries.

But she was taking pictures of secret government files on his desk, blithely ignoring him as he entered the room. That was not fine! She was a nice-looking woman for fifty-seven, which was a year younger than him (he was pretty familiar with her dossier from their previous scuffles). She was clearly a woman to be reckoned with. But now this brazen broad had gone too far, and his patience with this elegant international delinquent had reached its end.

"Hold it right there, Ms. Volkova. How you got into my secret safe, I don't know, but your larceny is at its end. You clearly took a covert impression of my door key at our last encounter to engineer this little caper."

"Dr. Barclay J. Dixon, my old friend. Copying your pitifully insecure door key was only a tiny portion of my motives then, which were intended to fulfill even this pentagenarian's biological urges."

He smiled. "Okay, that sounds realistic."

"I also did not expect you to return this soon," the violet-haired spy said in a strong Russian accent as she looked up from the desk and set her camera down.

He pulled a translucent green plastic gun from his right pants pocket and pointed it at her. "I am not prone to violence, so no sudden moves, now. Please put your hands up and surrender peacefully, as I don't wish to harm you."

She raised her hands and laughed. "You will shoot me with a child's water pistol if I do not comply? That is somehow supposed to frighten me? How juvenile—but that's exactly what I would expect from someone of your maturity level and pubescent intellect."

"How little you know, my dear—it's *not* a squirt gun. It contains a strong sedative and truth serum, which I will have to use on you if you get too violent, Ms. Alexandra Nina Volkova."

"You think you can overpower me, do you?" the smirking woman said.

He laughed. "Of course I can. I'm twice your size. Are you daft, *comrade?* Amalgam-Man has few physical superiors, and you are surely *not* one of them. You need a timeout, pretty lady."

"Really?" She pulled a foot-long chain from the left pocket of her leather pants and tore it apart like a comic book heroine. "Not so, Dixon. My country's strength-enhancement experiments have made me more than a match for you. Am I to believe you thought me unprepared to defend myself?" She laughed heartily.

He snatched the broken chain from her hands and did the same stunt. "It's just cheap pot metal, Ms. Volkova. Why would you think you could deceive me with such a stupid trick? Did you not remember that my cerebral cortex has more folds than normal, which imparts upon me far greater intelligence than others? You are hopelessly outmatched—both physically and mentally."

She shook her head and pointed to his pants. "I was under the impression your brain was in your trousers. At least that's where it was at our last encounter at the hotel."

She was brilliant and devious, so he was concerned that the chain trick was just a distraction, so he would underestimate her. He guided her to the leather sofa, sat her down, and pulled out a long cord of thick nylon rope from his bag, which he wrapped around her body several times and then tied in a secure knot.

She laughed as she squirmed slightly. "What shall be my peril this time, Dr. Dixon? Are there terrible tortures that now await me for attempting to steal your little treasures? Bamboo shoots under my nails? Chinese water torture? Tickling me to death?

Forcing me to watch Plan 9 from Outer Space?"

He patted her on the head softly. "Now you know I would never hurt you, but I do indeed have *special* plans for you, which absolutely will involve terrible tortures in the form of old monster movies." He laughed heartily in his deep bass voice.

"Oh, no. Will I enjoy the additional plans?"

"I certainly hope so, as I am skilled at many things, including giving pleasure to female spies. Meanwhile, just try to get out of that, Ms. Volkova. It may look like mere rope, but it's an aerospace-alloy fiber that's stronger than steel."

She laughed as she sat calmly and smiled at him. "Maybe I don't want to."

He shook his head. "You don't fool me with your reverse psychology, Ms. Volkova. You are attempting to trick me into letting my guard down, and you will try to escape or do other destructive things the first chance you get. I won't fall for your schemes again."

"You do know me well, Dixon. I have met my match at last. Or have I?"

He then pulled a set of bright orange female correctional institutional leg irons modified with Bengal tiger fur lining from his medical bag on the ottoman, which he deftly clicked onto her svelte ankles, leaving her able to walk in short strides but not run. The escape of this dangerous woman would mean disseminating all his secrets to a foreign power, the results of which would be devastating for national security and, perhaps, the world. He couldn't let America down, he had told the President at their recent meeting in the Oval Office.

"Can't break *those* chains, now, can you?" He laughed.

"Hmmm. You have planned my capture in great detail, Dr. Dixon," she sneered. "I was woefully unprepared for this, and I am running out of options for freedom. I now feel like I am on the chain gang in the Siberian gulag, although they would not bother with comfy fur lining, as the happiness of prisoners is not a priority in Russia."

"Well, your happiness is always my top priority, Ms. Volkova."

"I also sincerely hope that is not *real* tiger fur—I would have to notify PETA in that case, among the many other governmental agencies I need to notify about today's atrocities that surely are forthcoming. You will therefore be joining me in jail for your depraved actions."

"It's the finest synthetic material available. I must say, they look very sexy on you, with those black high heels and shiny leather pants. Yowza."

She looked at her feet and smiled. "I reluctantly must agree. My black pants, shoes, and orange shackles with tiger-fur accents result in a strangely stylish Halloween-esque fashion combination appropriate for mid-October. Purple is more my color, though."

"Sorry, those were out of stock. Your delicate, manicured hands will also become calloused from working on the Siberian rock pile in such freezing temperatures."

"The only rocks I shall ever touch are diamonds or emeralds. What do you call your luxury prisons—Club Fed? Tennis and golf every day suit me."

"I doubt they will supply diamonds and emeralds, and there will be no Club Fed for the likes of you, stunning scoundrel. I will, however, make your stay here far more pleasant than the gulag. Your shackles also match the hue of the stylish prison jumpsuit you will wear soon after our business here has concluded."

"Can I at least get *that* in purple?"

"I'll see what I can do."

She tilted her head. "And what is this 'business' you speak of? You are being rather vague."

"You'll find out, Ms. Volkova." He laughed.

"Humph, how depressing. How long will I be in prison, Dr. Dixon?"

"Are you kidding, lady? With what you've tried to steal . . . probably life without parole."

"That is a long time. Will the provided cuisine be tolerable to one of my high culture and social standing?"

He shook his head. "Hardly. I don't believe the women's federal prison serves caviar, lobster, roast duck, filet mignon, and gourmet coffee—your favorites. Get used to stale bologna sandwiches and Kool-Aid."

She rolled her blue eyes. "*That* is unacceptable."

"On a positive note, I can likely get permission for you to live here under house arrest, under my supervision, naturally. I am a talented chef who can serve you all those things to please you."

"It is very chivalrous of you to consider my nutritional needs."

"I will consider *all* your needs, Ms. Volkova. However, a cunning kleptomaniac like you must be securely restrained at all times, as you are too dangerous to be running around free and causing havoc to this great country."

"Oh, my. Even in bed? I must have my beauty sleep."

"*Especially* in bed. That should go without saying, and there won't be a lot of sleep occurring with me guarding you at all times."

She growled. "A life sentence of seeing *you* every minute, versus prison? A Hobson's choice." She paused for several seconds and frowned. "I will take prison, obviously, as it is the lesser of two evils."

"Suit yourself, although I will definitely feed you better." He then pulled a pair of dark brown heavy leather wrist cuffs with 24-karat plated gold buckles and a short connecting gold chain from the bag. "You will also have to wear these, Ms. Volkova. While you are lovely beyond compare, I hope you will understand I do not trust you."

"I would not trust me either." She nodded in agreement as he locked the luxuriously padded leather manacles around her small wrists while she, surprisingly, offered no resistance. He remembered she had been a champion girls' wrestler in the 121-pound weight class in the Soviet Union as a teen, and those small but mighty fists could pack a punch, he knew; in the right place, such a blow could be lethal to even him, and she was surely trained to know vital spots of impact. After all, even he was only flesh and blood. Therefore, he had expected her to put up more of a fight than this.

What was this lovely yet scheming woman planning? Did she have a secret, undisclosed weapon to destroy him at her leisure? Poison gas, tetrodotoxin, or perhaps she really did have augmented strength now and was merely playing possum with him? He needed to be on his toes here to avoid an untimely demise that could jeopardize the free world.

"There you go, Ma'am. I hope you like them as you'll be wearing them for a long time."

She looked at her hands, turned her head towards him, and smirked. "These particular boujee restraints look like they came from the hospital psychiatric ward. You are indeed perverted, Barclay Jarvis Dixon."

He looked at her in puzzlement. "They came from a very upscale behavioral health facility for rehabilitating incorrigible female spies and were custom-made to fit you precisely, my little delicate lavender flower; your point is what, exactly?"

"That you are locking me up like an insane person; I suppose a straitjacket is next." She wiggled her hands in them as she smiled in delight. "However, they *are* made of rich Corinthian leather with 24K gold accents and seem quite inescapable yet very comfortable, I must admit. I shall concede that you are a man who always procures the best of everything, whatever the nefarious purpose."

"Ms. Volkova, despite your antisocial actions today, I always have your comfort and penchant for luxury items in mind. Having these effective, high-quality products in my medical bag is necessary for any unruly enemy females I might encounter, and you are indeed insane to think you could succeed in stealing government secrets from me in broad daylight. Unfortunately, my bag lacks space for a nice cozy straitjacket. Maybe next time."

"Oh, dear. What exotic material would that be made of?"

"Why, the finest soft Egyptian cotton, of course. That would be quite appropriate for you as it would keep you out of mischief. On the other hand, such a garment might make certain, uh, 'activities' difficult. Decisions, decisions."

She shrieked. "I shall *immediately* report you to the medical board for the unauthorized items you have in your doctor bag and the unsavory 'activities' you surely have planned, you depraved Lothario." She looked towards the sunlit window in despair. "What warped things will you do to me? I can only imagine the licentious acts your famed cerebral cortex, with its extra folds, can conceive. Oh, is there no one who will come to my aid?"

He shook his head. "Nope. You made your bed, and now you must sleep in it, Ms. Volkova—pun intended. And just how will you notify all these government agencies about my misdeeds with no phone and your hands locked up in rich Corinthian leather?"

"I shall find a way with the covert, advanced, microminiaturized Soviet-era KGB devices secreted on my person. The Russian President is likely watching your antics as we speak, and he is not as forgiving as I. I also do not find your humor amusing, especially concerning activities occurring in beds, Barclay Dixon."

He easily lifted his well-restrained prisoner over his right shoulder and walked with her towards the doorway to his luxurious bedroom, where further shenanigans surely awaited.

He then heard the front door open and close. Oh, shit. *That* was not something he expected, as he froze in his tracks. What additional attacks would he have to withstand now? Could he handle another diabolical spy? One Ms. Volkova was a handful, and even he had his limits.

At that moment, a five-eleven, late-twentyish, bespectacled, freckled redhead rushed into the living room. He certainly didn't need another intruder, as one intruder in the home was enough to deal with. This one was quite a bit larger than Ms. Volkova.

"Hey, I just needed to come by to borrow some of your camera stuff. What in tarnation is all that noise, and what are you doing home at noon?"

Dr. Dixon and Ms. Volkova stared at their unexpected guest blankly.

"Uh, whoops! I know nothing, I see nothing!" the tall young female intruder said in a *faux* German accent as she put her hands over her eyes and ran out the door, slamming it behind her.

He then heard the young lady's car back out and drive off, tires squealing. She obviously had entered the wrong mansion. Well, mistakes happen.

"My, *that* we certainly didn't need. Not that we can do anything about it now." With his left hand, he pulled his cell phone from his pocket and dialed a secret number. "Mr. Secretary? Yes, as predicted, someone had broken into my spacious mansion. Guess who? Yes, she used her superspy abilities to bypass the alarm system, break open my safe, and take photos of secret documents entrusted to me by the President—can you believe that? Yes, sir, she is secured now and can't escape. What's that? When am I bringing her to headquarters for interrogation? That's really hard to say, Mr. Secretary. We've got some terrible weather here. Our connection is also breaking up. Sorry, I can't hear you! Mr. Secretary, I've lost you!"

She laughed. "It is sunny and seventy degrees outside, Dr. Dixon. Despite your severe moral shortcomings, I always thought you to be honest."

"One never knows about the weather in Beverly Hills," he said as he continued to carry her to the bedroom.

"You are manipulating this situation to suit your own primal needs."

He scratched his head with his free hand. "Again, what's your point?"

"That you will force yourself on me while I am helpless, Dr. Barclay Dixon."

"I will not, as I have the highest ethical standards, and I wouldn't abuse my prisoner in any fashion; however, if you would gain comfort in your current situation from my companionship, I would not refuse you, as you are quite beautiful."

"Define 'companionship' in greater detail, Dixon."

"It has a broad interpretation."

"You would not take advantage of me in my current state? That is so gentlemanly of you. Well, in that case, I have no choice but to surrender my body to you to do to it what you will, even though it surely will entail excessive debauchery."

With his great strength, he then placed her gently on the bed.

"None of your martial arts tricks, although you might find it hard to kick me now."

She nodded and sighed. "I will not, as you still have your water pistol."

"You betcha I do. Yet, I have a much larger and powerful squirt gun, which you shall see in a moment, should you permit such an activity."

She looked at his groin and gasped in horror. "Oh, no. It looks quite dangerous. *Please* do not shoot me with it."

"It is quite powerful, Ms. Volkova, but it won't injure you." He lay down beside her on his luxurious king-size bed as he stroked her violaceous tresses.

"It had better not. The Geneva Convention states: No physical or mental torture, nor any other form of coercion, may be inflicted on prisoners to secure from them information of any kind whatsoever. Prisoners who refuse to answer may not be threatened, insulted, or exposed to any unpleasant or disadvantageous treatment of any kind."

"I was not aware you were so facile in international regulations. And I hope you will not consider your treatment unpleasant."

"That remains to be seen, Barclay Dixon. If I had only gotten out of your spacious mansion sooner, I would not have been captured and in this dire predicament." She looked at her fur-encased feet and spread them as wide as her chains would allow. "Perhaps you should unlock these orange tiger-fur thingies now, as I don't think this small amount of leg separation will fit into your dastardly plan, you cad."

He pondered her statement for several seconds. "Maybe you're right, for once. Now, where did I put the key?" At least he had a connection at the fire department if they needed to be cut or drilled off.

Or, she could probably get them off with a bobby pin or other thin piece of sheet metal, given her advanced Russian spy training.

AAAAA

Two days later, he and Evie had their weekly dinner at his house. Jayna had a late meeting at the hospital, and Robert was teaching an evening class, so they were on their own for the spaghetti and vegetarian meatballs that she prepared, since he, unlike his alter ego, was incapable of preparing anything his daughter could tolerate. Hot dogs and lunchmeat sandwiches were the extent of his talents.

"How are things at the university? Your research going okay?"

"Sure." She took a sip of iced tea. "Presenting a poster at a national conference in San Diego in a couple of weeks."

"Does Rob have a good group of kids this term?"

"I guess so." She looked at her coffee cup with a blank stare.

He took a bite of spaghetti. "There seems to be an awkward silence, which is unusual for you."

Evie looked down at her food for several seconds, which was atypical; she was always straightforward and never at a loss for words. "I'm fine."

"Come on, what's wrong?"

"Well, okay. Dad, I'm just so ashamed that I barged into the house unannounced the other day and rudely interrupted, uh . . . *whatever* that was I can never unsee. I didn't think you would be home, and I just wanted to get in, borrow some stuff, and leave. I saw Jayna's blue Camry in the driveway and thought you probably rode together to work in your fine new red vehicle, since you sometimes do that. I'm sorry if I embarrassed you both."

He laughed. "It's okay; it'll always be your house, too, and what's done is done. I guess I need to put a sign on the door, or a light, or something. I apologize if it shocked you. We went to the house in her car, obviously."

She laughed. "Dad, you are the famous creator of Amalgam-Man, whose outrageous alter ego knows no bounds for anything, so do you think that would've shocked me? What I saw was barely PG-13, anyway."

"I guess not. Sorry."

"I'm just so happy you have such fun with Jayna and have someone to play spy with."

"*Someone to play spy with?* Am I a boy who needs a playmate?"

She nodded. "Yes, Dad. You are a genius in many ways, but so juvenile in others, making you so special to me." She walked around the table and hugged him. "You were so depressed after you and Mom split up, and I'm so pleased for both of you that you're back to your old self, which is good, most of the time."

"Thanks, I think."

She went and sat back down at the table. "It's just that Jayna is very religious, though, and seems so conservative, like how she dresses. I guess I thought she would be far too prudish and proper to engage in Amalgam-Man's espionage roleplay scenarios by wearing a spy getup with a purple wig, leather outfit, and many other, uh . . . 'props' that seem a bit out of place for a highly Christian woman."

"You should know now that there's far more to Jayna than meets the eye. But what's un-Christian about our props? A water pistol? A purple wig? Fake secret agent documents? Gimme a break. The Bible doesn't say anything about props. I know, I checked."

She rolled her eyes and blushed. "Well, no, not those items, but I really don't want to discuss them . . ."

He shook his head. "I can see why you might think that, but that's a stereotype. Despite her shy exterior, she's extremely fun and imaginative. What we do is perfectly safe, respectful, loving, and consensual, to glorify the bond between two married people, and she has no objections to that. Some in the church might, but it's none of their business. And don't be so naïve to think this stuff is all my idea. Most of those 'props' are hers that she bought, not me. And I don't mean the clothes or wig."

She looked up suddenly. "Huh? Dad, I said I don't want to know about that stuff or your personal activities; they are your and Jayna's private business—"

"Your stepmother has an account at a large public safety supply house in Dallas for her other interests, common to many other Texans who value the right to bear arms. They deliver to law enforcement, correctional institutions, hospitals, and the occasional private individual known to them. They have a wide range of merchandise like body armor and items like—"

She shook her head and waved her hands rapidly. "I really don't want any more details about my wholesome bonus mom's shopping habits at the cop shop, please! I also hope you won't worry I will mention this to Rob. Absolutely not, as that was something private I *never* should've seen, and it isn't any of my concern. I know you were both just playing around."

"Thanks. It's easy to blame Barclay Dixon for things that are on the edge. Also, remember that my spouse, the 'prude,' also carries a fully loaded concealed pistol for self-defense, and, believe me, she knows how to use it. Pound for pound, she is quite formidable. She had three older brothers who taught her how to care for herself and throw a pretty good punch."

She covered her ears with her hands. "That is truly more than I wanted to hear! Let's change the subject, okay?" She took a bite of melon from her fruit cup. "Regarding another topic: how is the investigation going?"

"We're pretty sure we know who burned the museum: Sybil Tegler, a medical geneticist at the medical school. You might have met her at last year's faculty mixer."

"One of your faculty? No way."

"Not in my department, but she is one of the medical school faculty."

"What do you feel is the motive?"

"Sybil likes to live beyond the means of what an assistant professor makes and has a fondness for the better things in life."

"Kind of a female Barclay Dixon."

"Except she doesn't have the resources to back it up. She has a serious gambling problem, which came up a year or two ago due to her accessing online gambling sites from her office and undesirable folks on campus trying to collect debts. This all led to her divorce from a successful accountant who likely made much more than she did."

"Did they have kids?"

He nodded. "A teenage son. I also suspect Drake Fowler may have played some role in the fire; it seems rather convenient that a world-famous photographer would've exhibited at small-town Youngswood, which burned down the same night. There's evidence he's not as financially well off as one would think."

"You believe Tegler burned it down to split Fowler's insurance money?"

"Maybe. I did talk to Mrs. Raymond, who said the insurance company will cover the real camera, pending the arson investigation. But the real one is still out there, waiting to be sold on the black market to some private collector."

"But, Dad . . . this theoretical 'private collector' couldn't ever show it to anyone, because the 'real' camera is presumed destroyed. Does that make sense?"

"I think so. For some narcissistic people, mere possession of the prized item is sufficient. It would've cost less than buying it through the 'regular' market."

"Well, maybe that's the case. I know you are an expert on the abnormal criminal mind." She smiled.

"We haven't found anything to link Fowler to any of this, other than that he would benefit financially. It's also feasible he has no clue at all, and some insurance person is the middleman in this caper, but it appears he isn't as financially well off as one might think, and that would give him motive."

"What about the Biggerstaff Medical Sciences building? Did she do that too?"

"That is a bit more difficult to sort out. It would seem likely given circumstantial evidence, but somehow, I doubt it."

"Why not?"

"She would've destroyed her own research, although her career would surely be over anyway if she was convicted of burning down Youngswood. The university is self-insured through a fund, so there's really no money to be made by an individual for torching Biggerstaff, so the motives would be different."

"One of your hunches, I see. It does seem rather convenient for someone else to blame Biggerstaff on Dr. Tegler. Maybe that's it? After the museum burned down, another criminal saw an opportunity and the perfect person to blame it on."

"Exactly. Someone else did it, of that I am certain, and I have a couple of candidates in mind. Soon, I shall find out for sure."

"Just don't get yourself in a bunch of trouble in the process, Dad. I know that's likely not possible."

"Probably not."

AAAAA

Evie left to make the forty-five-minute drive back home to Columbus an hour later, and Jayna returned from the hospital twenty minutes after that. He went and greeted her at the door, kissed her, and they went to the den to relax for a little while.

"Did you and Evie have a good dinner?" Jayna asked.

"We did. She made spaghetti and vegetarian meatballs. You?"

"Egg salad sandwich for me. It was the only non-meat option available at the meeting. It was an exciting meal."

"Pharmacy and Therapeutics meeting go okay?

"Same exciting agenda as always. Not too much bloodshed. There is always some argument about which insulin pens to use, which depends on which manufacturer gives us the best deal." She took a sip of the decaf coffee he had given her. "Did Evie mention anything in particular at your dinner, Dan?"

"What? You mean about barging in on our afternoon delight two days ago?"

She blushed. "Of course that's what I mean. I haven't gotten it out of my mind since it happened."

He nodded. "She was acting really weird in that she was unusually quiet, and I had to drag it out of her. She was extremely embarrassed about it."

"Was she shocked at what she saw?"

"Not really, as she's used to my dramatic nature and love of the theater. It wasn't like we had our clothes off or anything."

"Not yet, anyway, thank goodness."

"I don't think anything like that would surprise her, but she mainly was stupefied that you would even want to do those things, given how evangelical you are."

She shook her head. "I don't know what religion has to do with it. We're married and are doing things that are mutually enjoyable to both of us that are consensual and loving, in the privacy of our own home, except when she came in, of course, so we need to make sure that doesn't happen again. We 'spiced it up' with some costumes, campy dialogue, and other accoutrements that some might find weird. But I don't answer to other people, only to God. The only things, in my opinion, forbidden in God's marital covenant are: abuse—either physical or psychological; adultery, like a threesome or 'switching;' disrespecting or demeaning each other; incest; or using pornography. We clearly don't do any of those things."

"I know you despise the latter, as I do. It's degrading and disrespectful to women. I guess I used to pretend it was cool to be one of the guys, and I pretended to like them when my dad had his girlie magazines around, but I was always offended by it."

"I know that about you, Dan." She kissed him on the forehead. "I also forgive you for writing Toxicology for the Unmotivated."

"Those young women were demonstrating important medical equipment and procedures, and were clothed."

She laughed. "Just barely."

"I believe she is also surprised how accepting you are today of Barclay Dixon when you used to really dislike him."

"He's a fictional character, and I don't believe I can truly 'dislike' him. I was just never impressed with him as a literary device because of his one-dimensionality. He wasn't interesting at all because he had no flaws, and no one can identify with such a character."

"You told us once how disappointed you were in him that he never evolved and only cared about himself, as readers want to see characters improve themselves, and that he never did. He used his wealth for outlandish cars, fancy women, and jewelry instead of helping the less fortunate."

"That's right. But he is you, Dan, and I do believe Barclay has evolved over time, as have you."

He scratched his head. "He has? Really?"

"Of course. He's your alter ego, and Volkova is obviously mine. We are only with each other, respect that relationship, and don't lust after others, which in God's eyes is the same as adultery. We pretend to be enemy spies, grappling or meeting in a hotel or whatever, but it's still just us roleplaying in our love for one another. We are always of equal standing, but one may have some 'authority' over the other in certain 'spy' situations, like when I 'robbed' your safe and you 'caught' me. I guess Volkova did 'sin' by stealing." She laughed. "Both characters gave up their alcohol and tobacco addictions, which they had in the book, for example.

"Even in our event two days ago, you, as Barclay, may have acted like you wanted to 'molest' and take advantage of me, but in reality, you were very concerned about my enjoyment and caring for me while I was in a pretend vulnerable state. You would never have abused or disrespected me in any way."

"Of course not; what a ridiculous statement. You are indeed priceless to me, the greatest treasure I could have. But it *was* me, not Dixon."

"You miss the point. Your contemporary interpretation seems different than the womanizing Dixon I recall from your original and subsequent books. He used women only for his physical pleasure and discarded them like rubbish when he was done; that was abusive. He had no interest in them as people or in helping them achieve their goals. They were disposable, and one pretty lady was the same as any other. God would certainly condemn the threesomes or foursomes or more he had. We won't even talk about your stupid play, which was ridiculous beyond belief."

"I guess what seemed so cool at sixteen is different now."

"Of course it is, Dan. I did some things in my youth I'm not proud of either, like breaking Marlon Gray's nose in a rage. We all evolve, which is what makes people interesting."

"Some of us devolve. I think my dad fit into that category."

"Agreed. But the games we play involve having complete trust in one another, and I don't think the "old" Barclay could've done that because he was too self-absorbed to care about anyone but himself. I'm the same woman whether or not I'm dressed like this or wearing a purple wig, leather pants, and other accessories, Dan."

"I think she was worried I thought she might tell Robert. She said absolutely not, that it was our private business."

"I think we agree on that. But even if Rob *had* seen it, he knows his mother is completely devoted to God and her husband, and he wouldn't worry, as he has complete trust in me. I make no excuses about our lives, as I believe we live in a Christian way, although others may disagree. Some Christians feel it's okay to drink, while I don't. Many are also probably critical of my interest in firearms and owning a handgun. I am a completely nonviolent person, but I have no objection to using my gun for self-defense to protect myself or my family. It is also an interesting sport. I never really enjoyed hunting, although Sam and the boys did."

"Well, you saved me once by shooting that piece of crap site visitor Roland Okdar. I also told Evie the Bible does not say anything about marital 'accoutrements,' as you say."

"It does not, as long as they are used to mutually please each other in a happy, respectful, and loving way."

"You please me every day, dear." He gave her a hug. "We have some leftovers from dinner if you want."

"That would be great, then it's time for bed. I feel a bit worn out from all the interruptions in the middle of the night."

"And during the day, too, it seems."

Chapter Thirteen

Dan Rudbeck's Office
Staffordsville University Hospital
1130 hours

Dan sat down with his old friend Ted Brannigan at the conference table of his large and cluttered office in the basement of the medical education area. He liked being in the middle of things, where the action was, and where residents, students, and others could wander into his office at will—when he was there, that is (he had many side interests that took him away; his assistant Yvonne was good at saying "you just missed him!).

He didn't like isolation, which is what many of the C-suite administrators preferred—someone guarding the area at all times to prevent such random intrusions. But if his door was open, people needed to feel free to enter. However, he realized not everyone could multitask as efficiently as he did.

The overweight, balding, reddish-haired Ted took a sip of strong black coffee. "Malgy, I still don't understand why you didn't take the American Board of Physician Education chief job.

That would've been the type of dream job you always wanted."

He nodded. "One would think that, yes. *'Wheresoever you go, go with all your heart.'*"

"Profound, as usual. But you always lamented that you weren't appreciated, and finally, someone did. The money would've been better, too. You always wanted to live the fine life, so I don't get it."

"The cost of living in Chicago would be double or triple here, at least, Ted. Parking costs and traffic are terrible. I decided I didn't need the hassle. Jayna is happy here, and Evie is less than an hour away. My modest home is fine for what we need, although we want to upgrade soon."

"Your ranch house doesn't quite meet Barclay Dixon's upscale standards. At least Jayna probably didn't come with all the junk you have."

"She still has the old house. Her son Robert stays in it occasionally when he's here. But Barclay will just have to live with it until we look elsewhere. I've learned that aspiring to be Dixon ain't all it's cracked up to be."

"That's impossible to believe." Ted took a slurp of coffee. "Is Evie still dating Robert?"

"Yeah. They're pretty serious, I hear. He's a high school fine arts teacher in Columbus, so they have much in common."

"Does she still make a lot from her paintings?"

He nodded. "I don't know how much, but probably at least a hundred and fifty thousand a year. I don't see how she has time to do it and do astrophysics research. I wish she would slow down sometimes."

"You're also still here, in the same office you've had for years, when you could've had an office up in the administrative suite."

"What, and be in a fishbowl? Why the hell would I want to be up there in that toxic environment? That life ain't for me, my good friend Theodore. I don't need to be all-important and have people always see where I'm going. The people who really need to see me—the residents and students—have free access to me up here, while they would be intimidated to go up to the administrative suite, which is full of assholes. Not all of them, mind you—but I have tried not to become one of those."

"Atta boy!" Ted slapped him on the back. "Now *that's* the Malgy I remember. Welcome back, pal. I thought we'd lost you to the

did you know that Sybil Tegler is half-Asian? Her mother is Chinese-American."

"Big deal, Malgy." Ted said snidely. "We all know that! What a stupid statement, especially from one who idolizes Confucius. Unlike you, I hear she can actually speak Mandarin Chinese. What's your point?"

"Speaking of alcohol, my point is that I ran some other tests on her from the Palatine ER sample. Specifically, aldehyde dehydrogenase enzyme levels."

"Yeah, ALDH2 and other enzyme deficiencies are common in those of Asian descent, as I explained on Rudbeck's Rounds. Again, so what? That radio show was for the public, as all of the med students or residents already know that fact. She clearly doesn't have that mutation, with her recent history of drunkenness. She'd be dead long before reaching that state."

He shook his head. "That's what her medical record says, but it's wrong. Sybil has very low ALDH2 levels, so there's no way that she could've tolerated a BAC that high. She would've been hammered after half a beer, and those levels would be lethal."

"But we have the BAC from the emergency room and the deputy's PBT to prove it. Didn't you say Charlie did enzyme tests on her biopsy?"

"Exactly. One of the tests was falsified, so it must've been the biopsy, as I used some 'extra' blood from the glucose challenge test that I had the medical student collect."

"No kidding." Ted slurped his coffee.

At that time, he was greeted by his ex-wife, Lt. Eppard, and good friend Jake Fisher, who entered his spacious office.

"Wow." He stood up to greet them. "To what do I owe this visit from Staffordsville's greatest minds?"

"Thought we would come to see you for a change, Rudbeck, since you're always coming to us," Eppard said. "Lots of stuff to discuss. Holy mackerel, I gotta find a place to sit down with all the junk. I haven't been here in a while." The three new guests sat down at his six-seat conference table after pushing some papers, assorted photo equipment, and his miniature Lost in Space Robot B-9 aside. The latter was useful in meetings when he disagreed with something; he would punch a button on his robot, giving a dire warning: "Danger, Will Robinson! Danger!"

"So what's up, guys?"

"Yvonne said you were here, and we thought we'd just pay you a visit to get caught up on things," Charlie said. Yvonne Harper was his long-time administrative assistant—the gatekeeper for the famous Amalgam-Man, whose time was incredibly valuable. Yvonne was also an expert at covering for him when he was out on projects unrelated to his administrative duties, which was often.

"I was just telling Ted that I ran ALDH levels on Tegler's blood from the Palatine ER. She is deficient, although her electronic medical record states otherwise."

"What are you saying, Malgy?" Charlie asked. "The test on the biopsy was negative."

"So, either my test is wrong, which I doubt, or there's another reason. The deputy also did a roadside breath test at about the same level as the lab draw. He did the standard sobriety tests, and she looked like she was going to fall over, and he then did the horizontal nystagmus test, which was normal."

HGN was a field sobriety test used by law enforcement to assess potential impairment, particularly from alcohol or drugs. It involved observing a person's eye movements as they follow a moving object with their eyes, while keeping their head still. A positive test was when the eyes failed to follow the moving object smoothly, and jerky eye movements were observed when the eyes were at their furthest movement point. There was really no way to fake the test to make it look positive, as it was a fundamental neurological reflex.

"How do you know?" Eppard asked. "You weren't there, man."

"No, but the Axon bodycam recorded everything. While she was in the Palatine ER running her blood, they had some time, so Wolford did those tests since he didn't feel it was safe to do on the road."

"You can see enough detail in that video to determine that her horizontal nystagmus test was normal?" Eppard asked as he picked up an uneaten donut from the conference table. "I've obviously seen a ton of those, and I have doubts about that."

He nodded. "Yes. I would testify that the video is available for any official to examine. Her test should've been markedly abnormal. Here, I'll show you myself." He pulled up the video segment on his large monitor as Eppard watched for several minutes.

"Huh. I agree that the quality is quite good in the bright hospital lighting and that it looks normal to me, Rudbeck," Eppard said. "I haven't done those in a long time, though, not since I was a patrol officer."

"What does this new information mean, Confucius?" Charlie asked.

"I didn't think much about it at the time, but for some reason, she had an enormously high BAC and was showing no physical effects."

"No effects? But you and Wolford said she was about to fall over, and you can see her staggering in the bodycam video on the road. There's no way Tegler could've been the arsonist because she was at home in a drunken stupor until your antifungal agent eradicates the yeast, which you said could take a week or two. You even have a visiting nurse going over there every day," Charlie said. "You even testified in court to that effect at the hearing for her public intoxication ticket."

"That's clearly what she wanted everyone to think. She could've easily faked the first tests—heel to toe and straight leg raise, but not the nystagmus." He hit himself in the head. "And I know what I said in court, but I was wrong."

"Amalgam-Man was wrong? Say it ain't so," Eppard said, pretending to cry. "My hero has feet of clay."

"This time, he was. It was a perfect setup. How could I have ignored that initially?"

"I still don't get how she could have a BAC that high and not be dead. But you're basing this assumption on a bodycam video from a rookie sheriff's deputy doing field sobriety tests?" Eppard asked.

"I am, because rookies will do it right, knowing they must prove themselves and not make mistakes. Is that accurate, Brian?"

Eppard nodded. "I see your point."

"He did it in the well-lit ER, not out in the dark, so the detail was pretty good." He thought for a moment. "She must've had access to the investigational ethanol receptor blocker hydroglippane; it's the only possible way."

"*Hydroglippane?* Never heard of it," Charlie said.

"It's an investigational ethanol receptor—GABA-A—blocker in the brain. In sufficient concentrations, it would block any effect of ethanol even with a sky-high blood alcohol content."

"Why would she have done that, Malgy?" Ted asked.

"To have an airtight alibi for when she burned the museum down. If she was supposedly incapacitated by her rare 'ailment,' it seems unlikely anyone would suspect her as a culprit. I know I suggested it when she was in the Palatine ER with Wolford, but she must've been playing dumb and had known about that disorder for a while so she could plan how to fake it."

"Maybe, but why would she have any special expertise in arson? As I recall, female arsonists are pretty rare. Burning stuff seems to be in male DNA, except for your wife," Jake added.

"Six percent are female, yes. But Sybil would know because her father was a firefighter and arson investigator in Dayton. Sandy found out that information."

"Huh? Having a father who's a firefighter makes one an arsonist? How'd you arrive at that astounding conclusion?" Eppard asked sarcastically. "Speak to me slowly in simple words as you might to a child, so even I can understand the rudiments. I know my walnut-sized brain lacks your higher cortical reasoning."

"Such blatant derision hurts my feelings." He shook his head. "Sybil would therefore have the means to gather information on how to burn down buildings."

"*What?* That information is also readily available to anyone with an Internet connection," Eppard roared. "Most kids have absolutely no interest in their parents' occupations and have no idea what they do. I'm also sorry to hear that theory as it applies to Chief Arnold's two daughters; they seem destined to become pyromaniacs, so we'd better start tailing them now. I guess being the kid of a cop makes them predestined to become crooks, then? I'd better watch my son and daughter since they are surely headed for a life of crime. Finally, poor Genevieve doesn't stand a chance, given her father's myriad incurable issues. Sorry, Dr. Boisseau—even your fine genetic material can't counteract his near-lethal mutations," Eppard said, pointing at him. "All I can say is, I'm sorry."

"That's true," Charlie said seriously. "Evie is doomed."

"That's another of your ridiculous theories, Rudbeck. Jeez."

"Perhaps, but earlier, I also had Charlie run enzyme levels from Sybil's small bowel biopsy; they were normal, while the ones I had the residents run from the hospital samples showed almost no aldehyde dehydrogenase type 2 activity, the most common mutation. So, those were obviously faked, as was the yeast infestation. The biopsy clearly came from another patient."

"Well . . . I have to admit that's weird," Eppard said.

"Anyway, hydroglippane is an experimental drug, you said. Where would she have gotten it, then?" Charlie asked as she munched on a tiger tail doughnut, as sugar flakes flew everywhere.

"Don't know, Charlie. Some pharma contact perhaps Jayna can discover. I think Karmahut is in Nashville, which is not that far away. Obviously, something I need to find out, though." He slurped some strong black coffee. "I do remember that I took her from the Palatine ER to the main hospital myself since she was too drunk to go to the police station.

"But she insisted on stopping at home first, which a medical transport or the police wouldn't have let her do. I let her, even though I told her the hospital would have whatever medications she needed. Clearly, she needed to get her stash of oral hydroglippane, which would've worn off in half a day had she not taken more.

"I was a bit amazed how she was able to find her spare key and get into the house while being so drunk that it would have killed some people. She didn't even know her name when she was arrested, yet she had sufficient cognition to know my name and call me. Wildly inconsistent. My initial theory was that she had auto-brewery syndrome, which gave her an extremely high tolerance to alcohol because she was exposed to it constantly. Her records say she doesn't have ALDH deficiency, but she had it changed somehow; she's severely deficient in that enzyme, as many Asians are. The truth is that she wasn't drunk at all because the hydroglippane blocked the ethanol receptors in the brain."

"C'mon, Malgy," Charlie said. "This seems to be an awfully complex Rube Goldberg endeavor just to create the illusion that Sybil Tegler was chronically intoxicated and incapable of doing the arson herself. It's outlandish for even you. You're postulating that she was there and set the museum fire on her own after the event?"

"Of course, don't you see? It just makes it so improbable that she could be a suspect because no one could believe anyone would go to that amount of trouble. Even I was fooled by it initially."

Charlie snickered. “Even you, the master detective? Impossible.”

“Sure, laugh, Charlie, but remember that I always win out in the end.”

“You do? I was unaware of that fact,” Charlie said.

“Well, it’s true, and this time I shall prevail.” He took a bite of a doughnut. “She clearly researched the basic security and learned that the cameras recorded locally, and the files would’ve been destroyed.” He thought for a moment. “Or maybe not. Jake, is there any way to possibly recover surveillance camera footage from Youngswood?”

The wiry Jake took a bite of his Everything bagel and opened his eyes wide. “From a storage medium in the building itself? It would depend on how it was stored, Malgy. If it were on a mechanical hard drive, it might be easier to recover than a solid-state drive, paradoxically.”

“Really? I would’ve thought it would be the other way around.”

Jake shook his head. “Nope, some of those older systems were built like tanks with better environmental tolerances, and some old platter hard drives were pretty robust. If it was a newer one, then it’s probably not recoverable in a fire of that magnitude.”

“That clinches it,” Eppard said sarcastically. “Another one chalked up to the intrepid Amalgam-Man. Never mind that we have a whole bunch of gaping holes to fill in before this can even begin to be a prosecutable case, but such mundane details are of no concern to him. Those menial tasks are left to the mere lackeys like me and the prosecutor.”

“I shall find those clues, Lieutenant. Dr. Boisseau will verify my tenacity in that regard.”

“I will verify that one hundred percent,” his ex-wife said dryly. “Tenacity is not always pleasant to his friends and colleagues, however.”

“I just want to stay and play with all of Rudbeck’s gadgets,” the police lieutenant said. “Some of this stuff looks pretty cool.”

“Be careful, Eppard. Some of it is also dangerous, and I don’t want to be responsible for any damage to a police lieutenant. You will need to sign a waiver of liability.”

Chapter Fourteen

Buckeye Behavioral Health Partners
Columbus, Ohio
1003 hours

The next morning, he drove to Columbus for his bimonthly meeting with his therapist, Dr. Deanna Palmer. Deanna was a well-known clinical psychologist specializing in dealing with physicians and other high-end academics; they could be difficult to handle. He once had a personal coach—Elizabeth Beckwith—and she had helped him somewhat (when he listened to her, which wasn't often), but she was not a psychologist or psychiatrist—someone who could help him with his inner dysfunctions.

He had seen Deanna for about nine years—right after his divorce from Charlie. He knew he had grown immensely since then and had come to terms with much of his inner turmoil.

Deanna, a somewhat stocky brunette woman in her late fifties, came into the office and extended her hand as she handed him a cup of coffee. She was wearing a flower print dress and flat shoes. "Dan, how are you?"

"Fine, Dee. Got a lot of stuff going on down in Staffordsville. I don't know if you've heard about any of it up here."

She sat down with her cup of coffee and took a sip. "Yes, it's been on the news, and that's pretty unbelievable. The arts museum and a university science building both burned up in a two-week period. What's the connection there?"

He shook his head. "I don't readily see one, but it's unlikely they were both coincidental."

"Do the police or fire departments have any idea what happened?"

He nodded. "We have some clues."

She turned her head sideways. "How's that? 'We' have some clues?"

"Right. I do some consulting for the police department on an invited basis, although I sort of invited myself into this project, given that I am over the university building and we were at the museum the night before, as Evie had an exhibit there."

"Well, I just hope you don't get in over your head, but I know you likely won't listen to me. I know how your interests jump around. On the other hand, I know you're good at solving puzzles and digging up information. However, you've worked very hard to be in your current position; I just hope you have enough gas left in the tank and don't neglect your own work."

"I listen to you far more than I did to Elizabeth, my executive coach. I think she gave up on me."

"Not surprising. Do you still have your radio show? Rudbeck's Rounds?"

"Yeah, but I moved it from biweekly to monthly, and it's now only twelve minutes instead of twenty. I don't know how much interest there is today in hearing featured local healthcare guests; I even had Jayna on there once to talk about the pharmacy, which wasn't terribly exciting. I probably need to go to a podcast or something on a channel, but Evie would have to help me with that, as she does with my photo equipment blogs. She doesn't have as much free time as she used to."

"How is Evie, by the way?"

"She's great. Of course, she's the spitting image of her mom, but her personality is more like mine, with many male-brain traits. She loves her work and has developed an interest in dark matter in central Alaska, of all places."

"I have no idea what dark matter is."

"It's pretty important stuff out there that you can't see."

"She also has become quite the artist. Some of her pieces go for $10,000 or more."

"Evie is clearly financially independent, although you wouldn't know it by her car or clothes. She dresses like an impoverished college student, looks young enough to pass for one, and most of the time acts like one. She has gotten pretty serious with Jayna's youngest son, Robert. He's a year younger than her and teaches high school art at an upscale private school in Columbus, so they have that in common."

"You think it will go anywhere?"

He nodded. "I think so—this is the longest she's ever dated anyone, and they really like each other. They spend most of their free time together."

She nibbled on some mixed nuts that were on the coffee table. "Do you see Charlotte much?"

He nodded. "Maybe once a week. Our offices are on the same floor, so I stop by fairly often when I need something."

"You get along with her husband okay?"

"Jeff? He's fine, although we don't have a lot in common. We all go out together occasionally. We've played golf as a foursome a couple of times. They beat the pants off us, as they're both excellent athletes and we're not. I have strength but not much else."

"How is Jayna?"

"She's fine. The anniversary of Sam's death just came up, and she was very tearful about that. I told you what happened, right? He got COVID and developed fulminant pneumonia and died within a matter of days. He wasn't conscious, so one of her biggest regrets was that she and the boys didn't get to say goodbye. She set up a special room in the house for his things that she can remember him by."

"You're a good husband for supporting her in that way. Is her work going okay?"

He nodded. "Yeah, she likes being the director of the pharmacy—she now has responsibility for the retail outpatient practices in addition to the hospital stuff. It's a pretty big job, but it was a promotion over what she had in Dallas. She's exceptionally well organized, unlike me. I know I talk about how well I multitask, but usually, some task gets shortchanged."

"She and Charlotte get along okay?"

He nodded. "They don't have a lot of common interests, but they usually have lunch together once a month or so. Jayna loves her three sons, but I know she always wanted a daughter, so she is very close to Evie. I guess she and Charlie have her in common, so that's probably what they discuss. I hope they don't discuss me."

Deanna laughed. "I know she is very evangelical. Have you adopted any of that?"

"I try to go to church with her most Sundays, and we do some Bible reading in the evenings. I also sing with her in the choir, mainly because I'm the only true bass around. God and Christ have added a dimension to my life I didn't have before. We try to lead our lives according to their teachings. There wasn't much religion in the Rudbeck household while growing up. I think our family could've used some. I used to doubt the existence of God, but being a scientist, I finally realized that things likely wouldn't have turned out in such an orderly fashion without the existence of a supreme being. Matter, left to its own devices, tends to be in a more rather than less disorganized state. Thinking that complex biological organisms developed by random mutations isn't logical."

"Do you have time for each other? For fun?"

He smiled. "We have a good time. Evie said it's good I have someone to play with since I am somewhat childlike in mentality."

"Hmmm. Play with? Like tennis, pickleball, or golf?"

"Well . . . more like other types of games which take place indoors. She isn't that athletic, and we don't have much time for things like golf."

"Board games are fun, too. Scrabble, chess, and trivia games. You're surely great at the latter."

"Jayna is a great Scrabble player, but those aren't the types of 'games' we play." He laughed. "Don't worry. Everything is very gentle and loving."

She raised her eyebrows. "I . . . see. That's good, Dan. Knowing your wild imagination and affinity for various gadgets, I'm sure those encounters are quite elaborate."

"Jayna is very demure on the outside, but she is also quite creative and can be fun. She also seems to understand and tolerate male behavior well, likely from growing up with three brothers and having three sons. She can be surprisingly rambunctious at times."

"I am thrilled you have that kind of relationship." She took another sip of coffee. "So, how's good old Barclay Dixon these days? It's been a long time since you've written anything about him. Is he still as obnoxious and womanizing as ever?"

"I thought I had given him up, but I have considered another novel where he is older, has settled down, and is much more politically correct. Over the years, I have become less tolerant of many of his chauvinist qualities."

"The ultimate bachelor, settling down? That seems hard to fathom."

He smiled. "It's a major paradigm shift for the Amalgam-Man, kind of like real life."

"But with so many lovely ladies to choose from—how will he pick?" She laughed. "I mean Dixon, not you, of course. I don't think you had 25,000 conquests."

"I'm not sure, but I have some ideas. He has developed a certain fondness for a violet-haired enemy spy from The Sulphur Shadow."

"That sounds interesting, and I would like to know more later. But how are you doing? I know you used to have a lot of problems with sadness over your childhood and how you never got to rectify the issues with your dad."

He nodded. "Yeah. We had a lot of conflicts that were never resolved. He crashed his truck and was killed after he spun out on some ice. I'm sorry he died that way, but I'm glad he didn't hurt anyone else. A vehicle was as deadly as a firearm in his hands." He took a sip of coffee. "I also want to try to have a better relationship with my sister, Beck. We were never all that close and became more distant after Mom died."

"I remember you have a pretty close relationship with your cousin Sandra."

He smiled. "Sandy has always been my best buddy, and we often hang out and offer emotional support for each other. It's not a big deal these days, but being a lesbian in the 80s wasn't without challenges for her. Her family was always accepting of it, but not everyone else was. I stomped a few heads in high school when guys called her names."

"Oh, dear. I'm glad she had you as a sort of big brother."

"She does have an older brother, but he was out of high school by the time we were there. She is the best friend a guy could have. I talk to her about everything. She's one tough lady."

"I know you had a lot of regret over what happened between you and Jayna in college."

"I did; I finally realized I treated her terribly. They would call it 'ghosting' today. We had no cell phones or social media then, but I could've called her or written letters. I just disappeared because I went off the rails with my own problems."

"You did the best you could at the time, dealing with your dad's issues, and you can't go back in time. Fretting over that serves no useful purpose, Dan. I'm sure she's forgiven you, so you need to forgive yourself. She would want that for you."

"Dee, I didn't do the best I could. I was selfish, and I could have told her what was going on and let her decide whether to stay with me. I owed her that much. She might have decided to move on, but at least then she would've had closure to our relationship and not wondered if it was something she did that ruined it. She told me she didn't date for two years after that."

"But in the end, you got back together. Did Confucius have any quotes about that?"

He nodded. "Yes. He believed regret stemmed from actions taken without proper consideration and due diligence. I certainly was neither considerate nor diligent, Dee. But I'm thankful every day that she came back into my life. After all these years, I think it took her a while to trust me again. I can't believe she forgave me for that."

"The human heart has an immense potential for forgiveness, Dan." She leaned forward and put her right hand on his left shoulder. "You're an amazingly kind person, and I know you're sorry about the past. The trauma you went through as a child isn't something that goes away, and I know you were ashamed of your dad."

"I was. I thought that by ignoring things, they would go away. It was just kicking the can down the road."

"But you've turned things around, and it wasn't within your power to change him. You're extremely well-respected in your community and a man of integrity who uses his time to help and mentor others. You have a wonderful daughter and wife, and you are one of the fortunate few to have a friendly relationship with your ex. It's hard to ask for more than what you have."

"I often wonder if I should've taken that big shot job in Chicago after I solved that ransomware scandal regarding the education board. Five years ago, something like that was all I wanted."

"I know we've talked about it, Dan. I think we concluded that the things you were seeking were always within you, and having that job wouldn't have made you any happier."

"Yeah, I know. *Success depends upon previous preparation, and without such preparation there is sure to be failure.*"

"Confucius?"

"Of course. Who else?"

"Also, remember that you have a lot of political clout where you are currently and the freedom to pursue many of your eclectic interests. That might not be tolerated as much on the national stage. In these politically unstable times, consider your blessings right here. It's always tempting to look where the grass is greener."

"Yeah, I know. I'm better off where I am. I am indeed a lucky fellow."

"I know you used to be sad much of the time. I really hope that is better these days."

"It is, Dee. I occasionally get a bit tearful, but Jayna encourages me to try to remember God and all He has given me, which helps. I was in a bad place after my divorce, and I was depressed for a long time. I also want to try to be a better sibling to Beck. She just went through her second divorce and is having some financial problems."

"I know you will try to help her."

"I will do what I can, but she still thinks of me as her little brother and is somewhat reluctant to accept help. I know she's coming down sometime in the next few weeks, largely to visit friends in Columbus and here, but we'll spend some time together."

"I hope that happens soon, Dan. Siblings are important. We have a relationship with our siblings longer than with any other person."

Chapter Fifteen

Dan Rudbeck's Office
Staffordsville University Hospital
0745 hours

Jacob David Fisher was damn good at finding information mere mortals could not, which gave him the moniker "Jake the Rake," which meant he quickly could rake up and gather seemingly unrelated information from publicly available databases and make sense of it. It was amazing how much of that was publicly available to someone who knew where to look on the Internet on public watchdog sites and university email servers. Fire Chief Arnold had joined them in his office, as she wanted an update on the latest information.

"Fowler's credit score was in the crapper. He needed the money, Malgy. I told you at an earlier meeting that he had declared bankruptcy more than once."

"How is that even possible, Jake? He was one of the most famous modern photographers in the world. He must be worth at least twenty million dollars."

"Maybe at one time, but even the well-heeled can mismanage their money. He's had three divorces and pays a ton of alimony, wastes money on expensive cars—"

"Unlike us. I've had only one divorce from someone who makes more money than I, and I definitely don't spend money on cars, although my new wife did gift me one recently."

"Thank goodness, as that old vehicle was falling apart."

"You're a fine one to talk, with your old Buick."

"I have no pristine image to maintain, and there's nothing wrong with that car. I keep it in top shape. My Buick also doesn't have terminal leprosy like the old vehicle you drove for eighteen years, so you're a fine one to talk. You spend money on other stuff, though. The details are beyond the scope of this discussion."

"My possessions are important items for my investigations and other activities. Anyway, Sybil likes potato chips. She said that during her carbohydrate challenge. As in boatloads of them."

"So? I have been known to partake of them myself. Big deal," Jake said.

"Not ten thousand bags of them. Sandy, when you said the building was 'burnt crispy' when you called me the other night, I thought of the British colloquialism for potato chips: 'crisps.'"

"They're not just chips?" she asked.

"In England, chips are like French fries, and crisps are potato chips."

Sandy slapped herself in the face. "I forgot you are an international connoisseur of fine comestibles and have had tea and crumpets with the President. What about Canada?" she asked.

"Poutine, of course."

"Ah, yes. I had those fabulous gravy fries once. France?"

"*Frites,*" he replied with his limited French vocabulary, which was shameful given his daughter and ex-wife were fluent speakers. In contrast, Barclay Dixon was fluent in ten languages. "*Papas fritas* in Spanish."

"We're getting a bit off course here, Danny, but that's nothing unusual for you."

"An unusual factoid likely unknown to the common person unfamiliar with crime is that potato or corn chips are an ideal accelerant. They have immense caloric density due to their high fat content, are virtually untraceable, and they're cheap, readily available, and not restricted for purchase in any way."

"Well, they should be a restricted purchase for you," Sandy said, poking him in the gut. "A controlled substance rationed out in small amounts."

"Hey, I've lost weight recently. Let me show you the immense incendiary potential of the lowly potato chip."

He pulled up a video on his large conference table monitor of Russian superspy Ms. Alexandra Nina Volkova, igniting the contents of ten family-sized bags of potato chips with a dummy underneath. "In this controlled experiment, each chip burned for an average of 146 seconds, with little residue. That's way better than wood chips or any other common item."

"Almost as efficient as matter and antimatter, and way cheaper," Jake said, chomping on a cookie. "Fuel for our trips to Mars."

"Hey, stop it. The concept started in prisons since inmates can access them if they buy from the commissary."

"Nice to know you are up to date on correctional facility arson and riots," Sandy said.

"Survivalists also use the small bags of chips to assist in starting fires. Adding magnesium particles also helps. They can also be used as food, obviously."

Sandy rolled her eyes. "Yes, I also remember that you are *such* a rugged individual, living off the land, which is how you built your stellar he-man physique. I think you used them more for their nutritional value than starting fires in the wild, though."

"Hey, I have worked hard lately, so don't give me such a hard time."

"But why is my old childhood friend wearing a purple wig and holding a blowtorch?" Sandy put her hands over her eyes. "On second thought, I don't want to know any more."

He shook his head. "Don't ask questions you don't want the answers to."

"Wait a minute, she's now married to you. That's explanation enough because prolonged exposure to you has irreversibly mutated her DNA. She clearly has adopted her own alter ego after reading your novels. She's the Russian lady who was out to get you when you two weren't rolling in the hay. Whoops, sorry, poor choice of words, Danny."

"It's okay, we're married now, Sandy. She's often out to get me in real life whenever I irritate her or do stupid stuff, which is quite often. Ms. Volkova likes to get into mischief, as I do. But look at that dummy burn! He has sophisticated thermal sensors to detect rapid temperature changes, which we can analyze momentarily."

"Too bad you burned him up. And I can see that Jayna still likes to burn things, likely due to having three brothers and three sons who surely liked to burn things, as it's coded in male DNA. I also see that you still like to burn dummies. At least he didn't get launched off the tenth story of the hospital for the annual resident movie."

"Yeah, I try to forget that."

Sandy shook her head and scowled. "No, you really don't, and as a firefighter, it embarrassed me to no end that you did something so idiotic. The captain heard about it and asked me if I had helped you with it. Can you believe that, you big dummy?"

"Hey, it was all planned. 'Bubba' was on a guide wire and was extinguished as soon as he hit the pond at seventy miles an hour. There was no danger."

"*No danger?* Are you nuts? I like fun as well as the next gal, but some old man or lady could've had a heart attack from seeing a flaming man plummeting to his doom. Do you realize the permits and planning required to do something like that legally outside of a movie studio?"

"I am not a member of the Property Masters Guild, so no. I also did not have access to a movie studio, Sandy."

"Well, it's plenty. You're secretly proud of all the politically incorrect things you've done, and you'd be fired today if you still did that stuff." Sandy took a drink of diet cola. "You aren't the only one in your circle who has done irresponsible things."

"To whom are you referring, Fire Chief Arnold?"

"Oh, come on, we just watched a video of her. I know you still have the Super 8 movies you took when, in high school, Jayna burned up Marlon Gray's giant stash of adult magazines in the track and field area after no one would deal with him and his porn. It was a time of boys being boys, and the coaches just laughed at her when she and the other girls complained about those periodicals lying around the student lounge in perpetuity.

"Being very Christian, she was greatly offended at such sexist trash, and all the girls cheered as she loaded them on a wagon, took them to the shot and discus area across the street, put them in a pile, and ignited them into a glorious blaze after dousing them with lighter fluid and throwing a lit match on it on a cold February day. Marlon was mighty pissed and confronted her; he then set a Bible on fire in retaliation while yelling, 'you burn my books, Blackwell, I'll burn yours.'

"But burning God's Word went too far for the demure Jayna, who then broke the dude's nose with a single punch. The cops threatened to arrest her, but no one would say anything, as she became a schoolwide hero by standing up to a bully. Marlon also would've never lived it down by admitting a girl half his size kicked his ass good, so he swore to the cops that he slipped and face-planted on the concrete. What an asshole."

"I do have those old movies, of course, as I was there too. Playing the punch back in slow motion makes me very cautious about irritating her. But think about what I said—has a snack chip factory ever caught on fire?"

She thought for a minute. "Yes, a potato chip factory in New Brunswick, Canada, burned down a year ago, as I recall."

"See! I was right."

"But that doesn't prove it was the cause here, Danny, and there were exponentially more chips at that factory than there could've possibly been at Biggerstaff or Youngswood. There were so many things wrong with that medical school building—like the wiring—that I can't prove your potato chip conspiracy with certainty."

"Just because you can't prove it doesn't mean it's wrong. And nothing was defective with the arts museum building's wiring."

"Yes, but just because you think it's possible doesn't prove it in court. You know that arson can be difficult to arbitrate."

He raised his right fist. "Look, I talked to the museum director. She said she didn't ask for a COA for the camera, which was probably a replica, based on my analysis of the parts I found in the museum remains. Fowler took advantage of a small-town museum director's graciousness to just take his word to pull this off. Amalgam-Man has been right before. He will prevail again."

"And he's been wrong many, many times before. Like the time you thought the Methodist church's coffee roasting business was a front for a meth lab, and you sent the cops out there."

"*The man who asks a question is a fool for a minute, the man who does not ask is a fool for life.*"

"A fool nevertheless, Confucius. That says it all, Danny."

"That wounds me deeply. There were very high temperatures involved and chemicals in the trash, which could've been used to make methamphetamine."

"Yes, coffee roasting requires very high temperatures, duh. They had that business to raise money for their church mission. You should have known that when you set off your own fire alarms, roasting your coffee."

"Barclay Dixon could afford his own microprocessor-controlled coffee roaster. I couldn't."

"And it smelled bad, too. Charlie had a fit when she got home, with the kitchen smelling like a bonfire. Back to the church—those chemicals are also routinely used to extract caffeine to make decaf. And why were you going through the trash of a church, anyway? How embarrassing. I went to that church, too, and I denied sharing any DNA with you."

"So, I made one mistake. You're not perfect either, Sandy. Don't be so arrogant."

"No, I'm not, but I can find other examples other than that. But I know you mean well." She patted him on the shoulder.

"*Our greatest glory is not in never falling, but in rising every time we fall.*"

"Thanks, Confucius. You must have a lot of glory as often as you fall."

AAAAA

Jake Fisher's Office
IT Department
Staffordsville University Hospital
1020 hours

"What do you think, Jake?" he asked as he took a sip of diet orange soda as they sat in Jake's office in the information technology department. Jake was in IT now, but he was a former wizard in all aspects of audiovisual systems and had quite a technical arsenal. Jake had also helped him edit his politically incorrect resident movies back in the day, although he was in a different office then, and times were different now. The ambience was still the same today: two great minds working on a complex project unrelated to their real jobs. This one was pretty serious, though.

"These hard drives are a mess, Malgy." Jake took a bite of a peanut butter cookie as they looked at Jake's dual high-res 32-inch monitors. "There are fragments of video on the hard drive, which is in pretty bad physical shape, and it's amazing we found anything at all. However, the drive's electronics are surprisingly robust, given that this system seems to have been built in the late 00s out of old computer parts—a Frankenputer, if you will."

"But the museum wasn't nearly that old. Why use an old home-brew system like that?"

"Probably because someone wanted to save money or was a hobbyist who just had those parts around. I've seen your basement—you could make ten such computers out of your spare components. They can have amazing longevity as long as someone around can maintain them, but there's no tech support for Frankenputers. They are just a server for video files and don't need to have the latest technology, especially if they're not connected to the Internet. People just buy a new one every three years and discard the old electronics."

"I guess there are more of those systems around than we think."

"Yes. People think solid-state drives are more resilient, but not always, as in this case; the heat would've easily destroyed them." He clicked on his mouse. "Here's what I've been able to piece together."

They watched a poor-quality video of a darkly clad figure pulling a large bag along the floor. The individual then took out several smaller bags, opened them, and spread the contents on the carpet, covering it.

"The detail is lousy, but those look like potato chips," Jake said. "Just like you maintained."

"Yes. I can't tell who that is with the mask, but it appears either to be a slender adult female or an adolescent male, about five-five or five-six. Given our suspicions, I would bet on the former." He thought for a few seconds. "Tegler is about five-six, according to the police report."

"Big deal. So are millions of other women, just saying."

The video then stopped. "Only fourteen seconds of it, come on. We can't even see her lighting it on fire. Isn't there more?"

Jake shook his head. "No, that's the only intact fragment I could find from that night, and we're lucky to have that. Lesser mortals would have come up empty, so look at it as a glass half full, Malgy. Some other stuff from earlier in the evening shows nothing except some exhibits being taken down. This limited segment supports your potato chip accelerant theory, but isn't absolute proof that Sybil Tegler did it."

"Well, it's at least something, and it's a female who matches her physical characteristics. It's just more to add to our growing evidence. If that is Sybil, she must have connections at Karmahut Pharmaceuticals in Nashville, which has hydroglippane in Phase 2 clinical trials. She must have gotten some of it."

"So, yet another individual is involved in the grand conspiracy. Is that an oral medication?"

"Yes." He nodded. "The early prototypes were parenteral, but they developed a prodrug that is well-absorbed in the gut and converted to hydroglippane in the bloodstream. I assume the target audience would be alcoholics who can't stop drinking . . . but this inhibits its effect on the receptor." He thought for a moment. "And her ALDH deficiency is irrelevant, as it wouldn't make her sick since it never binds to the receptor."

"That sucks. Drinking to excess without the buzz. Kind of defeats the purpose."

"Huh. That doesn't sound like much fun for most people. It doesn't sound like a deterrent, but it's a step in the right direction. Better than disulfiram, which inhibits aldehyde dehydrogenase and causes a reaction like those with ALDH deficiency."

"You just need to find the connection. Knowing you, those clues will bc forthcoming.

Chapter Sixteen

Burk's Steak House
1142 N. Madison St.
Staffordsville, Ohio
1830 hours

He pulled into the parking lot of the upscale steak house, Staffordsville's best restaurant. He used to come here fairly often, but not much any longer since Jayna became a vegetarian. Burk's had superb steaks and chops, but not many vegetarian options.

He walked in and was greeted by the hostess. His sister, Becky, had arrived and was sitting at one of the preferred tables in the back that he had reserved. He didn't see her all that often as she lived in Minneapolis now, and the last time she was here was at his and Jayna's wedding a year ago.

He hugged the five-ten, dark-haired, sixty-four-year-old, slightly overweight woman as she stood. "How're you doing, Beck?"

"I'm fine, Danny. It's good to see you again. Sorry it's been so long. Wow, I walked in here and the hostess asked me if I was with you and brought me back to this table."

"I do have a few connections in town."

She looked around. "It looks like it."

"Anyway, how was your flight? I would've picked you up at the Columbus airport, or Evie comes up here at least once a week, and she would've done it."

"That's okay. I wanted to visit some friends in Columbus and needed my own rental car."

"You didn't have to stay at the hotel, you know. Jayna and I would've been happy to have you."

"I know, but I didn't want to be a bother."

"You would never be a bother for us. We have plenty of room."

"Charlotte is doing okay?"

He nodded. "She's great. She and Jeff still live in the old house."

"You two still speak to each other?"

He smiled. "Of course, Beck. We've remained friends, and I stop by and see her about once a week since her office is nearby. We also consult on some cases since our responsibilities overlap a bit. We sometimes have some playful banter in the office, but I usually lose those arguments. She and Jayna also have a friendly relationship."

"Not everyone could do that. I can't imagine having that kind of relationship with either of my exes. I don't ever want to see them, let alone once a week." She smiled. "Our communication occurs mainly through our attorneys."

"She's Evie's mother and will always be a part of my life, even though that part has changed. I can't change that.

"Sandy is doing okay?"

"Yeah, she's pretty good. She has twenty-five years in the fire department and will probably retire in a few years, so she and Laurie can travel to Europe."

"That's great. I've always been so proud of Sandy. It wasn't easy to be her in the early 80s. She was always proud of her sexual orientation and never tried to hide it."

"Yes, I always admired her for that." The server came and took their orders. "Annie and Isaac doing well?"

She nodded. "Yeah, they're living nearby." Ann was a nurse at a large Minneapolis hospital, and Isaac was a construction worker in St. Paul.

"Their kids?"

"Trisha is expecting, which will make me a great-grandmother. Can you believe that?"

"Nope, and you are fortunate, Beck. I am still waiting to be a grandfather."

"So, when is that going to happen for the famous Amalgam-Man? Is Evie still dating Jayna's son?"

"Yeah, they're pretty much an item. They go everywhere together and seem to have a great time. He's a fine arts teacher in Columbus, and she's pretty artsy, obviously. I wouldn't be surprised to hear wedding bells soon. Being grandpa would be cool." The waitress came and took their orders. "Are you doing okay?"

She looked up from her salad. "Sure, why wouldn't I be?"

"I know the breakup with Tim had to be difficult."

"It was actually better than with Richie. We agreed to divide everything, not that we had a lot. It's over, finally. I know you remember how much paperwork is involved."

He took a drink of diet cola the server had brought. "Yeah, I do. Financially?"

"I'm doing all right, Danny."

"If you need something, please let me know. I mean it."

"I know you do. I'm fine, really." She took a bite of the bread the server had brought and sipped iced tea. "I did stop drinking, though. I decided I didn't need that anymore. It was tough to admit I had a problem."

"That's great, Beck."

"I know you never drank, Danny, and I'm glad for that. I know it was terrible for you growing up with everything Dad did. All the trips to the jail to bail him out in the middle of the night. That must've been embarrassing."

"It was terrible for both of us. And for Mom. She became so depressed she hardly ever left the house, even after he died. I wish she could've gotten some help."

"Yeah, but Dad didn't have a lot of interest in me, which I used to resent—but then I realized it was probably for the best that he left me alone. I'm sorry I left right after high school. In some ways, I felt like I deserted you and Mom."

"You don't have to be sorry for anything. You did what you had to do to stay sane with all that dysfunction, and there was no future for you here. I'm sorry that things with Mom and Dad turned out the way they did—Mom wasn't a very strong person and couldn't stand up to him."

"It was just sad how Dad ended up—crashing his truck into a tree after spinning out on some ice. I'm sure he was probably drunk."

"Drunk and on pills of some kind, most likely. They found a bottle of booze in his glove box. At least he only killed himself and not someone else, too. I always worried about that, especially if he had killed or seriously injured a pregnant woman or child, so it was the best possible outcome in an unwinnable situation. I know that may sound terrible, but it's how I feel."

"Yeah. I just hope he's at peace now." She took a bite of her salad. "Hey, I heard about those two big fires. You know anything about them?"

He nodded. "Both of them. We were at the museum the night before it happened, and the university building was one that I'm over."

"Do they know what caused them?"

He shook his head. "Not sure, Beck. I'm working on some things with the police, but we don't have all the pieces yet."

"What?" She smiled. "Are you part of the police now? When did that happen?"

"Sort of. I work as a special consultant to the department on certain cases where my expertise is needed. This is one of those times."

"That's really neat, Dan. I'm so proud of you and everything you do for the community."

"It's good to be wanted and needed. Sometimes I can be a pain in the butt, though."

"I sure believe that, as you were definitely that when you were a kid. So, when are you coming up my way?"

"That's something I need to plan for spring. Jayna would like the mall, and Evie and Rob really like baseball, so they could take in a Twins game or two."

"Well, we need to plan that, and maybe that first grandbaby will be on the way by then."

"Beck, let's wait until they get married first."

Chapter Seventeen

Staffordsville Police Department
Staffordsville, Ohio
0930 hours

"I understand you've waived your right to counsel, Dr. Tegler," Lt. Eppard said as they sat in the interrogation room with Sybil. "You understand your Miranda rights as I've read them?"

"I do, Lieutenant. I don't have anything to hide."

"That's good. I want to show you some things." Eppard showed her Jake's pieced-together fourteen seconds of video footage from the burned museum security cameras on a large computer tablet. "For starters, is this you, Dr. Tegler? Dragging huge bags of potato chips into the arts museum to use as an untraceable accelerant?"

She laughed. "That's preposterous; there must be more than a hundred pounds of chips. Where would I get that many?"

"Please answer 'yes' or 'no,' Dr. Tegler."

"No, it's not me, Lt. Eppard, that's ridiculous. Spreading potato chips around like that looks pretty stupid."

He pulled out receipts from Hughes Food Supply. "Sybil, it may look stupid, but we're not, and I can prove where you bought enormous amounts of potato chips from a wholesale food company in Columbus over the last several weeks—far more than any single person could actually consume."

"So what? Many people use that commercial food service because of their prices, and I like to buy in bulk. That doesn't mean the person in that low-quality video is me."

"Most of those chips would be well past the expiration date before you could eat them, Sybil," he said. "It would take you ten lifetimes to use those up, so don't use thrift as an excuse."

"Is there a law against buying that many chips?"

"No, but there's a law against using them for nefarious purposes," Eppard said.

"I can also show you that I bought many other things in those quantities, like coffee. Did I use that to do something bad, too? That doesn't prove I used those potato chips to burn down a building or for other 'nefarious purposes,' as you maintain with your typical embellishment. I donated the extras to a food bank."

"Then you should have a receipt for that," he said.

"I think I have it somewhere. I would want the tax break."

"Sure, you're always complaining about how little money you make, Sybil; I can't imagine you wouldn't want the tax break."

She sighed. "They also took my name, so you can check it out at First Harvest."

"I doubt you donated anywhere near the excess amounts you bought. You did that just to give yourself an alibi for why you bought so much, to show you gave at least some away."

She took a sip of diet lemon-lime soda. "And I was far too drunk to have done anything like that. I'm better now, after a week on the fluconazole, but look at the police video from when I was arrested several days before the fire. You were there in the Palatine emergency room, too. No way could I have had the coordination or mental faculties to do that."

"Wrong, Sybil. My sophisticated gait analysis software proves with ninety-five percent probability that the perpetrator in this video is you." Forensic gait analysis technology did exist, but he didn't have enough video information to make a detailed analysis. The police could lie, so why couldn't he?

"Hey, Rudbeck is right, Dr. Tegler. His cyber-technology is

top-notch."

"We also know someone engineered the blowout of one of the front right tires of that Bowling Green bus at around 2200 hours the night you were picked up by the police."

"That's crazy. How could someone have done that?"

"Radio-controlled transmission of a small directional C-4 charge. We found the trigger about two hundred yards before the place where the bus broke down. That's where you triggered it; when it stopped, you conveniently boarded the bus and were told to get off because you were in the wrong place."

"How could someone do that? It's impossible."

"Is it?" He pulled out the small plastic evidence bag containing the transmitter he had found in the bushes at the mentioned location. "This has your fingerprints all over it, Sybil."

"How do you have my fingerprints? I'm not in the system."

"Ah, but you are, as good old TSA PreCheck had them on file. For a suspected arson case, it's not too hard to track down. And, the ABC tow service guy, Eddie Phillips, said you paid him to do it, in cahoots with a guy at a shop in Bowling Green, where it was actually placed because it had to be in the tire at the football game, because it had to be inside when it left. We're still determining that individual's name."

"Yeah, criminal mischief at that level is a felony, Tegler, maybe even attempted murder or manslaughter. That bus could've turned over and seriously injured or killed a bunch of people," Eppard said as he pointed his right index finger at her. "The prosecutor will have a field day with you. If its origin had been in another state, you'd also be looking at federal charges."

She hesitated for several minutes, then took a sip of water. "Okay. I admit to burning down the museum to help split the insurance money with Drake Fowler."

"Several million dollars' worth, at least," he said. "Maybe more."

"Yes, I know I could go to jail for that. But I had nothing to do with Biggerstaff."

"You *could go to jail?* Are you kidding? That's aggravated arson, Tegler. Five to ten in the state pen," Eppard said. "You said in the bodycam video you wanted a mugshot and orange jumpsuit, so you'll be getting your wish. What about the Bowling Green bus?"

She nodded. "Yes. I was told it would be safe, and they would just need to pull off on the side of the road, and there was no chance of injury since they were all dual tires."

He pointed at her. "Well, you were misinformed. How did you do that at the game? Someone would've noticed, and the driver likely stayed with the bus. We talked to Kathy Graves, the lab tech with whom you went to the game, and she said you couldn't have been away from her long enough to do anything to the tire. She also said you were acting perfectly fine until you disappeared after the game, and she couldn't find you because you needed to begin your trek down Highway 128 to find the broken-down bus and meet up with Deputy Wolford on his predictable patrol path. You conveniently left your small backpack containing your phone and wallet on your seat, knowing that Kathy would take it home with her, since part of your game was not to have it when confronted by the police, which promoted the aura of drunkenness you desired to convey."

She shook her head. "You're right—the tire was placed on the bus before it even left Bowling Green. It was a good tire, except for the modifications."

"Huh. Modifications that could've gotten a whole busload of people killed. So you needed some help there as well. More people to talk to," Eppard said. "There was a small block of C-4 in the tire the whole 155 miles from Bowling Green. It could've accidentally gone off." It was actually quite rare for C-4 to go off accidentally, but she didn't need to know that.

"I swear I didn't think that could happen, and it didn't. It blew out right where it was supposed to, and they got off the road safely."

"Lucky for you. The potato chip accelerants are suspected of having caused both the arts museum and medical building fires," he said. "Neither the arson dogs nor the vapor trace analyzer detected anything at either site, as we didn't find any typical accelerants like gasoline, kerosene, diesel fuel, turpentine, butane, isopropanol, or others."

"And that makes me the culprit for Biggerstaff, too? Potato chips aren't a controlled substance. Anyone could've bought them. I tell you I didn't do it!"

"Excuse me if your explanation doesn't hold water, Dr. Tegler. If you don't mind my being blunt, you don't seem to have much credibility. Very few people outside of large restaurant owners would've bought potato chips in such massive amounts. Why couldn't you have burned down both buildings?" Eppard asked.

"I already declared I used them for the other fire, but I wouldn't have burned down my own building that might've had people in it—at least give me some credit for that. A large portion of my research is gone now."

"My research is gone now—awww, how sad, Tegler. Makes me wanna cry. No, you just burn down museums containing millions of dollars worth of valuable items. *That* seems to be okay, though? Give me a break, lady," Eppard asked. "Lie at one thing, lie at another. You're in a heap of trouble."

"But how did you fake the carbohydrate challenge test, Sybil?" A pause for several seconds. "Look, I'm a pretty smart guy, and I'll figure it out sooner or later; I've come this far with minimal clues. You could deceive the deputy's PBT by putting hand sanitizer in your mouth as it doesn't distinguish the type of alcohol, but that wouldn't work for a police station breathalyzer or blood ethanol level."

Eppard pointed at her. "Yeah, your best chance for any deal is contingent on your being completely honest with us. You clearly had at least a half dozen accomplices."

She took a gulp of water. "It wasn't easy. A small expandable neoprene bladder was placed in my stomach, releasing twenty milliliters of ninety-five percent ethanol every half hour for four hours. It's still in there."

"Does it still contain ethanol?" he asked.

She nodded. "Probably. We didn't know how much we needed, so he added extra."

"And the blood alcohol level went up, not because of the carbohydrate load and auto-brewery syndrome, but due to that. The high blood alcohol content also didn't have any effect on you because of the hydroglippane, of course."

She looked up at him. "How do you know about hydroglippane?"

"I told you I was on top of things; I'm a well-known medical toxicologist, Sybil, so how did you think I wouldn't know about investigational drugs that block toxic substances, especially the most common toxic substance of all? You also have ALDH deficiency and would've died with even a fraction of that ethanol in your system if something wasn't blocking it."

"ALDH? What's that?"

He laughed. "Don't insult my intelligence. You're a medical geneticist, so don't play dumb with me, Sybil. It's the most common human genetic mutation."

"You think I have that enzyme deficiency?"

"I know you do. Given that you're half-Chinese, do you think I wouldn't check that out?"

She shook her head. "Only half of the people of Asian descent are affected, and my medical records state that I don't have it, so you're wrong."

"Sure, the official record from a year ago says that because you either paid someone to falsify the records or used someone else's blood to do the tests a year ago, so you've been thinking about this project for a while to plant the evidence. Since you don't drink anyway, no one would ever know the difference, and knowledge that you had that genetic abnormality would make it very unlikely you could've been believably drunk. But I don't always believe what I see, and I did my own studies.

"I then thought back to some faculty parties and how absolutely nuts you went when you discovered someone spiked the punch, which was often. I thought initially it might've been a religious objection, but the real reason was that if you'd ingested even a small amount of spiked punch, you would've gotten extremely sick. Therefore, you consumed only sealed containers of non-alcoholic drinks. Tell me that isn't true."

She looked at him with her mouth wide open. "I don't believe it. How the hell did you determine all this, Rudbeck?"

"I'm skeptical about everything I examine. But someone had to help you do this . . . not only to endoscopically insert the bladder in your stomach, but to falsify the biopsy results and get you the drug, in addition to all the others like the fake medical records. My guess is that the actual microorganisms in your gut are *not* those that cause auto-brewery syndrome.

"You also played dumb in the Palatine ER about auto-brewery syndrome, like it was something new you'd never heard about."

"That's right, it would've blown everything if I knew about it beforehand."

"But even before I got this other information, I had my suspicions that you knew about it, which was essential since you had to make all these arrangements with the gastric bladder and such. I contacted the main university library in Columbus and, with Lt. Eppard's help, ordered a printout of all your literature searches using your university credentials. Turns out you researched auto-brewery syndrome eighteen months ago and downloaded over a dozen articles on the topic. So this endeavor was all premeditated with prior knowledge of the illness, which gave you all the information you needed to plan how you were going to fake it."

Sybil shook her head. "How did you ever figure this out, Rudbeck? The tests came out perfect."

He nodded. "Yeah, *too* perfect, but you missed one thing that I did initially as well. Deputy Wolford did some sobriety tests while you were in the Palatine ER."

"Sure, I remember. I was staggering around and completely failed them on purpose."

"Of course you remember because you couldn't feel the effects of the alcohol. You could fake the heel-to-toe and one-legged stand tests, but *not* the horizontal nystagmus test. It was all recorded on Deputy Wolford's Axon bodycam, and the latter was completely normal."

"I don't know what you're talking about."

He pulled out a photo of an attractive blonde woman, perhaps in her late thirties. "Do you know this individual?"

She nodded. "Of course. She's a first cousin on my father's side, Chloe Thompson."

"That's correct. Do you know where she works?"

She sighed. "She's a sales representative for Karmahut Pharmaceuticals in Nashville."

"That's right, Sybil. And do you know what drug Karmahut makes?"

"They make many drugs, I'm sure. I don't keep track of them unless it's some kind of gene therapy, like the new cystic fibrosis drugs or therapy for an inborn error of metabolism. I'm a basic scientist, not a clinician, Malgy."

"Well, one of their drugs in investigational trials is hydroglippane sodium, a drug we've discussed that blocks the ethanol receptor GABA-A."

"Just because my cousin works there doesn't mean she would have any access to the drug."

"She might know someone with access to it. We're working on

finding out who. She's a beautiful divorced woman. I'm sure she might've had several suitors among the clinician-investigators."

"I wouldn't know about Chloe's dating habits." She crossed her arms. "I'm also not saying anything more without my attorney."

"Probably a good idea, but we'll figure it out, Sybil, and you've said plenty already. I will quite soon determine how Dale Stephens did an off-the-books procedure and falsified records. You would've required propofol for sedation, and we'll track that down, too, with my pharmacy connections. And then that person will be going down along with you. Add someone at a tire shop in Bowling Green and your cousin Chloe in Nashville as well, and we've got a regular rogues' gallery of conspirators."

"Didja hear that, Dr. Tegler?" Eppard asked as he leaned across the table at her. "You've got Rudbeck on your tail. That's bad news."

"Yeah, so what? People laugh at him all the time because he jokes around and likes to help the underdog, which I surely am. Some people don't take him seriously. Why do you think I had the deputy call him rather than someone else? I knew he would believe me and come out there."

"Take *this* seriously, Tegler: you screwed up and called the wrong dude. He's the big, ugly, scarred, one-eyed junkyard dog who doesn't give a crap what happens to him and will never back down. He will exhaust every last erg of his energy before he's done, and then come back for more."

"Lt. Eppard, did you just use 'erg' in a sentence?" he asked, smiling. "Outstanding."

"Hey, I did, so you're rubbing off on me, sadly."

"I'm aware of the hyperbole that constantly surrounds the ridiculous Amalgam-Man, but what's your point, Lieutenant?" she asked.

"That you're in a shitload of trouble, Ma'am."

"Tell me something I don't know. I think I do want to call an attorney now."

"Sure thing, lady. Knock yourself out. You're welcome to do it from here."

They left the interrogation room, leaving Sybil behind to call her attorney, and walked to Eppard's office. The lieutenant sat behind his desk in one of the chairs across from him.

"*Big, ugly, scarred, one-eyed junkyard dog?*" He frowned. "What the hell?"

Eppard pointed a yellow pencil at him. "Hey, I was paying you a compliment, Rudbeck. You're a tough guy who's been in some scrapes, and no one should mess with you because nothing scares you, because you have nothing to lose."

"Tough is okay, but *ugly?* I'm no movie star, but come on."

"What? You want to be some wimpy pretty boy like your alter ego Dixon? I've seen you sparring in the gym with some of our guys. You'd kick his sissy ass."

"Okay, I guess I see your point."

"And damn, Rudbeck, I'm impressed by you for once! Maybe there's some latent cop in you after all, making up that shit about the 'gait analysis' or whatever. The forensic work for the exploding tire was a masterpiece of detective work, as was your going out in that field with your metal detector looking for that transmitter."

He shook his head. "Well, forensic gait analysis does exist. Most human beings have minor idiosyncrasies in their gait that are unique and reproducible. Had we more footage, then it might've been more accurate. We don't have enough information from that burned-up drive Jake analyzed to implicate Tegler at Youngswood directly."

Eppard pointed at him. "But you got a confession from the woman with your bluff, at least for the museum. It sure makes my life a whole lot easier."

"She did actually take a bunch of chips to First Harvest Food Bank, as they record all transactions, in case someone dropped off something toxic or something."

"Really? Why didn't you mention that?"

"She didn't need to know that. She used her real name to support her story of donating chips. There was also a photo of her license plate from the surveillance video. She took just a small fraction of the chips she bought."

"You're becoming more cop-like every minute. You've come so far, and I'm proud of you, and I can almost tolerate you these days. You've become kind of an adopted son, although you're older than me, and not nearly as nice-looking."

"Thanks, Dad. I appreciate it. Can I give you a hug?"

"Don't you even think about it." Eppard took a swig of black police station coffee. "Do you think she burned down Biggerstaff, too?"

He thought for a few seconds, then shook his head. "I don't think so."

"Why not?"

"What would she have gained by that? She could've been in cahoots with someone to get Fowler's insurance money for the camera for sure, but there's no motive for Biggerstaff. She had much to lose by torching that, such as her research."

"Come on, Rudbeck, she would've left the country after she got her illicit payout. She didn't give a crap about her research."

"You may have a point, Brian, but that doesn't motivate her to burn Biggerstaff. Most scientists do care about their research, believe it or not. I believe that this is a much more complex project than the museum."

"It would need to have been someone who knew her or was in close proximity to her, who likely also works in Biggerstaff. Someone who might have been able to figure out her plan and then blame it on her. She's probably brilliant since she's a professor, but a great criminal mind she surely isn't, and even the smartest crooks eventually get caught. So, who else is in that building near Tegler who would've done that, Rudbeck?"

"Well, on that floor was Robertson, obviously, but he's dead. Ken Barton in histology and Lenny Peterson in cell biology are nearby. I don't see them having any interest in that."

He then thought about the chair of biochemistry, who seemingly had a lot of research funding without a lot of products to show for it. Jack Meach was a full professor, so he didn't need to be promoted, but almost all of his grants had been fully funded, while most investigators maybe had only a third funded. And, while Meach was relatively well-known, he wasn't a superstar of that caliber by any means. Lucky? In these tough financial times, unlikely.

This could mean that some of his research was falsified to get lucrative research grants, and the fire was a perfect way to destroy most of the evidence and cover his tracks. But maybe that wasn't the only reason.

He had an idea and needed the help of his favorite pseudo-private eye, Jake Fisher, as he needed proof of his theories. And destroying most of the evidence might leave a small amount yet to be discovered.

"John Meach, the biochemistry department chair, would be my bet, Eppard."

"We don't have any evidence or motive for him doing that."

"Just be patient. I need some help from a friend."

Chapter Eighteen

Jake Fisher's 2013 Buick Regal
1800 Block of North Mathison Street
Staffordsville, Ohio
1820 Hours

"So, why do you want my help, Malgy-Man?" Jake Fisher asked as they drove in his 2013 burgundy Buick Regal down Mathison Street in search of wrongdoing. "Brannigan didn't want to assist? I also don't carry a gun like a genuine private eye, so why didn't you invite your lovely spouse?"

"Ted doesn't have your computer expertise, and Jayna knows nothing about this. An efficient spousal crime-solving team we are not. We would also likely argue about something stupid she thought I was doing, which would detract from the ultimate goal."

"Which is to waste time?"

"No, no. Solving crime."

"That's good, thanks for telling me. We are, however, likely to do some stupid stuff, like we are already doing."

"True, true."

"Does your buddy Eppard know about this?"

"I don't bother the busy lieutenant with the details of my crime-solving activities. It's better that he doesn't know, actually."

"Are we supposed to be incognito private eyes, driving around in my old Buick? Is that the plan, man? I just want to be sure I'm on board."

"We are. Two Ohio everymen out for an excursion. We won't attract attention."

"Got it, we blend in perfectly. And thanks for spilling your food and pop everywhere, pal. I thought I was done with little kids messing up my car, but you're worse than all of mine ever were."

"No one would notice in this old heap. And we're on a stakeout. Eating in cars is what private eyes do. We should start smoking cigars, too, to add to the classic ambience."

"Good idea. Stakeout at the steak house. Funny."

He nodded. "No one will suspect us. We're far too average to notice."

"Right, no one in town knows you, one of its most visible inhabitants. Your bass voice, for example—so indistinctive. And what is it we're looking for?"

"That." He pointed out the window to the couple coming out of Staffordsville's finest restaurant—Burk's Steak House.

"So what? Lots of people go there. Who's that? Dr. Meach? The biochem guy?"

He nodded. "Yeah, that's my buddy Jack. I told you his car was in the lot. Dummy didn't even think of using another car. What an amateur."

"I doubt he thought he would be tailed to Burk's by wannabe private investigators. Hey, you think he burned up the med school building, don't you?"

"That's the theory. I think he wanted to kill Johnny Robertson and cover up some illicit research stuff he was doing."

"Wow, that sucks. You have some evidence of that?"

"Some circumstantial stuff. We need more of a motive, though."

"Who's that pretty lady he's with?"

"That's Cheryl Robertson—Johnny's widow. It looks like they're out for a night in town. Exactly what I was trying to find out."

"Awww, Malgy, that's just two people out for dinner, and that doesn't necessarily mean anything, even if he is a scumbag. Maybe he's taking her out to console her or something."

He choked on his soda. "Yeah, 'consoling'—right. The only 'consoling' will involve a motel room somewhere."

"Come on. This isn't your novel with its cheap no-tell motels."

"Barclay Dixon only stays in the finest opulent five-star hotels, I'll have you know."

"Sorry, man." Jake patted him on the shoulder. "I didn't mean to insult your hero."

"Rumor had it that Cheryl was always gone, probably stepping out on him."

"Perhaps Johnny paid too much attention to his research rather than to her. I heard that his car was always in the parking lot all night because he was sleeping in his lab, probably drinking most of the time."

"Cheryl's pretty attractive, and Robertson was about twenty-five years older, you said, and was morbidly obese and in shitty health, so how in the hell did he score her as a wife?"

"Johnny was better looking when he was younger, and he married Cheryl when she was a student at the university who took one of his introductory classes. He had some money, she was enamored of him, I heard, so she rode the gravy train for a while. After about ten years, the gravy train started breaking down, and she began playing the field. By that time, he spent most of the time in his office eating, drinking, and probably taking drugs."

"Did they have any kids?"

"No. Hey, pay attention—they're leaving! Follow them." He pointed out the rolled-down passenger window.

Jake punched him in the arm. "What am I, your chauffeur? Don't give me orders, Dixon. What do I get out of this road trip, anyway?"

"The pleasure of solving a complex crime, and some fine eats."

"Working Guy's Buddy burgers, yippee, what a treat from the big spender here. Burk's has takeout, so we could've had a couple of prime ribeyes with onion rings."

"Sorry, Jake, but that might've taken too long. I just want to see where they're going. Nothing illegal about that."

"Jake the PI always works within the law. So, do we go in after we don our disguises we didn't bring, or do we wait out here?"

"Meach would recognize me instantly. You, probably not. Why don't you go in and take a seat at the bar and see what's up?"

"Oh, that sounds like a lot of fun."

"Come on. I sure can't go in and do it."

He finished his cheap WGB meal as Jake went in to see what they were doing. In the meantime, he answered some leftover emails from work (as he was a master of multitasking) and completed the remainder of his sandwich and drink. Fifteen minutes later, Jake came out.

"Well? What's the scoop?"

"They were sitting together in a booth and were pretty chummy. She sure didn't look upset and in need of consoling."

"Probably celebrating the death of Johnny with Burk's finest champagne."

"Yeah, they were, but that doesn't prove anything."

"No. We just need to wait here on the stakeout to see where they go afterward."

"Okay, buddy. Your wish is my command, as always."

Fifty minutes later, the couple left and took off in their car, with the 2013 burgundy Buick Regal in hot pursuit, as Jake was careful not to follow too closely. Meach and Cheryl eventually pulled into the parking lot of the Deacon Motel on the edge of town—not the worst place in existence, but something below what Meach could likely afford, given his side research deals. Cheryl was a striking blonde of about forty-five, a good twenty-five years younger than her deceased husband. How she and Johnny ever got together was not readily apparent; he wasn't the most attractive or personable fellow.

"Two people just out for dinner, huh?" He took a bite of his half-pound cheeseburger and sipped diet root beer as he inhaled an onion ring. "Here's what I think—Meach is on the same floor as Tegler and could easily have bugged her office or something to figure out what she was up to. He has the intellect and the means to have burned up Biggerstaff, and he tried to blame Sybil for it, because it would've been so easy. He also incessantly complained about how terrible that building was."

"So did dozens of other people, Malgy, including you. That doesn't mean he burned it down, as much as you'd like to think that."

"No, but he clearly is having an affair with his widow, and he knew that Johnny often slept in his office. He spiked his CPAP machine with alprazolam and burned the sucker down. Who knows, maybe Cheryl has something to do with it, too."

"We would have to prove he did that to his CPAP machine." Jake took a sip of coffee. "Do you think he just went in there and put it in the plastic humidifier water reservoir?"

"I don't think so. It would've been easy for him to learn which machine he used because it was always out in his office; he then obtained a spare reservoir for it, put the alprazolam into it as a concentrate, and then Johnny would have filled the rest with distilled water."

"Where do you get one of those reservoirs? The drugstore?"

"No. That model is pretty common, and it would've been easy to get one from any number of online medical supply vendors."

"Is it possible Meach has sleep apnea and uses the same model?"

"I suppose so, but unlikely. He's pretty skinny. One thing is that any of those supplies require a doctor's prescription, and Meach wasn't a physician."

"How easy would that be to forge?"

"Ridiculously easy, as long as he was paying cash and not using insurance. It's not a controlled item by any means. No one would likely check, and any physician's NPI (National Provider Identifier) number is public record."

"What about the police talking to Meach?"

"That may be coming soon, but Meach isn't Tegler. She pretty much spilled the beans when we confronted her, but I suspect Meach will be way too sophisticated and polished for that. He'll lawyer up and then he'll know we're on to him, so that's one reason we're not pushing it. We need more evidence and to find out some of that information legally. I'm not sure how to do that."

"What about the alprazolam?"

"That will be easier to track down, as it's a controlled substance. Fortunately, I know the director of pharmacy very well."

"I'm sorry for the director of pharmacy," Jake said.

AAAAA

Jayna Rudbeck's Office
Staffordsville University Hospital
1345 hours

"I've checked all prescriptions for alprazolam that have gone through our system," Jayna, wearing a tailored navy blue pantsuit, said as they sat in her hospital office at her small conference table after he barged in and interrupted another meeting she was having. "I'm bordering on violating HIPAA here, but I guess this is official police work, and you do have some official standing."

"You bet I do, dear."

"Okay, Detective Rudbeck. There are the scripts for John Robertson from Dr. Castleton, of course, but we knew that already from the information Charlie gave us after his death. Those tablets couldn't easily have been converted into liquid aerosol products."

"So, how do we find out where Meach got it?"

Jayna shook her head. "I have no idea. It's a common drug, and there are many other drugstores besides the university retail pharmacies, or he could've gotten it illegally, or online in some fashion."

"We need to prove that he had access to it."

"But he would've needed it as a liquid, Dan. The tablet would've left some residue of inert substances used as binders and might have clogged the machine unless he had the ability to extract the active drug."

"Well, he is a biochemist. He would have the knowledge and resources to do that."

"Possibly, but he would still need to get the pills, and it would be a lot of trouble and risk. But that leaves the hospital for a liquid preparation, but I've checked, and all parenteral alprazolam has been accounted for, not just here but in most of the Columbus area. He could've gotten it from other cities, though: Dayton, Akron, Cleveland, etc." She thought for a few seconds. "Unless—"

"Unless what?"

"Unless he procured it from a less regulated source. To that end, I would imagine there's a veterinary preparation of alprazolam."

"For some freaking dog or cat with anxiety? You've got to be kidding me."

"I'm not, and there are likely uses for them and larger animals who need sedation for procedures. And that would be much easier to get without all the restrictions of a human prescription. I'll contact my friend at the vet school at Ohio State right now."

"Okay. Now we're getting somewhere." He took a sip of coffee and stared at her across the desk as she remained motionless, like a slightly menacing blonde statue.

She stared back at him for half a minute. "Is there something else I can help you with, Doctor?" she asked, frowning.

"Just waiting for more of that information. Let's get going; there's a crime to solve."

She pointed to the door. "It's going to take me a little while! Please give me some peace and quiet and come back later."

"Yes, Ma'am." He smiled, left her office, and closed the door. He knew when he wasn't wanted and was being a bit obnoxious, which was nothing new. She also wasn't allowed to have her pistol in the hospital; she had to lock it up at the hospital police station when she came in and retrieve it when she left. So, she couldn't shoot him, at least.

He went back to his office to do some actual work and talk to his assistant, whom he had not seen in two days; he returned to the pharmacy office a couple of hours later to see what his spouse had found out.

"Any information yet, Miss?" he asked as he plopped down in one of her chairs and took a sip of coffee.

She sighed. "I know that the lowly criminal underbelly is your entire existence these days, Barclay, but I do have other work to do, sadly, as I lack the same privileged existence as you. Seriously, doesn't anyone ever wonder where the heck you go during the day and what you do with your time? Most of the time when I go down there, you've vanished into thin air, and Yvonne never saw you leave."

He nodded. "They probably do wonder, but AI does a good job of auto-replying to certain emails, and Yvonne takes care of the rest. I am a master of multitasking and stealth, like a shadow."

"You weigh two hundred and forty-five pounds. That's a pretty hefty shadow."

"Yeah, well, I can disappear from my private back exit up the stairs to my secret parking space, and no one would ever know I was gone. Bet you can't say the same. My vast arsenal of mobile devices also always keeps me connected."

"Except in the middle of the night when I have to answer your phone because of the roaring of your CPAP machine." She frowned. "Well, I did talk to my old college friend Frannie Richardson, a vet school professor. Meach researches the nervous system's response to hypoglycemia using animal models, usually mice. He purchases insulin and such to do his experiments."

"So what? I don't care about his stupid insulin."

"I'm only demonstrating that he's been buying pharmaceuticals for his research."

"Big deal. A lot of researchers do that."

"Let me finish, please. I thought you wanted my help."

"Sorry, please continue, dear."

"There's also a company in Charlotte called Southeast Compounders that makes alprazolam liquid for veterinary use. Meach purchased some of that under the patient pseudonym, 'Mouse Meach,' supposedly to decrease the anxiety in his lab animals before their death from hypoglycemia. We have the lab receipts to prove it."

"That's great, but it doesn't prove he put it in the CPAP water reservoir, and I doubt the amounts needed for a mouse would be similar to that for the morbidly obese Robertson. I suppose I could go through his trash, but it's unlikely there are any paper receipts since he probably bought the spare water reservoir online."

"What if he didn't buy it?" Jayna asked as she chewed on her yellow pencil.

"Where would he have gotten it then, hon? Stolen it from someone?"

"Well, there are a couple of home durable medical equipment suppliers in town. The hospital also has CPAP machines for patients who need them."

He frowned. "I'm well aware of that, as I often work with pulmonary patients."

"Yes, but you said the one Johnny used was a common model, so maybe the hospital uses the same one. You have several CPAP machines yourself."

"Yeah, so? One is for travel I keep packed in a bag, and another is a backup. Lots of people who can afford it do so."

"Do they all use the same humidifier water reservoir?"

"They do, as they're pretty standard. All the ones I've had over the years used the same fittings."

"There we go. Remember that buying online would have produced some kind of a paper trail and payment record, even if it was under a fake name. He could've stolen one from the hospital or gotten someone in respiratory therapy to sneak him one."

"Is there a way to track the inventory of the hospital's units?"

She nodded. "Yes, absolutely. That should be fairly easy to track. Barb Johnson in respiratory therapy can find out."

"Can you call Barb?"

She sighed again and saluted him with her right hand. "Of course, Doctor, sir. I am at your disposal at all times for your crime-solving needs." She looked up the number on her computer and made a call. "Barb? It's Jayna Rudbeck. I have a favor to ask, and I'm going to send a rather large visitor your way. Who? It's a surprise. I bet you can't guess who. Also, I'm sorry in advance. What do I mean? You'll understand in a few minutes."

AAAAA

Respiratory Therapy Department
Staffordsville University Hospital
1615 hours

He went to the second floor to the respiratory therapy department and met the director, Barbara Johnson, as he walked into the department.

"Hi, Barb, I'm Dan Rudbeck."

The fiftyish blonde looked at him and smiled. "I didn't know Jayna was sending the famous Amalgam-Man to my department. I am honored, Doctor. What can I do for you?

"We have a case going that might involve someone putting a drug in a CPAP humidifier water reservoir for illicit reasons."

"Oh, dear. What can I do to assist?"

"We don't know where the person got the reservoir and were wondering if it had come from your department. He might not have had a prescription."

"Do you know which model, Dr. Rudbeck?"

"Promatic X10."

"Maybe. We have a bunch of those models, and the reservoir

hasn't changed since the X6. Let me check and see if there was only a reservoir that was checked out." She looked at her computer for a few minutes and called someone on her office phone. "Rodney, can you please come in here? Right now, please. Bring the CPAP supply inventory log for September. Thanks."

Rodney Binford, the supply clerk, came into the office five minutes later. "What's up, Barb? Hey, what's Dr. Rudbeck doing here?"

"He has some questions. Did you give a Promatic X10 water reservoir to a Dr. John Meach a few weeks ago?"

Rodney looked at the clipboard and nodded. "I did; I didn't think it was a big deal. We have over fifty in stock."

"And you just gave him one?"

"He said he needed it for some experiment and offered to pay me for it. I told him not to worry about it, and I had no way to make such a transaction, so I just gave it to him, as the wholesale cost was only twenty bucks. It's not like it was a controlled substance or something."

"When did this happen?" he asked.

"About a month ago, Dr. Rudbeck. I have the inventory slip right here." Rodney pulled out his clipboard. "Here you go."

"Thanks. Can I get a copy of that?" Rodney went to another office to make a copy and returned two minutes later. "Appreciate the help, folks."

He returned to his office on the ground floor and called Eppard on his smartphone.

"Eppard. Is that you, Rudbeck?"

"Yeah. Brian, we have evidence of Meach purchasing alprazolam from a veterinary pharmaceutical supply house in Charlotte. Someone at the hospital gave him a CPAP humidifier reservoir—the same kind that Robertson used."

"Why would a legitimate business sell him a controlled drug?"

"He said he needed it for mouse experiments."

"Are you kidding me? Is that possible?"

"Possibly, but he purchased a quantity thousands of times what he would need for even a hundred mice."

"Damn, I didn't even know you could do that. Well, that's enough circumstantial evidence to arrest Meach on, Rudbeck. We have proof he had the drug and the reservoir and had no legitimate need for either one."

"The reservoir, no. He'll try to concoct some story about needing the drug for his rodent experiments, although the amount he bought is enough to kill ten thousand mice. Is it enough to convict him on?"

"That I don't know, never seen a case like this. I'll get right on it, but the prosecutor must be involved. Thanks for all the detective work."

"I'll send you copies of all the records."

Chapter Nineteen

Dan Rudbeck's Office
Staffordsville University Hospital
0830 hours

"So, you're saying Meach burned the Biggerstaff building down, and he's responsible for the death of Johnny Robertson?" Jake asked as they sat in his office at the conference table.

"That's my theory. He was on to Tegler's scheme and decided to blame it all on her after she was blamed for the museum fire."

"Why did Meach want to kill Robertson?"

"Jack was apparently having an affair with his wife. He had the means and motive to set the fire, either himself or with help, as Tegler's method was easy to duplicate. Robertson also might have files on his computer that implicate Meach accepting money for fraudulent research or something else."

"But the two fires were within ten days of each other. He wouldn't have had time to plan out everything Tegler did unless . . ."

"Unless he knew beforehand she would do that, Jake."

"You believe they were in it together?"

He shook his head. "I don't at all. They're two vastly different people, and I believe Meach spied on her in some fashion."

"Both of their computers must've been burned up in the fire. There might be some files in the cloud, though."

"I doubt he would put such sensitive information on the cloud, and someone could hack into that. The thing is, the day before the museum burned down, I received a package of *Rudbeckia hirta* seeds from an anonymous source. Inside were the seeds and a slip of paper with that number."

"You think Robertson sent it to you before he died?"

"Yeah, he must've known something was up, and he sent me that for insurance."

"Knowing you would obsess on it and not just discard it like most would. Clever."

He looked up a file on his phone. "-3280.8504. I remember I put it in my phone in case I needed it for something later."

"What do you think it is?"

"I don't know, Jake. It could be almost anything."

"A Swiss bank account number?"

He shook his head. "No, those are 21-character codes, beginning with CH. This number is only eight digits."

"I figured you would know about those. Could it be referencing a location?"

"Maybe, as that could be the product of a latitude and longitude. Our longitude is a negative number, in the 80s or so, and that could be what made the number negative."

"Our latitude is positive?"

"Yes."

"A huge range of numbers could yield that product, Malgy. We need something to narrow it down a bit."

"Wait a minute."

"What?"

"There was something else. Asking how many work hours are in a year."

"That's 2,080, isn't it, for a forty-hour work week?"

"Yeah, but how is that important?"

"Maybe it's a divisor."

He pulled out his phone again. "Dividing -3,280 by 2,080

doesn't provide anything useful. But what if the 2,080, or 2.080 more logically, is the ratio of the longitude to latitude?"

Jake shook his head. "It's still an enormous range of numbers, although that narrows it down. Still insufficient to go digging for buried treasure."

"The clue also mentioned 'ever since my birth.' Wonder what that means? Hey, can you find out when and where John Robertson was born?" he asked.

"That's a common name. What's his middle name?"

"Thomas."

"Age?"

"Seventy-one."

"Three by that name in Ohio, but the other two are younger than that. There's a John Thomas Robertson who was born in Lancaster, about fifteen miles from here," Jake said thirty seconds later. "Born December 5, 1954."

"12-5-54. That doesn't seem to mean anything initially, but I can get the computer AI bot to try some scenarios. Is it possible to find the exact place of his birth?"

"I can look through online birth records. It'll take me a few moments."

He took a swig of coffee and munched on a doughnut for several minutes. "Anything?"

"It looks like he was born at 1125 Baxter Street in Lancaster, according to his birth certificate," Jake said.

"Can you get the longitude of that residence?"

"Sure. -82.6072. Latitude is 39.6945."

"If we divide the longitude by 2.08, we get 39.7156. Or if we multiply the latitude by 2.08, we get -82.5650, logically accounting for the negative longitude, though," he said.

"What about the other number? Divide -3280.8504 by -82.6072," Jake said.

"39.7156."

"Well, that might be the latitude of whatever it is we're supposed to find. What is it?" Jake asked.

"GPS map says it's a field right off Highway 33 near Lancaster."

"That's where we need to go to uncover our next clue, then."

"I guess I should talk to Eppard first. I don't want to start digging around in another county without permission, or we could get into trouble. Hopefully, their law enforcement will extend some police courtesy to us."

AAAAA

Fairfield County, Ohio
Highway 33
0910 hours

The next day, he, Jake, Lt. Eppard, and Fairfield County Sheriff Kyle Warner went to the exact spot they had determined from the mathematical clues: longitude -82.6072, latitude 39.6945, which was a deserted field about a quarter mile east of Highway 33. This was assuming they had interpreted the clues correctly, of course.

They all shook hands with Warner. "Thanks, Sheriff Warner, for accommodating us on such short notice. I know this seems like a bizarre request," Eppard said.

"It's the weirdest I've seen, but I'm happy to help out, Brian. Luckily, we contacted the property owners, and they have no objection to us looking around this area as long as we exercise reasonable caution and don't destroy everything. Are you absolutely sure about this? Why would someone bury an item way out here?"

"We double-checked our numbers, Sheriff," he said. "The coordinates pinpoint it to an area of approximate radius thirty yards. We believe it to be a clue to a complex mystery involving the two large building fires a couple of weeks ago in Staffordsville."

"No kidding. What is it you're looking for?" Warner asked.

He shook his head. "Not exactly sure. Likely something containing documentation, probably a portable hard drive or hard copies of something."

"You have the proper instrumentation?"

Eppard laughed. "That's a funny question, Kyle. Rudbeck here has the finest instrumentation known to man. If it's findable, he'll detect it."

"Okay, then. Let's go, Jake. You guys can watch if you want."

He and Jake took his sophisticated, military-grade metal detector and combed the field for approximately twenty-five minutes until they found something.

"Here. The metal detector found something about six inches underground." He dug into the soft grass with the shovel he had brought. "Yes, there's definitely a dense metal object here." They dug up a small metal ammunition box. "The ammo box made it easier to find when whatever's inside could've just been placed in a plastic or cardboard box if they wanted to hide it. Robertson wanted us to find this."

"Well, what is it, guys?" Eppard asked. "The suspense is killing me."

Jake opened the ammo box. "It's a portable USB-C solid-state computer storage drive. Two terabytes."

"What the hell's on it?"

"Let's go back to the car." Jake put his laptop on his car hood as the others watched.

"Be careful, man, that thing could have tons of viruses on it."

Jake frowned at him snidely. "I'm not a dummy, Malgy. I'm using a secondary laptop and know what I'm doing. The drive is encrypted anyway."

"Can you break the encryption?"

"Not easily. We need to think of what the password might be."

"It has to be something we would know since Robertson directed us to this."

He thought of the package the clue came in. "Try *Rudbeckia.* The clue came in a package of flower seeds. It's not something anyone else would likely know, but Robertson knew I would."

"Come on. Can it really be something that simple?" Jake asked.

"Try it."

Jake entered it and waited several seconds. "Holy crap, *Rudbeckia* is the password, Malgy."

"Well?" Eppard asked.

"Give me a few minutes, Lieutenant." Jake perused the documents for several minutes. "Damn, Malgy. This drive has tons of documents linking Jack Meach to several offshore payments for what appear to be falsification of study results for drug studies. It's like Robertson knew he would die and wanted you to have the information."

"He wasn't the healthiest fellow. If he wasn't burned up in the fire, he probably wasn't long for this world, given his medical problems and substance abuse issues."

"There's more, Malgy. Some emails and other documents from a Dr. Dale Stephens which connect him to Meach."

"Stephens—the guy who put the neoprene bladder in Tegler's stomach so she could fake auto-brewery syndrome. But that had to do with the museum fire, not Biggerstaff. This proves that he was involved in both capers and that Meach knew about Tegler's plan, although she surely didn't know that."

"So, this is absolute evidence that Meach took money from illicit sources and gives him a motive for also killing off Robertson in the fire. Thanks, Rudbeck, you've come through once again. How the hell you did it, I don't know."

"This is the darndest thing I've ever seen," Sheriff Warner said. "I wish we had a Rudbeck on our payroll."

"That's the irony, Sheriff," Eppard said. "Rudbeck does all this for free, for the good of the human race. He's almost like a son to me. Right?"

"That is correct, Lieutenant. I go where I'm most needed, even though I may not be wanted."

"And there is only one Amalgam-Man," Eppard said. "Thank goodness. One of him is one too many."

Chapter Twenty

Staffordsville Police Department
Interrogation Room
1423 hours

Jack Meach was finally arrested for aggravated arson of the Biggerstaff Medical Science Building and the felony murder of Johnny Robertson and was brought into the interrogation room for questioning. He was accompanied by his attorney, Andrew Pulaski, a defense attorney from one of the big Columbus firms, as he and Lt. Eppard came into the room and sat down.

Meach laughed. "Jesus, the police department's hard up to have idiot Rudbeck here. What's his role? Comic relief? Be nice to retards week?"

"Dr. Rudbeck is a special consultant to the Department and has been working on this case," Lt. Eppard said.

"That's a sad state of affairs," Meach said as his attorney grimaced and whispered something in his client's ear.

He kept his composure and stared at Meach. Just keep it up and dig yourself a big hole, he thought to himself. He wasn't going to let this imbecile make him mad. He would, instead, find a way to get him to explode.

"We maintain Dr. Meach's innocence, Lieutenant Eppard," Pulaski, a small, wiry man in his late fifties, said. "While we acknowledge the terrible things that have happened recently, you don't have any direct evidence to hold my client. It's all circumstantial."

"Is that right? Let's examine the facts. Your client has motive and means to burn that building down," Eppard said.

"Motive?"

"Fraudulent research. He wanted to destroy evidence," he said.

"What proof do you have of that, Dr. Rudbeck?" Pulaski asked.

"To start: testimony from two graduate students who said Meach offered them money to falsify results in the logbooks. Both of them quit."

"That is very convenient. If it's true, then why haven't we heard from those two students recently?"

"They claim Meach threatened them if they said anything. A department head vs. two graduate students: not much of a competition, and the world of research in that area is fairly small; they would've been blacklisted. Also, the financial logs don't match. Meach is skimming off the top for his lifestyle, which is far out of sync with his salary."

"So why would he just burn the building down over that? Stuff a couple of grad students said? He could've destroyed evidence without burning a whole building down."

"Perhaps, but the consternation that fire would create would overshadow anything to do with his research. Few people would care about it with that going on."

"Even if he did destroy his research, which we're not admitting, that doesn't prove he burned that building down."

"Well, maybe this will convince you. Second round." He handed the attorney printed copies of the files on Robertson's hard drive, which he and Jake Fisher dug up in Lancaster.

"What's this, Rudbeck?" Meach asked.

"Copies of files we discovered from Robertson's computer. Copies of emails from you that you deleted from your own computer. They clearly implicate you in fraudulent research and accepting money to falsify results. The money was deposited in offshore accounts."

"I will have to examine these," Pulaski said.

"Hey, be our guest, Counselor. Let's move on to the death of John Robertson," Eppard said. "He was poisoned by the drug alprazolam, which someone placed in liquid form into the humidification reservoir in his CPAP machine. We have the residue from that drug in a partially melted reservoir from the fire."

"That doesn't prove Dr. Meach did it."

"There's also evidence of Dr. Dale Stephens being involved in this from those documents. He has also been implicated in the Youngswood museum fire," he said.

"My client has no comment on Dr. Stephens."

"Okay, then, why did he purchase liquid alprazolam from a veterinary supply house in Charlotte?" he asked.

"I used it for my rodent experiments. I study the effect of insulin on animals and the neurologic response to hypoglycemia. It's very stressful on the mice and rats, and this helps them."

"Oh, I'm so glad you're concerned about poor rodents and making their last moments more comfortable, Meach. You're a wonderful humanitarian."

"Shut up, Rudbeck." Pulaski put his hand on Meach's shoulder to try to calm him down before he said something incriminating.

"The minimum amount you could've ordered from there is a 10 mL ampule or a third of an ounce. You ordered ten thousand times that amount. I checked with the veterinary school—the amount of that preparation you'd need for a rat would be 0.1 mL, less for a mouse. So, either you way over-ordered, or you had some other intention for that drug. If you were going to run out and you needed more, you could've ordered it."

"Just because he ordered more than was needed doesn't prove anything," Pulaski said.

"It all adds up, Meach." He pulled out several high-resolution photographs of Meach with Cheryl Robertson at Burk's Steak House and going to the Deacon Motel. "What about this, Jack? Looks like you didn't waste any time after Johnny was gone. The restaurant was nice, but the motel seemed a bit substandard."

Pulaski laughed. "Just because Dr. Meach and Dr. Robertson's widow went out to dinner and a mediocre motel afterward doesn't mean Dr. Meach killed him."

"Pretty tacky, though."

"Being tacky isn't illegal."

"And where did you even get the reservoir, Meach? You don't have sleep apnea."

"That's not any kind of illegal item."

"You collect them or something, Meach?"

"Maybe. There are weirder things to collect."

"No, I have proof that a hospital's respiratory therapy department clerk gave you one. I can't see any legitimate reason for you to have that."

"None of this proves my client had anything to do with burning down the Biggerstaff building. Your theory is that someone used potato chips as an accelerant, similar to your proposed method of burning the Youngswood Arts Museum. Yet, the surveillance video shows a female figure, about five-six, spreading the chips around Biggerstaff on several floors. That person cannot be Dr. Meach, and the size matches the person you've accused of burning the museum—Sybil Tegler."

"We never said Meach did it alone, but he had access to the building and motive to destroy it and kill Robertson. We have yet to determine who this individual is, but we don't believe it to be Tegler."

AAAAA

Dubois County Courthouse
Superior Court #1
State of Ohio vs. John Charles Meach
Bail Hearing
1102 hours

He and Lt. Eppard were at Meach's bail hearing the next morning. Thanks to his detective work, much evidence to implicate Meach in the postulated arson of the Biggerstaff building had been discovered, and a quickly convened grand jury indicted him unanimously.

"The state requests remand, Your Honor," Dubois County Prosecutor Harold G. Utterman stated. "He is accused of heinous crimes that have devastated this community, and we're concerned he will flee the country."

"That's unreasonable, Your Honor," Meach's attorney Andrew Pulaski stated. "The evidence against my client is circumstantial. We believe he has ties to the local community and is not a flight risk. We request release on recognizance given that this is his first offense."

Utterman shook his head furiously. "The state disagrees. There is significant evidence Dr. Meach accepted payments from various sources to falsify his research and engineered the poisoning of Dr. John Robertson, who died in the fire. These payments, which in aggregate were over twenty million dollars, were deposited in offshore accounts which Dr. Meach would have access to. He therefore had the motive to burn his lab down and has the means to disappear for a very long time."

"The authenticity of this evidence has not been confirmed, Your Honor."

"I am happy to share those documents at this time, Your Honor."

"Bail is granted in the amount of $500,000. The defendant will also surrender his passport."

So Meach would get out with $50,000 paid to the bail bonds agent. He could surely afford that and swing a private flight out of the country to bypass the airport and customs to get to a country that would not extradite him eventually. Given Meach's likely dismal future, he just worried about what such a conniving and desperate person might do.

AAAAA

Jake Fisher's Office
IT Department
Staffordsville University Hospital

"Some lady similar in build to Tegler did it, Malgy," Jake said proudly as they sat in Jake's office, drinking diet root beer and eating pepperoni pizza. "The Biggerstaff videocam footage is stored off-site at another building, and the connection wasn't lost until the cables were burnt. It's good quality."

"Great. What does it show?"

Jake pulled it up on his dual monitors. "Same as the museum footage, but longer and in higher quality. I'll show you the highlights."

"Tegler says she didn't do it. Somehow, I believe her."

Jake paused for a minute. "The figure is obviously female and wearing a dark outfit like before, but that still doesn't prove it's Tegler."

"The thing is, the security cameras in the Biggerstaff building would've been easy to cover up, but this person didn't. Why forget such a basic detail? It's almost as if she wanted to be seen so we would think she was Tegler."

"That makes sense, Malgy. That person wouldn't know if we had video from the Youngswood museum or not, but it would make sense she'd want to emulate Tegler, assuming it really *is* someone else."

"I doubt my 'gait analysis' trick will work again. There isn't enough video from Youngswood to do a good comparison with this."

"I assume you think it's someone else?" Jake asked.

"It has to be. There have to be some other accomplices involved here. They clearly burned up Biggerstaff, unsure if we had the original footage."

"But no way for Tegler to prove it wasn't her. Too bad your 'gait analysis' technique isn't real."

"But it is, Jake. I just bluffed at the police interrogation to get her to confess; we don't have enough footage from Youngswood—only fourteen seconds. However, we have much better footage from this encounter, and we can compare it to existing footage of Tegler from the bodycam video and other videos I shot when she was in the hospital for her carbohydrate challenge. And I have one other person I want to compare it to."

"Who, Malgy?"

"Cheryl Robertson. Our intel indicates she is about the same height and age as Tegler, although Tegler may be twenty pounds heavier. She could've been the one who helped Meach set fire to Biggerstaff."

"Would Meach have known enough about gait analysis to pick someone approximately the same height and age as Tegler?"

"Maybe. Or that could be just a coincidence, Jake. Need to get more information to be sure. We have the video of them coming and going from the steak house and motel, and it should be easy enough to get more."

AAAAA

Forensic gait analysis (FGA) was a method used to identify individuals based on their unique walking patterns, especially in criminal investigations where other biometric identifiers are unavailable. AI algorithms could help match suspects to crime scene footage, even when faces are concealed, by analyzing video footage and comparing gait features with reference data.

FGA studied an individual's walking style, including characteristics like stride length, speed, and swing phase. AI algorithms then analyzed video footage to extract these gait features and compare them to databases of known gait patterns. This process could help identify suspects in crime scenes, even when facial recognition or other biometrics were unavailable.

Deep learning algorithms could be used to analyze large datasets of gait patterns, making identification more accurate, even with poor video quality. Artificial intelligence could automatically extract relevant gait features from video footage, like stride length, swing phase, and other movement patterns. Artificial intelligence algorithms could then compare extracted gait features with databases of known gait patterns to identify potential suspects.

AI could facilitate real-time gait analysis for various applications, including wearable devices, rehabilitation monitoring, and fall detection. Gait patterns were more difficult to disguise or manipulate than other biometrics like fingerprints or facial features. It could also be performed at a distance, using surveillance footage, without needing close proximity or cooperation from the suspects. Gait patterns were relatively unique to each individual and could be used to identify people even in crowded environments.

Chapter Twenty-One

Dubois County Medical Examiner's Office
Staffordsville University Hospital
0840 hours

"Malgy, my forensic gait analysis expert in Washington verifies with 97% certainty that the person in the Biggerstaff video is Cheryl Robertson and not Sybil Tegler, based on the video files you sent. The signature matches Robertson's with high specificity," Charlie Boisseau said as they sat at her office conference table with Lt. Eppard. "There are some slight differences in gait between Asian and Caucasian populations, presumed to be genetically determined."

"But Sybil's only half-Chinese," he said.

"What are these differences, Dr. Boisseau?" Eppard asked.

"Significantly larger heelstrike transients, stride length, maximum loading rate, and significantly faster walking speed are seen in the Caucasian populations."

"Whoa! You're sounding like Rudbeck. What the hell does

that gobbledygook mean?" Eppard asked.

"It is quite technical, Lieutenant, but Robertson's gait matches the Caucasian standards, while Dr. Tegler's is more in line with the Asian group. Since they are approximately the same height and weight, we don't need to correct for that variable."

He took a sip of black coffee. "So, she helped Meach set fire to the building. That makes her the culprit for both that and felony murder."

"What's the motive for her to do that? I know she was estranged from her husband, but come on," Eppard said. "Seems a bit extreme."

"Money, Brian. You saw the deposits to the Grand Caymans yourself. And, guess whose cousin works at Karmahut Pharmaceuticals as a drug rep?"

"Tegler?"

"Yes. Chloe Thompson works there. She might have been able to get hydroglippane sodium for Sybil."

"So many people involved," Charlie said, taking a sip of Earl Grey tea.

"Yeah, we all know everyone talked about burning down the building for years. Hell, I probably said something like that myself."

"Did you secretly do it, Rudbeck?" Eppard said, laughing. "Do we need to bring you in for questioning?"

"The common denominator in both is Dale Stephens. He's the one who falsified the biopsies and implanted the ethanol reservoir in her gastric antrum, and we have evidence he also was involved in Biggerstaff. Meach knew about both but didn't directly aid the Youngswood arson."

"Where the hell did he get such a device?"

"He has a background in medical devices and biomedical engineering. It likely isn't that complex of a device to create; it's just a small neoprene bladder with some simple electronics and hydraulics to push the ethanol out when it receives a radio signal."

"I do remember that I asked her who she wanted as a gastroenterologist, and she was pretty quick to mention his name. But why? The dude makes about nine hundred grand a year, so why the hell would he do this?"

"And his wife spends most of it. Look at the car she drives and her jewelry."

"I know, but . . . even I'm skeptical that Tegler could coordinate this all herself. She never seemed to be that organized."

"Money can be a great motivator. '*Wealth and rank are what men desire, but unless they be obtained in the right way they may not be possessed.*'"

"Nice to know. We found the actual samples; they were typical intestinal flora. The yeast was planted in the samples from another patient sent to the path lab. Since those were from a patient with normal ALDH activity, those enzyme studies were normal."

"Tegler. Meach wanted to frame her to make it look like she did it, knowing that we probably wouldn't go to the expense of DNA testing."

"I believe you, but why would he do that?" Charlie asked.

"Because all his research was leading nowhere and was likely falsified, which would be discovered in time. This was the best way to get rid of the evidence. He took all that grant money, and would have to pay it back and be disgraced for all time. But now he can say it was all destroyed with the associated sympathy, and then he could move on to something else. He had found out about Tegler's plan from Stephens and used this as an opportunity to frame her for a second, similar crime."

"Stephens—what a piece of work. Her BAC was 0.42 percent, at which point most people would be dead. She was taking the ethanol receptor blocker. Hydroglippane would have blocked the effects of the drug, but would not lower the BAC."

"Well, time to go back and put it in the file on Meach. I don't think he's made bail yet."

AAAAA

Eppard called him two hours later while he was sitting in his office. "Brian? What's up?"

"We put a tail on Meach after his bondsman put up the bail, as we were worried he might do something stupid after he got out. He lost Detective Baker already. We don't know where he is, and he's not at his house or the lab. His secretary says he hasn't been there for days."

"What about Tegler?" he asked.

"No one has seen her for days, either. She was supposed to be back from her 'treatment,' although we know it was all faked."

"Do you think they're in on it together?"

"I doubt it, but there may be some connection. I don't know what, though. I believe Meach to be truly evil, while Sybil is just an unfortunate individual consumed by gambling and other debts who tried to get a payoff. What Sybil did was bad, but the implications of what Meach did are far-reaching and could damage millions of people."

"How's that, Rudbeck?"

"Falsification of research reports could lead to some hazardous drugs being introduced into human studies. Changing the results could result in drugs being marketed that would otherwise have been quashed."

"What about the other way around? Could there be good drugs that these false reports make look bad, so that they never get to the market?"

"Absolutely, Brian. For example, one company knows that a competitor is bringing a new, novel drug to market that is superior to anything they have. Producing false reports about cancer in mice or something, then gets it killed off before it even gets to human trials."

"That's horrible, Rudbeck. I can't believe doctors and researchers would do that."

"Welcome to the corporate medical world, Eppard. I've seen just about everything, but this one takes the cake."

Chapter Twenty-Two

An hour later, he received an incoming video call from an unknown source on his tablet while sitting in his office. He didn't recognize the number.

"I know you've been looking for me, Rudbeck."

"Give it up, Meach, and turn yourself in. We have evidence of you possessing liquid alprazolam and a water reservoir for Robertson's CPAP machine."

"Great, I know all that, idiot, but you won't be able to do anything about it."

"I can do a lot about it. You're going to prison."

"Well, maybe, maybe not. You like escape rooms and complex mysteries, Rudbeck? Try this one for size. Sybil Tegler is being held in a warehouse somewhere in town, as, like me, she is still out on bail awaiting her court date. You were right that I learned about her trick to fake auto-brewery syndrome. The reservoir is still in her stomach, partially filled with ninety-five percent ethanol, and there is a radio receiver that will trigger it in two hours unless you find her by then."

"So she gets drunk. There can't be enough alcohol in there to kill her."

"A normal person? Of course not. But, as you know, she can't metabolize alcohol, and no longer has the receptor blocker in her system, as I've had her long enough for what was in her system to have metabolized, so she will die within minutes when that radio goes off. And it won't be a peaceful death. Those byproducts that build up will be quite painful. You want that on your conscience?"

"ALDH deficiency? She doesn't have that, per her medical records."

"You know as well as I those are false, so don't insult my intelligence."

Dammit. "I can't believe you could be so depraved as to do that, and for what? What can you possibly gain from doing this to Sybil?"

"OMG, how corny, but the type of reply I would expect from the dumb-ass do-gooder Amalgam-Man. Maybe I like to see pain and suffering. And, if the alcohol doesn't kill her, two hundred thousand volts will go through her body in what is essentially an electric chair."

"What the hell do you want, Meach?"

"I've always hated you, Rudbeck, which is why I want you to suffer the guilt when she dies."

"What's your damn problem, Meach? Why do you hate me, anyway?"

"You're fucking blue-collar white trash and you don't deserve to be in academia like me. You've lucked into everything, and here you are staying at the White House."

"Maybe you don't know what it means to face adversity and come from humble beginnings. You're going to find out about adversity soon when I kick your scummy ass. There won't be enough of you left to scrape off the sidewalk."

"But what do I want? Hell, Tegler isn't worth two cents, so I won't get anything from her. I only want the satisfaction of getting rid of you, as you're a piece of shit. You always hold yourself up as this altruistic hero, so let's see what you're really made of. Most people would just walk away from this, but I know you'll just plunge headfirst into danger to save a loser."

"You're the loser, Meach. No way you come out of this in one piece. And why do this? If they pay at all, it'll take months to get the insurance money, given significant evidence of criminal wrongdoing, and you won't get any of that. Tegler's the one who orchestrated the Youngswood fire."

"I have other things I'm going to do if you don't meet my demands."

"You're nuts."

"Am I? There's an explosive set to go off somewhere in town that no one but me knows about, that will kill thousands of people downtown. Do you really want to risk that?"

"How do I know you and Tegler aren't in cahoots and you're just making this up?"

"Fair enough question, asshole." He put on a video of Tegler, who was shackled into a heavy steel chair, with tape over her mouth, wearing a purple wig. "I thought I would make her look like your fictional girlfriend. Maybe this is fake, maybe not. Are you going to roll the dice on this, Rudbeck?"

"I still don't know that it's real. She could've faked her kidnapping."

"Are you willing to risk that?"

"Maybe. Assuming you're being truthful, you are using a fellow arsonist as your bargaining chip? That's kind of lame, even for you. Do you really think the authorities are going to let you out of the country using a confessed fellow arsonist as a hostage?" Of course, he cared if Sybil died, even though she committed a serious crime; his ethics would never allow him to let another person suffer, but he didn't have to let Meach know that.

"I do. You also can't notify the police. I will detect whether you do that from my monitoring. If you do, Tegler will die instantly. You and your great family can solve the mystery since you're all so wonderful and talented."

He didn't believe that Meach could detect that, but he didn't want to take chances. "You said an escape room. You mean there will be clues, with some chance for success?"

"There will be clues, but you'll never figure them out, and I hope you die in the process. Here is your first one. 'What room can no one enter?' Goodbye for now, Rudbeck. I'll contact you if you figure out the first clue. Remember what I said about no police."

"That's easy," Jayna said. "A mushroom."

"Okay, yeah, but how does that help us?"

Evie thought for a couple of minutes. "There's a Portobella

Street near the warehouse district on the southwest side of town. That would be an ideal place."

He pulled up a Staffordsville map on his phone. "Portobella Street is only seven blocks long, but that doesn't help us very much, given our limited time. We need the Amalgam-Man exoskeleton. It has heat-sensing probes that can detect a person and other features we might need. I just wish I had a helicopter to fly in on like last time."

"Sorry. Not in the budget," Jayna said.

The lightweight carbon fiber lithium battery-powered exoskeleton would protect him from modest damage, and it had its own respirator. The original armor came from a Ukrainian robotics engineer, Ivan Vladimirov, who swapped the prototype at a Dayton electronics meet for a huge quantity of vintage East German Zeiss optics four years ago. Why such an engineer was in Dayton, Ohio, was unknown, and why he would give an advanced robotics suit away for $25,000 worth of Zeiss Jena optics seemed odd.

Ivan's father, Viktor Vladimirov, was rumored to be a former Soviet bionics and robotics expert with a shadowy past, and he couldn't find out much about either Viktor or Ivan. He could call his friend, Vice President Robby Benton, but he suspected he was the one probably *behind* eliminating any public information on Viktor Vladimirov, and one didn't dig into such details and remain healthy. He didn't ask where the suit originated, but the Russian military probably abandoned it, and creating another one might be challenging. He and Evie knew enough about electronics to do all the necessary medical adaptations and minor repairs.

He wanted to use the sophisticated thermal camera inside; its high-efficiency probe of his and Evie's design could easily distinguish a human being from inanimate matter. It was a prototype he had tried to market to the fire department, but it was too impractical and expensive to mass produce, and it would need to be reverse-engineered. However, it could be thrown off if the ambient temperature were the same as body temperature.

After stopping by the house to get the suit (which he kept charged in case of emergencies, of course, in a special room), he put it on and they headed to the southwest end of town, towards Portobella Street. Thankfully, there was sufficient room in the

Expedition to accommodate the large man plus his suit. He was sure to get looks from other motorists on the way.

Meach appeared on the tablet again several minutes later.

"Here's your second clue, Rudbeck. What kind of pins are used in soup?"

Evie thought for several seconds. "Terrapins, of course, which can be used to make turtle soup. That's pretty dumb."

"Turtle? There's Chelonian Distributors right at the end of the street in about five blocks. That must be it."

"These corny riddles are almost too easy, Dan," Jayna said. "Be careful. You're the one who did him harm, so this is likely a trap. He doesn't care about Tegler."

"I will be, and, believe me, I will do him even more harm soon with my fists. The suit isn't bulletproof but insulated against gases and the like."

"So, we can't use the police or Sandy. That leaves me, Jake, Jayna, and Evie. Jake is the cyber expert, Jayna is for weapons, Evie is science and tech."

"What is your contribution, Dad?" Evie asked.

"My expert leadership, resource coordination, and advanced technology, of course. Jake, where are we as far as figuring out where Meach was when he called?"

Jake shook his head. "Impossible to tell where he was. He was routing his call through several other nodes around the world. He could be a mile from us, or on the other side of the country. He seems to have some idea what he's doing."

"Yeah, well, so do we. An 800 MHz radio transmitter triggers the gastric reservoir, I had learned. Evie, can we jam it somehow?"

His daughter shook her head. "Not universally, no. You would need enormous power even to cover a city block, let alone an entire small city like Staffordsville. We would have to confine it to the room she is in, at best."

"My suit can generate an electromagnetic pulse with a radius of several feet, but I can only sustain it for a few minutes."

"We also don't want to do something to trigger it accidentally."

"So, where the hell do we start looking?" he asked as they pulled up to the Chelonian Distributors warehouse, which distributed small electronics goods. They got out of the red Expedition; Jayna gave them each a Kevlar vest from a bag in the back of his vehicle, and she donned a size small for herself. They walked to the front of the building from the gravel parking lot.

"Bulletproof vests?" Evie said. "Where did you get these?"

"I am a resourceful person. No law against owning body armor, unless you are a convicted felon or using it to commit a crime."

"Thanks for the mini-law lesson."

"Hey," Jayna said. "I bought them from Dallas Personal Defense Supply, so I'm the one who's resourceful. Never know when you will need protection."

"Your thermal camera," Evie said. "Try that."

"I can try, but I don't want to shoot the probe in as it might trigger something, and there's no entry anyway." He looked towards the building from the outside. "Too much interference. Nothing. I have to get inside."

A large older model brass padlock locked a single steel door at the entrance. There were some garage-style doors on a loading dock next to it, but they were also made of steel, which didn't seem like a way in.

"I don't think we can break this down, and there's no other way in. No windows."

"Did we bring bolt cutters?" Jayna asked.

"The suit has some small ones, but it likely won't break something that large. It's designed for paramedics and other heavy equipment that would be on the scene. Sorry, didn't have a lot of time to prepare for this. I'm not the best locksmith, but I must work on that skill."

"Can't Jayna just shoot it off like in the movies?" Jake asked.

Jayna shook her head. "No, that doesn't work with a handgun on a heavy brass lock. It would just ricochet off and possibly kill one of us. You'd need a big shotgun or a rocket launcher for that. Didn't happen to bring either of those today on such short notice."

He tried to pull the lock open, but the suit wasn't built for strength; he could possibly exert about twice his normal strength. "Need to work on the servomotor power."

"Remember the escape room: brain supersedes brawn. I have an idea." Jayna found an old energy drink aluminum can on the gravel by the door and took out a set of metal shears from her small backpack.

"What are you doing, Jayna?" he asked. "Why are you cutting

up that old can? We don't have time for that foolishness."

"Same principle as the escape room with the shim."

"I'm not following. That lock isn't a handcuff."

Jayna nodded. "In a way, it is. Most common locks work in a similar fashion. You'll see."

"Okay, but don't cut yourself, and hurry up."

"I won't and I am." She put on some work gloves from her backpack and cut it into a long strip with a smaller strip protruding down. "Most common padlocks use a spring lock to engage the shackle. It's possible to use a thin piece of aluminum or other metal to jam and unlock it."

"Are you sure you can do that?" Evie asked.

She nodded. "With older locks like this one, maybe."

"You know whether or not a lock is old or new?" he asked.

"Yes. My dad and uncle always collected old locks, and we went to a big show in Columbus every year to look at them. This model is about twenty to thirty years old."

"I didn't know people collected them," Evie said. "I guess they could be interesting."

"I've done this before as a kid and fooling around with my boys, as I saw it done for demonstrations at the shows." She put the small piece of metal into the extremely thin space between the lock body and shackle, and twisted it for about thirty seconds, and it popped open.

"You are truly amazing, just like at the escape room." Wearing his high-tech exoskeleton, he opened the door leading to a large room in the three-story building. He scanned the building and did see a small mass of temperature close to 100 degrees Fahrenheit on the second floor, which had to represent a human being—unless it was a decoy. Meach was crafty, for sure, and it wouldn't be hard to create a manikin of the same temperature.

"She's on the second floor. I'm going up alone."

"No, you're not, Dad. We're doing this together."

"There could be poison gas or something, and I'm the only one who has protection."

"No, you're not." Jayna pulled two small breathing apparatuses from the bag she had brought. "Sorry, there isn't one for Jake. Didn't know he'd be here."

Jake smiled and nodded. "That's okay, I'll stay out here and watch for intruders. I did bring an aluminum baseball bat, which

I'll get out of the car. No one will get past me."

"Well, let's go then. I'm the lead." They ran up the stairs to the second floor and came to a wooden door. He broke into the room and saw Sybil locked in the chair, as seen on his thermal camera. He thought about firing a laser into the room camera, but thought better of it, realizing it might trigger an event and wouldn't help her or accomplish anything positive. He pulled the duct tape off her mouth.

"Thank God. Rudbeck, are you in that thing? Get me the hell out of here."

"In a minute, Sybil. First things first." There was no timer, so he didn't know how long they had left. It probably wasn't much.

The first thing he did was remove from his gauntlet a hypodermic syringe filled with a parenteral form of hydroglippane, which would hopefully negate the effects of the alcohol in her gastric reservoir, in case Evie's radio jamming didn't work. She turned on the UHF transmitter jammer, which should prevent the reservoir from being activated.

"What did you just inject into me?"

"Intramuscular hydroglippane, which should take effect immediately. It will render any alcohol in your system harmless in case your ethanol reservoir is triggered."

He pulled against the locks holding her hands to the steel chair with his Amalgam-Man armor, which imparted strength about twice normal. About the electrocution threat—he looked around for some type of electrical conduit he could disrupt and didn't see anything, meaning that the wires were under the chair. Either that or it was an empty threat. Knowing Meach, it was likely real.

"Damn, these things are strong, and I've never seen any locks like these." He had hoped that she had been restrained with something simple and familiar like zip ties, rope, or handcuffs, which he could remove easily, but these metal clamps didn't even have a keyhole, so how did they come off? Each of the two clamps had a green metal button rigidly fixed in place to a quarter-inch steel shaft. Each button had a stylized "BH" logo in yellow letters. "Jayna, you used to go to lock shows. What are these?"

Jayna shook her head. "Beats me, never saw anything like that, Dan."

"Get me the fuck out of here, Malgy!" Sybil yelled.

He thought back to his escape room adventure for a minute and remembered Evie's magnetic lock, something he had seen a few months ago in a German medical catalog. Then he pulled it up on his helmet's computer readout, as his exoskeleton had 5G cellular speeds. "The 'BH' stands for 'Baumhauer.' It's a German manufacturer of medical restraints for hospital patients."

"Well, there has to be some way to get them off if they're used for patients," Evie said.

He found more info from his files via his readout; it was a good thing he always saved his downloads. "The locking pins are quarter-inch hardened steel, and it would take some specialized cutting tools we don't have right now to get them off without hurting you. It would take the fire department." He thought for a minute. "But you know the Germans—they tend to engineer everything highly. As I see from a technical brochure, these locks are magnetic and require a special magnetic key to release."

"Then do it, dammit!" Sybil yelled. "That suit must have a fucking magnet in it somewhere!"

"It's not as simple as just putting a rare-earth magnet or strong magnetic field over it. The online manual says six magnets in the key have to be aligned at exactly the right polarity to work, but the exact details aren't there. It seems a bit overkill to me for a patient restraint. Most patients don't know enough about—"

"Rudbeck, we don't need a lesson on magnetism right now!" Sybil yelled as she tried to remove herself from the chair.

"Pacemakers," Jayna said.

"What about them?" he replied.

"Aren't they programmed magnetically?"

He thought for a few seconds. "Yeah, good call; that may be the only solution. The AM-1 suit is capable of over two dozen emergency medicine protocols, and one of them is programming pacemakers, which use similar magnetic polarities. This is because there could be some emergency in the field where paramedics would need to reprogram under the direction of a physician. The pacemakers use complex set patterns to prevent accidental reprogramming by casual magnetic interference."

"Well, magnets are simple devices with either a north or south pole," Evie said. "By cycling through dozens of combinations quickly, we should arrive at the right one to open these crazy locks."

"Assuming we have enough time. Evie, six magnets with two polarities—how many combinations?"

The tall redhead thought for a few seconds. "6! or 720."

"Shit, that's a lot. Here goes." He programmed the cybernetic armor's multipurpose probe for pacemaker programming, cycling through the different polarities quickly, about six per minute, as he held the device over the green lock.

When he reached number 77, the lock became loose and pulled away after a one-quarter twist.

"Now we need to do the other one."

"Assuming it has the same key code."

"I don't know. We'll see. He applied the transducer with the same polarity combination, and it pulled off immediately. He then opened the metal straps holding her body to the chair and threw her out of the way onto the floor.

The Amalgam-Man suit had saved Jayna three years ago with his novel carbon monoxide antidote. Its unique technology had saved another person.

Just as Sybil had been freed, he felt the electricity go through his suit, since he was still touching the chair with his right hand. The suit was many things, but entirely invulnerable to electricity it wasn't. It was designed for paramedics, so it was mainly designed to prevent smoke inhalation and provide timely antidotes, an automated external defibrillator (AED), medical device diagnostics, and other medications to patients out in the field. Greater resistance to electrical shock would be an AM-2 armor feature.

He then lost consciousness as the world became enveloped in darkness.

Chapter Twenty-Three

Dr. Barclay Dixon woke up sleepily, seeing an empty side of the bed to his left that had been slept in. The bedsheets and drapes were light lavender, and the walls a bright purple. Only one person had a color scheme like that. But would this person be friend or foe today? Or a bit of both, as usual?

The familiar purple-haired woman came in from the adjoining bathroom and smiled at him. She was wearing a set of shiny magenta pajamas and took a sip of what smelled like hot chocolate.

"Ms. Volkova. Why am I here? What have you done to me and how did I get here? Drugged me in some fashion? I knew you were not to be trusted."

"Why, Dixon. Do you not remember? We are married now, so it's 'Mrs. Dixon,' not 'Ms. Volkova.' We do things that married people do. Do you remember some of those?" She kissed his heavily-muscled, hairy chest. "Things like pleasing you, as my bed has many accessories made of rich Corinthian leather you will enjoy. And you can always trust me."

"What? The worldly Amalgam-Man, married? This could

never be. You must have tricked me in some fashion to get my money."

"Money is not important to me, my love. You are."

Money not important to the incredibly vain and materialistic Alexandra Nina Volkova? This could never be.

"You surely have something bad planned for me, knowing you."

"If you insist, I will surely do something to you, Dr. Dixon, but only something you will like."

"I can only imagine the things you have in mind."

"Perhaps, my husband. But first, a spiritual passage." She pulled out a small Bible from the bedside stand. He thought all Russians were atheists! "*She does him good, and not harm, all the days of her life.* Proverbs 31:12."

He found it hard to believe that Ms. Volkova—now Mrs. Dixon, apparently—only wanted to do him good, but she might have even been rehabilitated. He said earlier that she had to be under house arrest under his supervision, although it looked like she was the one in charge here. Maybe such an arrangement would be enjoyable.

He then saw a cloud of smoke with a faint sulfur odor. A massive, middle-aged Chinese man emerged and stared at him intensely, his mood inscrutable.

"*Confucius?* What are you doing here, sir?" he asked. "This doesn't look like the kind of establishment you would frequent."

The man pointed at him angrily. "Silence, Barclay Dixon. Speak not until spoken to. Where I go is not of your concern."

"Sorry, I had forgotten how big you are."

"That's right, you'd better know I can whip your sorry tail, insolent clod. I have returned to discuss your progress since our last meeting. Do you remember that?"

"That was a couple of years ago. I was dying of terminal cancer from smoking and various sexually transmitted diseases from having slept with 25,000 women, and I had lost all my money due to poor investments, and had liver failure from too much booze. I was on Skid Row."

"That is correct, dull dolt. You were paying the price for your immoral, selfish lifestyle, and those ailments were only a dream. However, it seems you have taken some of my prior comments to heart, changed yourself, and evolved into something better."

"I have, wise Confucius?"

The massive, wizened man nodded. "You have given up your unhealthy addictions and seem to be faithful to the violet-haired female in the room, although some of the peculiar activities in which you and the lavender lady engage are perplexing to even Confucius, but I do not keep up with the latest romantic trends. Nevertheless, it is a start, but you still have far to go on your journey, Dixon. There may be hope for you yet. Goodbye until our next meeting." The large Chinese man disappeared in another cloud of smoke as quickly as he came.

AAAAA

He then looked up to see the inside of a familiar Staffordsville University Hospital room and Jayna, Evie, and Charlie sitting by his bed; the shade was down, so it was impossible to determine if it was dark outside or not. He had no clue how much time had passed since he became unconscious after being nearly electrocuted at the Chelonian Distributors warehouse.

"Ms. Volkova. You're still here."

"Yes, I'm still here, Dan." She grabbed his hand. "I've been here for a while."

"Have you been dreaming again, like last time?" Charlie asked.

"I guess so, but what . . . the hell happened? Where am I?"

"The hospital, Dan," his wife said. "You were electrocuted by Meach's death trap, which would've killed Tegler had you not intervened. Your suit protected you from most of it, but not all. If not for the suit, you'd be dead."

"Confucius was there again. He said there was hope for Barclay after all, that he had evolved but still had far to go."

"That's great, Dad. It's always beneficial to have a stamp of approval from Confucius."

"But Ms. Alexandra Nina Volkova and Dixon were married. The scheming Ms. Volkova had kidnapped me and was holding me prisoner in her soft lavender bed with its many accessories made of rich Corinthian leather, and she was about to—"

"Yikes!" Evie waved her hands rapidly. "I told you I don't want to know your business with Ms. Volkova, Dad, even in a hallucination. What I saw at the house was enough."

"No, let me finish. She was quoting the Bible—Proverbs. Distinctly different than the Ms. Volkova of The Sulphur Shadow."

"But not different than the real one," Jayna said, smiling. "Maybe you can write a sequel where she gets redemption for her misdeeds. Everyone deserves a second chance. Remember, you got one." She gave him a hug.

"At least that's better than what happened in your last hallucination with him, when he had gone bankrupt and had end-stage cancer from smoking, HIV, and liver failure, and had slept with 25,000 women," Charlie said.

"Well, it stopped at 25,001. And he gave up drinking and smoking. It does seem that being married to Volkova would be a pleasure."

"Luckily, you are." Jayna kissed him on the forehead.

"The AM-1 armor? Is it intact?"

Evie nodded. "It appears to be, Dad. It is a pretty tough piece of hardware. It rebooted after you were shocked, but then came back online."

"That's good. It might be hard to get another one." He took a sip of bottled water. "What about Sybil? Is she okay?"

Jayna nodded. "Yeah. She's fine. She's here for observation, and another gastroenterologist needs to remove the reservoir in her stomach, as the medical board has suspended Stephens. You saved her, Dan. Just like you saved me two years ago."

"How long have I been here?"

"About five hours. You've been in and out, until you finally woke up."

"Geez. I hope I don't have any brain damage."

The three women looked at each other and broke out laughing. "Dad, how could we tell, given your baseline abnormal behavior?" Evie said.

"I'm serious, Evie, the brain is no laughing matter."

"I would say everything is back to normal," Jayna said.

AAAAA

Lt. Brian Eppard walked into his room an hour later after the women had left to get something to eat for a late dinner.

"Shit, Rudbeck, are you okay?" Eppard said as he sat in the visitor's chair across from the bed. "You've been out of it for several hours."

"That's a loaded question. I probably lost a few more neurons during this caper. Luckily, I have many to spare." He took a bite of his substandard hamburger. "I could use one from Working Guy's Buddy right about now. I want to go back to my dream."

Eppard nodded as he took a sip of coffee he had brought. "Yeah, that burger looks pretty bland. I do remember you saying something about Dixon having more folds in his brain than normal, which imparted vastly superior intelligence, hence your great cognitive abilities, which helped in this case, and gave you some spare neurons."

"Thanks. My brain appears to still be recovering."

"But I gotta tell you—this was the weirdest thing I've ever seen. The plot was so convoluted that no one besides you could see it. We couldn't have solved this without you."

"I'm glad I could help, Brian." He took a sip of apple juice. "What happened to Meach? Did you arrest him?"

"He's dead, Rudbeck. I couldn't tell you because you were still unconscious. We went to apprehend him at his home after your family contacted us about the Tegler kidnapping and what happened to you. Fisher could determine his location, and he was always in town. He'd shot himself in the head shortly before we got there, which is when he apparently realized you'd saved Tegler but might've died yourself."

"No shit. Meach probably hoped I was dead."

"Very likely, but we'll never know. Meach was involved in a lot more than just burning down Biggerstaff, as you know. You and Fisher were responsible for uncovering that he was taking money on the side for falsifying results of clinical trials for drug companies from that data drive we dug up in Fairfield County."

"Yeah, I suspected as much all along. Meach also said he had an explosive set to go off somewhere in town—was there any evidence to support that?"

Eppard shook his head. "No, that must've been a bluff. I don't think he was an expert in explosive devices, although using Tegler as a hostage didn't show the greatest brainpower."

"Maybe not money-wise, as no one would give money for her, sorry to say. I think he was out to get me most of all. He seemed to blame me for most of his woes, and he became desperate after his master plan went south. I'm sure he had a few psychiatric diagnoses we weren't aware of, but we'll never know now. We'll have to convene the search committee for a new biochemistry department head."

"Aww, he's just jealous, that's all. Hey, we're rounding up everyone else—the corrupt GI doctor, Fowler, Tegler's cousin at the drug company who had supplied her the drug, the tire guy, the tire shop in Bowling Green, and a few others."

"Cheryl Robertson?"

Eppard nodded. "We have her in custody. She denies spreading the potato chips around Biggerstaff and lighting them, but we have enough evidence to offer her a plea bargain in exchange for her testimony against the others. We think she knows a lot."

"Two greedy people—Tegler and Meach—had planned the same crime involving different buildings, with Meach trying to blame Sybil for both after he found out about her plan."

"Yeah, it's pretty bizarre. If Sybil hadn't planned the museum fire in the first place, this wouldn't have happened."

He spied the clean, new bedside urinal hanging from the rail. "Hey, we've been working too much, and it's time for some fun for a change, so watch this, Brian." He picked up the plastic urine receptacle. "Showtime."

"What are you up to, man? No good, I can see."

"Just wait." He proceeded to pour the remainder of the apple juice (which resembled urine) from the bottle on his lunch tray into the small plastic urinal. He then crumbled up a biscuit and put the pieces into the container, which formed a cloudy yellow suspension with floating white particles.

"Dang, Rudbeck, what in the hell did you do that for? That's gross."

"Just check this out. One of my favorite tricks to pull on the youngsters." The young student nurse came in several minutes later and picked up the small plastic urinal he had put back on the bed rail, which was now filled with apple juice and bread crumbs.

She looked at it and shrieked. "Oh, no, Dr. Rudbeck, that urine looks terrible! I'm calling Dr. Foley right away."

He took it from her and looked at the cloudy suspension. "So it does. What do you recommend?"

"We probably need a urology or nephrology consult."

"Nah." He opened the lid and chugged the contents. "I just

need to run it through again, that's all." He smacked his lips. "Rather tasty, at that."

"*Yiiiiieee!*" The twenty-year-old student turned white as she yelled and ran out of the room. "That weird doctor just drank his own pee! Mrs. Crenshaw, help! What do we do now? He's going to die!" he heard from the hallway.

"Damn. Are you wasted on some painkillers, Rudbeck? That was freaking nuts!"

"No, I am perfectly lucid. Fun, though, right?" He laughed.

The police lieutenant shook his head. "If that's your idea of fun, you need some therapy, man."

He nodded. "Probably true. I will tell Dee Palmer at my next appointment."

"I'm going to need some therapy after what I just saw."

The charge nurse, hard-boiled Betty Crenshaw, came in several minutes later with the nursing student. The overweight, fiftyish nurse was scowling as she stood over him.

"Aimee, this miscreant is a known obnoxious character who apparently hasn't changed since he was a resident here in the early nineties. I am so sorry you were assigned him as a patient. No nurse deserves that terrible fate, but unfortunately, we have to serve everyone. It's the law, right, Lieutenant?"

"No comment. I wouldn't blame you if you punched him out or threw him out the window, Ma'am," Eppard said. "I won't look."

"He isn't going to die, right, Mrs. Crenshaw?"

Crenshaw patted the young woman on the arm. "No, Aimee, he isn't going to die, although he may wish for that after I get through with him. Better yet, I will tell his wife, ex-wife, and daughter about what he did when they return from lunch. They will pummel him to a pulp."

"Maybe it was too over the top," he said.

Crenshaw crossed her arms. "Dr. Daniel Rudbeck, you are unbelievable, and you owe this nice young lady an apology."

"Aimee, I am truly sorry for my little joke. I thought it would be funny."

"It scared me to death, Doctor! Why would you make such a joke? It's not funny!"

"You obviously don't know him very well," Crenshaw and Eppard said in unison.

AAAAA

"Well, it's time to go, Dan," Jayna and Evie said as they packed his belongings at noon the next day. "We must supervise you so you don't walk out alone."

"I said I would behave this time."

"We need to make sure and apologize to all the nurses who had to care for you as a patient."

He nodded. "That's true; they deserve a medal for dealing with me."

Mrs. Betty Crenshaw came in with his wheelchair. "I really am sorry to see you go, Daniel. It's been an unforgettable experience, as working with you always is."

"No, you're not sorry, Betty. Do I have to be in that stupid wheelchair?"

"Daniel, don't make me get violent. If you disobey Mrs. Rudbeck, you'll get a whooping you'll never forget."

"Yes, Ma'am." They gathered his items, and Jayna wheeled him out of the medical unit to the elevator. However, they exited on the second floor rather than the lower level.

"Where are we going, lovely ladies? This isn't the way to my secret exit and parking spot. I hope you parked there rather than in the garage; that is for mere peons."

"That's where peons like me park, but we need to make a side stop, Dan," Jayna said.

"The pharmacy isn't on this floor, and I don't need any medications, anyway, and I don't want anything to eat from this place. Let's go home."

"In good time." Jayna wheeled him towards the main conference room.

"Why are we going in here? The last thing I want right now is a stinking meeting."

"Stop complaining, or I'll call Nurse Crenshaw."

They entered the main conference room as at least a hundred people yelled "surprise" in unison. A purple banner at the front of the room read, "Our Hero, Amalgam-Man."

"What's this?"

"Everyone heard about your heroism this time and wanted to throw you a going-home party, Dad."

"Why?"

"You deserve it. You risked yourself to figure out those crimes," Jayna said. "If not for you, Meach would still be at large and doing illicit research. Tegler was a lesser criminal, but needed to be brought to justice as well. You helped a lot of people, which is what you do."

"You both risked yourself too in helping me rescue Sybil."

Evie nodded. "We did, Dad, but it would've never happened without your integrity, expert knowledge, and tenacity."

University Hospital CEO William Englert went to the podium to make an announcement several minutes after they arrived.

"We are all proud of our colleague, Dr. Dan Rudbeck, and his incredibly diverse skill set that allowed him to help the police and fire department solve not one but two crimes involving the arson of the Youngswood Arts Museum and the Biggerstaff Medical Science Building." There was a round of applause. "We all owe you a debt of gratitude. There is another friend of Dr. Rudbeck's who couldn't be here in person but wanted to share her congratulations on a video her aide sent me."

He opened his mouth wide. Hell, no. It couldn't be.

Englert pulled up a video clip on the computer screen, and the blonde, fifty-three-year-old forty-seventh President of the United States came on the projection screen.

"I know you're having a celebration today for my good friend Dr. Dan Rudbeck," President Wendy Mendoza said in her deep Southern Appalachian accent from behind the Resolute Desk. "I'm sorry I couldn't be there in person, but I just wanted to congratulate you on your achievements and diligence in solving two significant crimes in your community within the last month. People of Staffordsville, you are all fortunate to have Dr. Rudbeck in your community, who uses his unique combination of talents to do good every day. Again, congratulations, Dan. The residents of your city and I owe you much gratitude."

Englert went back to the podium. "I certainly don't have anything to add to that. On behalf of all of us, Dr. Rudbeck, thanks for everything you do for us daily." The entire room stood up and cheered. "Dr. Rudbeck, would you like to make a few comments? We know you're a man of few words." The room roared in laughter.

He rose from the wheelchair and went to the podium. "I was truly surprised by this and want to thank you all. I thought my wife was taking me to a meeting. I don't have any comments prepared, naturally, but I'm just so fortunate to work at a place with so many friends and colleagues. As you may know, I had an opportunity to leave Staffordsville a couple of years ago for a job in Chicago, but turned it down, because I knew I would never have there what I have here. Again, thanks for everything, folks." He walked back to the wheelchair and sat down.

"Thanks, Dan. We have plenty of refreshments for everyone, so let's all enjoy. We'll have more comments from some of his other friends in a little bit."

"Do I have to stay in this wheelchair, Ms. Volkova?" he asked.

Jayna sighed. "I guess you can get up and get something to eat. After what you did, it's more than you deserve after terrifying that poor student nurse. Won't you ever grow up?"

"No, it helps keep me young. I'm also really hungry after three days of lousy hospital food. It can't be much better if this was from hospital catering."

"Let's go see, Dad. Maybe it is better."

He, Jayna, and Evie walked up to the food table, and his eyes opened wide at the featured selections. "I don't believe it—smash burgers and breaded tenderloins from Working Guy's Buddy! How did you manage that?"

Sandy came up behind them and patted him on the back. "They asked me what you would want for your party, and I told them there was only one choice for this man who can tolerate only the best international cuisine. I didn't know if Jayna would allow it, although they did make some veggie burgers too, and she finally acquiesced."

"Tell me which ones those are so I can avoid them, please. The carnivorous Amalgam-Man needs some real meat."

"I think he deserves a cheat day, Sandy, after all he's done," Jayna said. "You want some punch, Dan?" Jayna asked.

"Sure. As long as it's not spiked."

"Huh? What? At a hospital? Come on."

"Little inside joke. Never mind."

Chapter Twenty-Five

Beans N' More Coffee Shop
Staffordsville, Ohio
1015 hours

Several days later, he met Sybil Tegler in the small coffee house across from the hospital. He didn't seem to have any ill effects from his electric shock, but he knew that losing consciousness was not to be taken lightly. Sybil was still out on bond, awaiting her trial in four weeks, but she hoped to cut some type of deal with the prosecutor.

He took the coffee he had ordered from the barista and sat across from her in a rear, secluded booth in the back, as he didn't want people staring.

"Thanks for meeting me, Dan. Are you doing okay?"

"I'm fine, Sybil, I'm nearly recovered. How are you doing?"

She frowned and took a sip of her hot drink. "Well, not the greatest. I'm looking at second-degree aggravated arson, up to eight years in prison."

"And the business with the bus tire that could've killed two dozen people."

"That too."

"You may not get that much time, given that you helped us with some of the clues and Meach almost killed you."

"No, but my attorney is trying to cut a plea bargain for three years of prison time. I practically confessed everything I did with the arts museum, and the evidence about the Bowling Green bus isn't contestable. That's probably the best we can do."

"I guess everything costs, Sybil. I hope things work out the best they can, I really do."

She put her right hand on his left arm. "I also know I wouldn't be here if you hadn't saved me, even though you're the one who uncovered the evidence that will send me to prison. I know people make fun of your ridiculous fictional character and some of the crazy projects you have going on, but you really are a flesh-and-blood hero. You had nothing to gain by coming to rescue me, so why did you do it? Your family, too. You're all wonderful people."

"What, I was gonna let you die just because you burned down the museum and were part of an incredibly complex criminal conspiracy to defraud the Worthington T. Brick Insurance Company of twenty-five million dollars? Would I do that?" He put his hand over his heart.

She frowned. "I don't know the answer to that sarcastic remark."

"Well, that would be rather petty and not very heroic. I was just being truthful. I'm also going to have to retract my testimony in your public intoxication hearing, although the hydroglippane prevented real intoxication. On second thought, I'm just going to forget about that. Double jeopardy would likely apply there."

"And Meach clearly took advantage of your heroism."

"Maybe. It's who I am, Sybil. I can't ever change it."

"And I can't change what I did. I'll probably never work again, except at some menial job, if I can even get that."

"You still have your son and the rest of your life to live. That has to count for something."

She laughed. "Yeah, right, some life. The next few years will be at the women's prison in Marysville. Tommy won't even speak to me now, and I doubt he'll come to see me in prison."

"Give him a chance, Sybil. The human heart has a large capacity for forgiveness."

"Yeah, sure."

"I still don't know why you did it. The plot was so convoluted."

"You believed it for a while, didn't you?"

He nodded. "Yeah, I did. I probably wouldn't have even imagined you faked it and started this whole investigation if I hadn't looked at the police bodycam for the horizontal nystagmus test Wolford did in the Palatine ER. Part of my OCD. Deputy Wolford didn't have to do those tests, as the lab was going to measure your alcohol level, but, like most young officers, he did things by the book."

"I can't imagine you could've determined that from a bodycam."

"You'd be wrong. The resolution of those new Axon cameras is 1080p, but you're right that the detail wouldn't have been there if he'd done it in the dark. But he did it in the well-lit emergency room, which made the difference."

"I never thought anyone would even look at that or know what it meant if they did."

"But you could've killed someone in the museum fire, and then you would be looking at felony murder, like Meach, if he was still alive. You still are, Sybil. You need to make the best of things. I know it'll be hard."

"I did it for the money, I guess. Eighty grand a year for an assistant professor position doesn't pay the bills."

He frowned in disapproval. "We live in a small city in central Ohio, not in San Francisco, Washington, or New York City. You and Henry had a modest house on Belmont Street. What kind of bills do you have that you need that kind of money?"

"Easy for you to say. Physicians make way more than basic science professors. I wanted to provide for my son after the divorce."

He shook his head angrily. "Don't blame me for your gambling woes, as I went to bat for you a couple of years ago when you were in trouble for using the university computers, and you said you'd clean up your act; that obviously didn't happen. I doubt Tommy would've wanted the profits from your crime, either."

"Hey, come on, now, Malgy. That isn't fair."

He shook his head. "Sorry, but that's the way I see it—it was your choice to be a basic science professor, not mine, and I paid my dues. I'm sad you felt that way and couldn't live within your means, Sybil. We all make choices. But how in the hell did you think you were going to hide all that money once you got it? And what if Fowler decided not to give you your portion—what were you going to do? Go public and sue him? You didn't think this through very well."

"Stephens knew someone offshore who could take care of it."

"Yeah, Stephens . . . he was involved in Biggerstaff too and was in cahoots with Meach. He would've cheated you at the first opportunity."

"How do you know that?" She took a sip of coffee and a bite of her blueberry muffin.

"Documents Robertson had hidden that we uncovered that show his involvement in Grand Cayman payments to him and Meach for falsifying research reports. Meach knew about your museum project and worked diligently to frame you for Biggerstaff."

"I guess I owe you for proving I wasn't involved in that, at least."

"You don't owe me anything, Sybil. I did what I thought was right."

"But about choices—unfortunately, I will have to live with mine, and Dale, Fowler, and a bunch of other people will have to live with theirs, too. Chloe's career is ruined. She most likely won't go to jail, but she'll never get another decent job after sleeping with one of the hydroglippane principal investigators in order to get the drug for me."

"She made that choice, too. I'll do all I can to help you. I do promise to come and visit if you want."

"That would be great, Dan. I probably won't have anyone else who will come. I owe you my life, at least what's left of it."

"Make it count for something, Sybil. Help someone else. You are an educated person who can help someone in Marysville have a better life. Promise me that, at least."

"I'll try, Dan. It won't be easy, but I will."

Chapter Twenty-Six

One Month Later
Dan Rudbeck's Office
Staffordsville University Hospital
0955 hours

"So, what's the update on everything, Malgy?" Jake Fisher asked Jayna and him in his office while drinking coffee. "I'm missing all the excitement in our lives."

"Sybil Tegler pleaded guilty to aggravated arson of the Youngswood Cultural Center and criminal mischief for the Bowling Green bus. She accepted a sentence of three years at the Ohio Reformatory for Women in Marysville. With good behavior, she can earn a thirty percent reduction in that. Considering all that she did, that's actually pretty generous."

"Will her son go visit her?" Jake asked.

"Don't know. It's not very far away, but there are a lot of fences to mend there with her and Tommy. I feel bad for Sybil, I really do, but she deserves what she got. She was greedy, planned this for a long time, and could've hurt many people in the process."

"Drake Fowler?"

"His case is still in federal court since the fraud involved multiple states other than Ohio. He didn't have anything directly to do with burning down the building. Still, the insurance fraud is being prosecuted heavily by the feds because of the claim for the real camera when the one destroyed was only a replica. He will likely see some prison time. In any case, his career is ruined, thanks to me. Yay. I wish I felt better about all this."

"Cheryl Robertson?"

"Still trying to reach an agreement with the prosecutor. Likely a similar deal to Tegler's, with a longer sentence due to the felony murder charge. She wasn't the instigator, but did set the fire."

"Lots of others involved too, from the tire guys to Dale Stephens to Tegler's cousin at the drug company. You've done it again, my man. So, what's the plan with the building?"

"Rebuilding the Biggerstaff building after they demolish the old one. Demolition will take three months. A year and a half to create a new building, which will be two stories taller and have fifty percent more office and lab space, and a new library and computer center for the students."

"What will they do with the existing faculty who had labs there?"

"We'll have to find lab space in other university buildings. We still have some remote workers from the coronavirus pandemic, so we have some extra space which is scattered around. It's not ideal, but neither was the old building."

"How will we know the new building will be any better than the old one?" Ted asked.

"We are hiring a group of blue-ribbon contractors from Columbus who will bid on the project. And guess who will be supervising it?"

"Oh, no. You? What expertise do you have in such matters, Dan?" his wife asked. "You didn't tell me that. You have a hard enough time supervising projects at your own house."

"Now, that's not fair. I am good at organizing large projects and supervising complex arrays of personnel. Another thing I'm good at is my obsession with details."

"Yes, we know," his wife said as she took a sip of her latte. "Don't remind us."

"Fortune has given us another chance to make a better building. I know we can't count on any more Teglers or Meaches to burn down the new building so we can get a third one. Not in my lifetime, anyway."

"I sure hope not. That would force Sandy into retirement for sure," Jayna said. "Just don't name it the Rudbeck Building. That would jinx it for sure, and make Dan's head three times as big."

"My head needs to be three times as big to accommodate my huge brain with its extra cerebral folds."

"Brain volume decreases by five percent each year after age 40. Sorry, Dan, another fact."

"Well, it's good I have a lot in reserve, then. That brain loss will take a long time to become significant."

AAAAA

So what was next in store for the amazing Amalgam-Man? When would he start work on the fourth Barclay Dixon novel, "Purple Passion," which would detail his settling down with a rehabilitated Ms. Volkova, who was sentenced to life supervised by him under house arrest? It might be hard to believe he could settle down with just one woman, but he knew from real life that she was one heck of a package. Even Confucius was impressed, and that wasn't easy to do.

He hoped Evie would also settle down and marry Robert, and maybe he could be a grandfather soon. It would be good to have little kids to play with again, and he couldn't wait to see what new toys would be available.

He also looked upon his life and realized that he had achieved what he had desired, not what he thought he wanted, but what was really important. He could likely ride his friendship with the President to prestigious new positions in Washington, and he was even contacted about that, but he wasn't interested because he'd learned to value what he had. Confucius taught that appreciating what you had, whether it was abilities, knowledge, or friends, was a key part of living a fulfilling life. He seemed to have all three in abundance.

He again had solved a complex crime with his unique skill

set, combined with family and friends who stood up for him and did the tasks he asked, even though he could be very irritating and exhausting to deal with.

He stopped Meach from doing more damaging things, but he was sorry that someone like Sybil Tegler had turned to planning an elaborate crime because of her gambling addiction and inability to live within her means. Perhaps she could become rehabilitated as well. He would be there to help her when she got out. It would be the Christian thing to do, his wife would tell him, and Confucius would be proud of his protégé.

But enough of work; now it was time to find Ms. Volkova and arrange another play date in her plush lavender bed with its various accessories. He wasn't sure what deranged activities she had in store for him after their last encounter, but it would be exciting. He imagined that some of their "accoutrements" might be available in larger sizes at the Dallas public safety store.

THE END

www.ingramcontent.com/pod-product-compliance
Lightning Source LLC
Chambersburg PA
CBHW060625310726
48982CB00003B/673

* 9 7 8 1 7 3 4 9 3 7 2 6 8 *